RECOMMENDED BY
Roger
PLEASE RETURN

D0499093

What others are saying about Election Day

Jim Moore's *Election Day* is not only a clever civics lesson, but also a high-stakes thriller in which an unlikely band of political operatives struggles to keep the presidency out of the hands of a madman. — Ben O'Connell, Montana native and Washington, DC, political journalist

The unimaginable becomes inevitable in this riveting thriller by Montana cowboy legislator and lawyer Jim Moore, who takes the reader on a thrill-ride of unexpected and sometimes blood-chilling "what if" situations, arriving at a fantastic conclusion actually possible within the legalistic intricacies of the American election and Presidential succession process. — Bob Brown, former Montana Senator and Secretary of State.

Jim Moore knows the law, and he knows politics, and he's brought both to bear in this crackerjack of a read. — Craig Lancaster, author of *600 Hours of Edward* and *The Summer Son.*

Political suspense, constitutional crises, murder, mayhem and romance -- Jim Moore's book has it all. The bonus is that the whole crazy plot revolves around a decent, no-nonsense Montana cowboy. — Ed Kemmick, Reporter and columnist for the Billings Gazette and author of *The Big Sky, By and By*

ELECTION DAY is an entertaining story told by a gifted story teller—also an exceptional gentleman, lawyer, rancher, and Montana senator who could have found himself in the shoes of Bobby Hobaugh. It is a "must read" for political wonks wondering when the flaws of our presidential election system are going to catch up with us, students trying to stretch their minds about the oddness and origins of the electoral college, and anyone who enjoys a good mystery entwining interesting characters, politics turned on its head, and a surprise ending – all in a way that could honestly happen in real life. — Dorothy Bradley, former Montana legislator

As a former Chief of Staff for a U.S. Senator during the tumultuous 2000 Presidential Election that the U.S. Supreme Court ultimately resolved in Bush v. Gore, I did not believe the circumstances of an election could provide more drama or interest. But then I read **Election Day**. What a story! Jim Moore spins a fascinating tale based on facts that could actually happen and would make any other election contest seem like a bore. — Will Brooke, attorney

ELECTION DAY

Also by Jim Moore

Ride the Jawbone

a legal murder mystery set in Montana in 1902

Jim Moore

ELECTION DAY

A novel by Jim Moore

To Val —
Enjoy
Jim!

 Raven Publishing, Inc of Montana

Election Day
by Jim Moore

Published by: **Raven Publishing, Inc.**, PO Box 2866
Norris, MT 59745

This novel is a work of fiction. Names, characters, places, and events are the product of the author's imagination or are used fictitiously. Any similarity to any person or event is coincidental. Names of any public offices, building, new corporations, and publications are used fictitiously.

All rights reserved. Except for inclusion of brief quotations in a review, no part of this book may be reproduced or transmitted in any form or by any means without permission in writing from the publisher.

Copyright © 2012 by Jim Moore

Cover design by Craig Lancaster

Printed in the United States of America

Library of Congress Cataloging-in-Publication Data

Moore, Jim, 1927-
Election day / Jim Moore.
p. cm.
ISBN 978-1-937849-00-9 (case bound : alk. paper) -- ISBN 978-1-937849-01-6 (trade paper : alk. paper) -- ISBN 978-1-937849-02-3 (electronic edition)
1. Ranchers--Montana--Fiction. 2. Presidents--Succession--United States--Fiction. 3. Political fiction. I. Title.
PS3613.O5626E44 2012
813'.6--dc23

2012006219

For Kay
Our children and our grandchildren
My family – My life

Constitution of the United States

The executive power shall be vested in a president of the United States of America. He shall hold his office during the term of four years, and together with the vice president, chosen for the same term, be elected as follows:

Each state shall appoint, in such manner as the legislature thereof may direct, a number of electors, equal to the whole number of senators and representatives to which the state may be entitled in the congress....

The electors shall meet in their respective states, and vote by ballot for president and vice president....

The congress may determine the time of choosing the electors, and the day on which they shall give their votes; which day shall be the same throughout the United States.

Saturday, October 30, early afternoon

BILLINGS, MONTANA

Senator Forrest Blaine, patrician in both looks and manner, thanked the Secret Service man for holding the door as he stepped into the limousine. Leaning his head against the backrest and closing his eyes, he heaved a sigh. The visit with his old friend left him with a feeling of extreme weariness. At their last meeting, only two years ago, that friend had been bright-eyed and energetic, if a bit overweight. Now he was little more than a shrunken shell. The cancer was eating his life away.

As the limo moved away from the campus toward the street that would take him to the center of town, the senator's thoughts turned to the uncertainty of life. His friend would be dead in a month.

Deliberately driving that thought from his mind, he focused on the next of numberless campaign appearances—the one here in Billings, Montana. And then on to the one this evening in San Francisco. And then the next—and the next—and the next after that.

When the driver slowed to turn onto the street that would take him to the hotel where his staff was waiting, he opened his eyes and leaned forward in the seat. At that moment a sound—or something—made him jerk his head toward the passenger-side window. His eyes widened. All he was able to cry out was, "Waaa....."

1

Saturday, October 30, early afternoon

BILLINGS, MONTANA

The police officer manning the roadblock turned when he heard the blaring of the horn and stared, open–mouthed, at the runaway gravel truck screaming down the steep grade from the airport. He jumped away from his motorcycle, ran to the middle of the street, and waved his arms at the careening vehicle. Whirling toward the limousine approaching from the side street, he bellowed, "Look out!"

The driver of the limousine, looking the other way, continued his entry onto North 27th Street—into the path of the heavily loaded and out-of-control truck. Tires squealing, the truck careened toward the open grounds of the campus—too late! The weight and speed of the truck carried it into the side of the limousine.

Amidst a metallic explosion of grating sound, the police officer watched the limousine slam against a massive concrete pillar bearing the sign, "Montana State University-Billings." As the noise of the crash died away, he muttered, "Jesus Christ!" and grabbed the mike to his radio. No one could survive that crash, not even the candidate for vice president of the United States, seated in the back seat of the car.

A few minutes later, at the Crowne Plaza Hotel a dozen blocks away, Janine Paul, the young, attractive, and frustrated aide to Senator Forrest Blaine paced the floor and groused to Lance Caldwell, "I never should have let him go off to visit with his friend without sending someone along to keep track of time." She waved toward the large auditorium beyond the hallway where they stood. "There are over three hundred people in there waiting to hear him speak, and where is he? If he doesn't get here soon, he'll be late for the next campaign stop, and that's the important one."

She yanked the buzzing cell phone from her pocket, muttering. "He should be coming in that door, not calling to tell me he's running late." She held the phone to her ear and barked, "Hello."

It wasn't Blaine, nor was it either of the Secret Service men who accompanied him, but a high-pitched, panicky voice. She strained to hear—to understand. At last, she mumbled, "Thank you," and punched the off button. Dead phone in hand, she slumped onto the bench behind her and stared into space. She felt as if someone had punched all the air out of her. Senator Forest Blaine was dead.

Numbed by the news, it took a few moments for the consequences of his death to register in her mind. She rested her forehead in her hands and closed her eyes, overcome by a mixture of emotions. Grief slowly turned to anger, and she silently cursed the senator for his insistence on stopping in this dreary cow town.

At last Janine gathered her wits, shook her head, and pushed herself slowly from the hard bench. Lance, the youthful press aide, had left her side when her phone rang and was huddled nearby with a Montana state senator she knew as Ralph Phillips. They turned their heads as she spoke. "Blaine's had a wreck." She took a deep breath. "They said he was killed instantly. The policewoman who called couldn't tell me any more than that, except that the limo was demolished."

Phillips' face remained impassive as he muttered, "I'll be damned."

Caldwell—tall, slender, somewhat gangly, bespectacled and lightly carrying the extreme good looks of youth—stood in stunned silence for a moment, then gasped, "Dead? He can't be dead!" After a heartbeat he added, "What'll we do now? There are people waiting to hear him speak." His eyes shifted from Janine to the state senator. "And we're supposed to get him to San Francisco for his appearance at seven o'clock."

Janine rubbed her upper left arm with her right hand as she collected her thoughts.

"I have to call his wife. She must be told before she hears it on the news. This will be all over the air in minutes. I've got to let the Weldon people know right away." She paused as thoughts raced through her mind. How on earth had this happened? She rubbed her arm even harder.

Lance Caldwell interrupted her thoughts. "I'll call Marsha at headquarters and have her get a press release out right away. You know, associates in shock, all of that."

Janine nodded. "Yes, good. And then call our contact people in San Francisco. Tell them what happened and ask about someone to cover for the senator at the seven o'clock rally."

Lance stood staring at her, wondering if he should offer a word of comfort and then thought better of it.

Her voice had an edge when she said, "Go! What are you waiting for?"

As Lance hurried away, Janine mumbled more to herself than to Ralph Phillips, "We have to do something with the crowd." She peered through the open doors at the throng that was milling about in the spacious meeting room. Some had taken seats near the front. Others stood visiting as they waited for the announcement that Blaine had arrived. The wide speaker's platform, bearing a podium and enough chairs to seat the most important of the local party officials, was to the side of the room, out of her sight. Tall curtains were draped on each side of the platform and across to the meeting room entry. The arrangement would allow the senator to mount the platform without a need to wade through the mob. "One of us will have to go out there and tell them what happened. Might as well send them home."

Short, rotund Senator Ralph Phillips stood with his arms crossed on his chest. His hooded eyes gave him a sleepy look. "I wouldn't do that, ma'am. Senator Blaine may be dead, but Governor Warren Weldon isn't, and he's the man we have to elect president of the United States. This is Saturday and Election Day is Tuesday. The people out there will be as shocked as we are. They need to be reminded that there's still an election to win. We need to give 'em something to fire 'em up."

He jerked his chin to point across the room. "See that guy over there? The tall one in the brown suit and western boots? That man's the one to make the announcement. He'll give 'em a stemwinder of a speech that'll have 'em charging out the doors to spend the next three days hustling votes for Weldon. Give him a chance, and this gathering won't be a waste."

Janine peered across the open area outside the meeting room. A small group of local party officials were clustered together while waiting to greet the senator upon his arrival. The man Phillips described was among them.

"Who is he?"

"Bobby Hobaugh. He's the state senator from Miles City. One of the nicest guys you'll ever meet. And he can speak. Take my word for it."

Janine shook her head. "He's a nobody. We can't send a nobody onto that stage, for heaven's sake. If anyone's going to talk, it's got to be someone who's known."

Senator Phillips smiled at her, but his voice was firm. "Ma'am, perhaps you'll excuse an old campaigner for giving advice, but those people out there are all Montanans. Most of 'em know Bobby personally. He may be a nobody to you, but he's a somebody in Montana. And he's a damn good public speaker."

As Phillips talked, Janine looked at his gunmetal gray hair, combed straight back. Well dressed, but portly, he couldn't be more than five feet, five inches tall. The top of his head was just above her eye level.

She shrugged. "What have we got to lose? Someone has to do it. Why not Bobby whatever-his-name-is. Get him over here."

Phillips leaned to one side and called out, "Hey, Bobby! See you here for a minute?"

Bobby Hobaugh said something to the group he was with, making them all laugh. He sauntered over to join Janine and his state senate colleague, nodded in Janine's direction, and said, "Ma'am." Turning to his friend, he asked, "What's up, Ralph?" His voice was soft and difficult to hear over the din of the hallway crowd.

Janine looked him up and down. She guessed him to be about fifty years old, six feet tall, wide-shouldered, with the body of an athlete softened by age. The suit he wore was fine gabardine, walnut brown in color, and had the appearance of a tailor's fitting. The pants and the jacket tails were slightly wrinkled. A tie of chocolate brown offset a starched shirt of soft tan. The knot of the tie was slightly to the side of center.

After months of making certain that Senator Blaine's appearance was above reproach, Janine felt an urge to reach across and straighten it. Instead, she raised her eyes to the top of his head. His hair, what there was of it, was sandy colored. Finally her eyes rested on Bobby's rather round face. Smile lines radiated from the corner of brown eyes that twinkled when he spoke.

The words "nice looking, but not exactly handsome," crossed Janine's mind.

Phillips grasped Bobby's arm. "We just got a call that Senator Blaine had a car wreck. He didn't make it."

Janine interrupted to add, "The limo driver and two Secret Service agents were killed, too."

Like the others when they heard the news, Bobby took a moment to digest it. His face assumed a sober look as he said, "Well, I'll be damned. That's a hell of a note."

"Your friend here suggested you should be the one to tell the crowd. Maybe you could give a little campaign talk while you're at it. Something to make them feel they haven't wasted the afternoon."

Bobby looked at her with inquiring eyes, "What could I say? Other than to tell them that the senator's dead."

Phillips squeezed his friend's arm, "Bobby, just tell them about the wreck and that Senator Blaine didn't make it. Then give 'em your old 'the-world-will-go-to-hell-if-we're-not-elected' speech. I've heard you make that talk a dozen times. The crowd always winds up cheering. And then they go out and hustle votes for the candidate you're supporting. This time do it for Weldon."

Janine started to turn away and then spoke over her shoulder, "You two take care of it. I'll call Governor Weldon's top aide. He's not going to be happy, and he'll take it out on me. We've got to do something about the appearances Senator Blaine was to make in San Francisco and Los Angeles. And Phoenix. And Dallas."

"That's hell about the Senator." Bobby stared into the distance. "Who do you suppose Weldon will pick as his vice president?"

His short friend was quick to answer, "He won't pick anyone until the election's over. If he wins, there'll be a hell of a scramble. All those who were candidates for president in the primaries will be courting him. It'll be interesting to watch." He nudged Bobby and added, "Go collect your thoughts for few minutes. Then you're on. I'll tell the rest of the bunch what happened." He stepped aside and called out, "Hey, people, we've got some bad news."

Saturday, October 30, minutes later

ROYAL CROWNE PLAZA, BILLINGS

While Janine listened to Roman Burke's questions in his curt, flat voice, she wondered how he could be so callous about death, especially the death of the candidate for vice president of the United States. But then again, the man seemed to have no feelings. As campaign manager for the Republican presidential nominee, Burke was like an automaton with only one purpose—to elect Weldon.

"What are you doing about the situation there?"

"We have a gentleman talking to the crowd right now. He'll handle it."

"What about San Francisco? Have you arranged for a replacement speaker there?"

"God, Burke, I just heard that Blaine's dead. I haven't had time to do anything about San Francisco."

"We need the California votes, and we're depending on you to make sure this incident doesn't lose 'em. Blaine is also scheduled to talk in Los Angeles and then in Phoenix. Then in Dallas. We sure as hell can't lose votes in California or Arizona. Or in Texas for that matter. Get on it."

Before she could answer, the phone went dead. Burke had hung up on her. "That bastard," she growled to herself. "How am I supposed to get a replacement speaker in San Francisco when I'm stuck in this God-forsaken town in Montana?"

A Secret Service agent, who'd been with Senator Blaine from the start of his campaign, grabbed her arm as she stepped from the corner where she'd huddled for the phone conversation. "Ms. Paul, we'll be leaving you. Our task now is to determine how that truck got through the roadblock at the top of the hill. We need to inspect what's left of the limousine as soon as possible and scour the route that truck followed. It's important to learn immediately if this was something more than an accident."

Janine thought about the steep roadway coming off the rimrocks where the airport sat more than five hundred feet above the town. As she and Lance had descended the steep hill, she'd noticed the entrance to Montana State University on her right. They had gone ahead to the hotel to make sure everything was ready for Blaine's speech, while the senator took that side street to visit an old friend, the provost of the University. She shook her head, still envisioning what must have happened. After visiting his bedridden friend at his home, the senator's limo would have come back through the campus, the most direct route to the hotel, entering North 27th Street—right in front of the heavy truck that was barreling down that hill!

Janine had made adjustments to Blaine's whole campaign schedule so that he could see his friend—a friend suffering from terminal cancer—"one last time." Ironically, it had turned out to be the last time he would see anyone.

"Ma'am?" the Secret Service agent asked.

"Yes," Janine answered, jarred from her thoughts. "I understand. There's no need for security here, now that the senator's gone. But thanks for telling me that you're leaving. We have to decide what to do next to help Governor Weldon's campaign."

News of the senator's death swept the country on Twitter almost immediately. The traditional media followed in short order. A large television screen mounted on the rear wall of the room where the party officials gathered showed a blurred picture of the anchorman.

> Breaking News! CNN interrupts its regular broadcast for this special announcement. Senator Forrest Blaine, Republican candidate for vice president, is dead. We have just been informed that Senator Blaine was involved in a vehicular crash in Billings, Montana. It is confirmed that Senator Blaine is dead. No details are being offered at this time about the cause of what is currently being called an accident. We go now to Denver, Senator Blaine's hometown, to...

Janine turned from the television set, her jaw clenched. She'd hear more of this later—more than she wanted to, no doubt. Now she had to move. Lance would have to handle the reporters. In that brief telephone call, Roman Burke had emphatically described her task—not to let Senator Blaine's death harm Weldon's campaign!

She walked quickly to the entryway of the meeting room where Senator Phillips stood. A musty odor tinged the air. The smell seemed to come from the long curtains hanging on the side of the stage. It was an odor that seemed to underscore the fact that Senator Blaine was dead. The curtains muffled the sound of Hobaugh's voice so she couldn't understand what he was saying, but the reaction of the crowd filtered through. At first there was silence, then a low murmur, and then silence again. After a few minutes, laughter was followed by silence, scattered cheers, and more silence. Then a huge roar burst forth and continued even after she could hear the clatter of people rising from their seats. She walked up behind Phillips. "I guess you were right about his ability to get people pumped."

"You bet. Bobby can sure turn 'em on."

Janine's right hand returned to her left arm. "We've got to do something about San Francisco. Blaine is scheduled to speak at seven o'clock. We're expecting a huge crowd."

Before she could finish her explanation, Lance rushed in, concern written all over his boyish face. "The fight has already started in San Francisco between the Governor and Senator Ryan over taking Blaine's place as the speaker tonight. It seems like they both hope to impress Weldon and get a shot at the vice presidency. Our staffer there is desperate. Both of those guys are calling Weldon, pledging support and asking to step into Blaine's shoes. Weldon's people tell them we're handling it."

"Weldon's people! They expect us to take care of that problem and every other thing that could possibly jeopardize the election. Roman Burke has already warned me not to mess it up and cost Weldon votes." She paused and looked at Phillips as though she hadn't seen him before. "I'm sorry, I don't know why we're telling you all of this. It isn't your problem."

"Ma'am, you've got the solution to your problem coming off that stage right now. Take Bobby out there to the coast with you and let him do the talking."

"Are you insane? Your Bobby what's-his-name may be somebody in Montana, but he really is nobody in California."

"You're right. Bobby's a nobody in California. So make him into a somebody. Do you know what the people in San Francisco and everywhere else will be asking in the next hour? They'll be asking who Weldon will pick as vice president—if he's elected. To make Bobby into a somebody, get a press release on the wire saying that Weldon is focused on a little known but highly regarded rancher and lawyer from Montana. And be sure that it gets good coverage on the San Francisco television and radio stations, as well as on the Net."

Janine glared at him. "You really are insane. Weldon would never even think of such a thing. If he's going to announce his choice before Election Day, he'll pick someone he thinks can help him win—not a cowboy in a wrinkled suit from a state with no electoral votes." She thought a moment and then added, "No. Weldon won't decide on a vice president until after the election. Then he'll go with someone he knows and likes." A grimace crossed her face. "Weldon and his people would kill me if I put out the crazy notion that some nobody from Montana named Bobby Hobaugh is the man."

"Would they? What will Weldon say when the press asks? He won't deny it. That would make him and his organization look bad. He'll just say that Bobby is one of several he'll consider. And when he says that, Bobby's a somebody."

The look of skepticism on Janine's face remained, but Ralph could tell she was wavering. She raised both arms with frustration and said, "My God, we can't have him standing up in front of a crowd in San Francisco in those wrinkled brown clothes. Doesn't he have a better suit?" She glanced at Ralph's carefully tailored sport coat and his slacks that were pressed with sharp creases. "Something like you're wearing?"

"Oh, I suppose Bobby's got a black suit that he wears to

funerals. But he won't have time to go home to get it. It's 135 miles to Miles City, one way. If he's to be your guy on the coast, you better get him to the airport. We'll ask Bobby for his measurements, and then you can contact your people out there. They can order a suit to be ready for him. Better tell 'em to have a tailor standing by, just in case the suit needs altering."

Janine shrugged her shoulders and turned to the young man at her side. "Lance, get out a press release as Senator Phillips here suggests. What the hell, I haven't any better idea."

Lance said over his shoulder as he turned to leave, "It's your idea, not mine." After two steps, he turned and asked, "What's that guy's name, again?"

"Bobby Hobaugh." Ralph replied. "Be sure you spell it right. H-O-B-A-U-G-H. And his name really is Bobby—not Robert."

Janine yelled after him, "Be certain they cover all the northern California radio and TV stations with that release. We want everyone in San Francisco to know there will be a speaker in place of Senator Blaine, and that the speaker may be the next vice president."

Lance called back, "I know, Janine. I know how to do my job."

Bobby was smiling as he came off the stage. "Damn, those are nice people. Did you hear 'em, Ralph? With folks like this, no wonder we stay in Montana."

"Well, Bobby, you're about to leave Montana. You're going to California. This lady insists that you give the same speech to the good people in San Francisco in about four hours."

Janine scowled. "What do you mean, I insist? It's your

idea." She turned to Bobby and added, "Senator Blaine was to speak to a gathering there this evening. To avoid a fight among the locals over his replacement speaker, we need someone from the outside. Ralph suggested that you're the person to do it."

"Ah hell, Ralph. I can't go to San Francisco tonight. I have things to discuss with the manager at the ranch in the morning, and I have clients to see day after tomorrow. Besides, no one in San Francisco wants to listen to me."

"Call Margaret and tell her what's up. She'll square it with your clients and notify your ranch manager."

Senator Phillips glanced at Janine. "Margaret's his office manager. She handles things like this all the time."

He turned to his senate colleague and his face took on a serious look. "This is important, Bobby. The election may be on the line."

Janine put her hand on Bobby's arm. "Senator Phillips is right. It's very important, and we're making sure that everyone will want to hear you." She tugged at his sleeve. "Come on, let's go. You can call your office manager from the plane."

Bobby grabbed at Ralph. "Listen, friend, if I'm going, so are you. You got me into this. You can help finish it."

"Bobby's right, Senator Phillips. We need you there too. There'll be plenty of room on the plane. The Secret Service agents will stay here to try to figure out what happened." Her voice caught. She swallowed hard before speaking to Ralph again, "Let's get going. If your friend Bobby is going to be vice president, we have a lot to do."

Ralph grinned at Bobby's dumbstruck look. "Don't get excited. We'll tell you all about it on the plane."

3

Saturday, October 30, late afternoon

NEW YORK, NEW YORK

Incumbent President Arthur Simpson heard of Blaine's death while traveling in his limousine from one appearance in New York City to another. His first question to Tracy Wheat, his chief of staff, was, "Can we take advantage of this?"

Wheat thought a moment before responding. "We can raise the age issue again. After all, Warren Weldon is seventy years old. An email flash, a tweet, and a web posting to remind the voters that they won't know who they're selecting for vice president might have some benefit." He paused. "But we have to be careful, sir. There's the sympathy factor to consider."

"You're right about sympathy." Simpson thought for a moment. "How will the Republicans pick a new vice-presidential candidate? It's too close to Election Day for a convention."

"If this had happened sooner, their central committee would pick the nominee. But as a practical matter, they'd pick whoever Weldon wants. I think he'll just wait until after the election. If he wins, he'll choose his man. If he loses, it doesn't make any difference."

The President thought about it. "Well, get the postings out to our supporters and to the media. It's most important to put the age issue firmly in the minds of those who haven't yet decided how to vote. I think this election will be closer than the polls show. This might help." His jaw jutted out in a show of determination, "We can win it yet."

Saturday, October 30, evening

SAN FRANCISCO, CALIFORNIA

The news reports of the death of Senator Blaine had turned to speculation about the person Weldon might pick as his running mate. The television set in the suite at the Mark Hopkins hotel was tuned to ABC.

> A spokesman for Governor Weldon just announced that the Governor will not attempt to select a new running mate before the election next Tuesday. Senator Blaine's organization issued a statement saying if Weldon is elected, he may choose a little known state senator from Montana named Bobby Hobaugh. The statement gives no information about Hobaugh other than that he is a lawyer and cattle rancher and that he is highly respected in his home state. ABC is following the story and will provide more information as it becomes available. Other possibilities, of course, include...

Janine punched the off button on the television and followed Bobby, Ralph, and Lance to the door of the suite. "Well, we know the networks picked up on the press release. Now we'll find out if it had any effect."

The answer was obvious when Bobby stepped to the podium after the Governor of California introduced him as a potential vice president. Before him a sea of faces crowded the hotel ballroom. Not only was every seat filled, but people were standing elbow to elbow along the walls and in the aisles. Bobby, freshly shaved, wore a dark grey suit with a cranberry-red tie over a gleaming white shirt. The cowboy boots were gone for now, replaced by a pair of black oxfords that gleamed in the overhead lights.

Watching from the back of the room, Janine was pleased with his appearance. At least he was dressed like a candidate for high office. But appearance wasn't enough. Remembering the language Burke had used, she prayed that Hobaugh would not embarrass her. Burke's call had come two minutes after the press release about Hobaugh hit the air. He expressed his anger in colorful terms and made it plain that Weldon was outraged. He demanded that she get Bobby Hobaugh out of sight as soon as possible and told her not to issue any more releases. Those, he made clear, would come only from Weldon's organization.

Bobby had only spoken a few words when Lance whispered to Janine that Burke wanted to speak to her again—immediately. She stepped into the corridor outside the ballroom, away from anyone who might want to listen in on the conversation, and punched in Burke's number. As she waited for him to answer, she speculated about the purpose of the call. It surely couldn't be good, given the last conversation.

"This is Burke."

"Janine here. You called."

"Listen, the idea of that guy from Montana as vice president has really caught the attention of the media. It's so off the wall that the news guys have latched onto it and are ignoring everything Simpson is doing or saying. The bloggers are all over the story. Our side is getting all the coverage, and Simpson is getting a blank. He might as well not exist as far as the networks and the web are concerned. How long can you keep that cowboy going without messing things up?"

"Keep him going? An hour ago you told me to shut him down."

"I know. But the longer we can keep the reporters focused on our campaign, even if it's only on your cowboy friend, the less coverage Simpson gets. That's all to our advantage, with only three days 'til Election Day."

"Well, he's out there speaking right now. We've got a huge crowd. There must be five hundred people jammed into that room listening to him, and more people from the media than I would have expected. He's a curiosity, if nothing else."

"What's he telling them? He won't say something to hurt Weldon, will he?"

"He doesn't have a written speech. He just gets up there and talks. If the crowd's reaction in Billings is any indication, they'll all be pumped when he gets done."

"Watch him! And keep him away from those reporters. He could say something dumb in response to a question."

"Okay. I'll do my best on that. Lance is handling the media. Do you want us to go to Los Angeles and have him give the speech there?"

"Yes. Get on down there and then go to Phoenix. Keep the same schedule you had for Blaine. As long as the reporters are busy trying to find out about Bobby...what's his name?"

"Hobaugh. H-O-B-A-U-G-H."

"Right. Hobaugh. Anyway, the news people will be busy running after him, trying to find out all about him. Especially something bad. That'll keep the focus on Weldon's campaign and away from Simpson. But for God's sake, keep that guy under control. He could ruin everything with one wrong re-mark."

Janine stood for a moment looking at the dead phone. As usual, Burke had punched off without saying goodbye. Ralph Phillips had been right. Making Bobby Hobaugh a somebody had turned a possible political disaster into an opportunity to upstage the campaign of President Arthur Simpson. Warren Weldon had been ahead in the polls before Blaine was killed, so it seemed logical that the poll numbers would hold, with all the attention his campaign was getting.

She smiled as she started off in search of Phillips. After a few paces she stopped. Senator Forrest Blaine, a dear friend and a really fine man, was killed less than six hours ago, and already the attention of the media had moved from that trag-edy to speculation about his replacement.

She wondered, what kind of country is this?

4

Saturday, October 30, evening

ATLANTA, GEORGIA

"If Warren Weldon is elected, and I think he will be, he'll be able to choose the vice president. Do you agree, Tucker?"

Tucker, standing in front of the huge gleaming mahogany desk, arms at his side, answered, "Yes Mr. Tootell. It appears that the Republican National Committee will make suggestions. But the actual choice will be made by Weldon."

"Then it behooves us to influence that decision." The big man sat with his back to the window that overlooked downtown Atlanta from the 40th floor of the Tootell Tower. He leaned forward with elbows on the desktop, large hands clasped together. "We need to ensure that I'm his choice."

"Sir, I thought you weren't interested in being vice president. You always said it would be president or nothing."

Tootell looked across at Tucker for a moment before he said, "Vice president—and then president. He paused and then spoke again. "We need to learn the names of any others that Weldon might be considering. And find out all there is to know about each of them."

"Yes, sir. I'll have that information for you tomorrow."

"Thank you, Tucker. See that you do."

Tucker nodded as he passed Miss Lotus's desk in the small outer office. She glanced up at him briefly and then returned her eyes to the computer keyboard. After years of passing through that room, he was accustomed to her behavior. She never spoke to him.

Saturday, October 30, evening

SAN FRANCISCO, CALIFORNIA

The volume on the television set in the hotel suite was loud so Hobaugh could hear it from the bedroom while he changed back into his comfortable brown pants.

MSNBC was reporting from the top of the airport hill. A reporter, wind blowing at her hair, stood at the intersection of the road exiting the airport and the main roadway. She spoke as a camera scanned the area.

> "There've been reports that the Montana Highway Patrol officers manning the road block understood that the candidate had already arrived at the convention center of the Crowne Plaza Hotel and that the roadway was clear. For that reason they allowed normal traffic to flow again to the downtown area. The truck, loaded with gravel, was first in line."

When her face came into view again, she continued.

> "Apparently the truck brakes failed coming down the steep incline, and it rammed into and demol-

ished the candidate's limousine as it entered the main road from the university."

Ralph mumbled, "Let's see what the other news channels are reporting."

The CNN reporter was caught in mid-sentence:

"....that the hydraulic brake lines of the run-away truck were deliberately cut is, as yet, unverified. Speculation focused on two unidentified men reportedly seen loitering near the truck as it was being loaded with gravel at a near-by pit. One person who claimed to speak for the trucking company told our man on the scene that the men appeared to be unshaven and of a swarthy complexion. CNN is pursuing the story and will broadcast further details as they become available."

Lance shook his head. "The terrorist theories have begun. What will they come up with next, for God's sake?"

Ralph muted the sound with a glance toward Janine. "It's hell about the senator."

Ralph used the remote to click back to MSNBC. The woman speaking, blond and attractive Kathryn Lewis, turned to face the camera as a view of the crash scene disappeared.

"Speculation continues about the man who might be vice president if Warren Weldon is elected next Tuesday. Standing by is Holly Sanchez of our San Francisco affiliate. Holly listened to Bobby Hobaugh when he spoke at a pre-election gathering this evening. Holly, having heard him speak, what can you tell us about Bobby Hobaugh?"

Holly answered, "Well, Kathryn, he certainly can stir up a crowd. He said what you would expect in a political speech at this point in a campaign. After expressing very sincere sympathy and re-

gret for the tragic loss of one of the most honest and honorable politicians this country has
ever known, he turned to the standard Republican talking points. He spoke of the failings of
the Simpson administration, promised that the
Republicans would take actions to improve the
economy while strengthening the armed forces,
and praised Governor Weldon as the man to lead
the country to greater things. But the way he said
it was certainly impressive. These Californians
are not easily aroused by political rhetoric but
when Bobby Hobaugh ended his talk, there were
five hundred of them on their feet, yelling and
cheering. As an example of the effect he had, I
heard the comments of one couple as they left the
ballroom. 'We've got to get home and start calling everyone we know and tell them to vote.' The
woman added, 'Tell them to vote for Weldon.'"

"Holly, what does he look like, up close and personal?"

"I haven't been up close and personal, Kathryn,
but he's nice looking. About six feet tall. Slightly
bald. He has a quiet voice so you have to listen
carefully to hear him. It's a very effective way to
hold the attention of the audience."

"Thanks, Holly. Keep your set tuned to this channel, folks. We'll provide more information on
the election crisis as it becomes available. This
is Kathryn Lewis speaking for MSNBC from New
York."

Ralph clicked the remote, and the screen went blank.
He swirled his drink in the glass. Grinning, he said, "Bobby's
sure doing all right, isn't he? The news folks will be busy until
Election Day trying to learn as much as they can about him.

It wouldn't have worked if the election weren't so close. Three days is about the attention span of reporters, especially television reporters."

Janine nodded. "I hope you're right about the time frame."

Lance interrupted. "This isn't your average story. Don't underestimate it. It will continue to get close scrutiny until the election."

Janine nodded. "Our problem will be in keeping Bobby out of sight so he doesn't have to answer questions from reporters. They have a way of getting candidates to say something that sounds different than intended."

"Bobby's a quick thinker so he'll be all right. But, it's better not to take a chance." Ralph was seated on a settee by the window. "How are we going to sneak him out of this hotel without the reporters getting to him? They've got the place surrounded."

"In the morning we can lead Bobby out a basement door. I've checked it out. And we're safe on the plane to L.A. It'll be tough to avoid media at the airport, now that he's caught the attention of the country. I'll run interference. Lance will handle the media. Ralph, you stick with your buddy. If he tries to stop and talk, don't let him."

Bobby walked into the room, buttoning the cuffs on his shirt. "Listen, I don't want to talk to reporters any more than you want me to. All I know about the issues of this presidential campaign are the things I've read in the papers. Those news guys..." He paused and continued after a smile at Janine, "and gals—can trip me up any time, and I know it." He poured a glass of water and stood looking from one to the other.

"Remember, I didn't hire on to be a candidate for vice president. All I was supposed to do was talk to the folks in Billings. Now you've got me here in California, acting like I know more than I do." When he looked at Janine again it was without a smile. "I'll give my little talk in Los Angeles and Phoenix and wherever else Blaine was supposed to go. But that's it." He took a long drink from the glass. "Reporters from the newspapers and TV stations will all be in Miles City tomorrow morning if not before, bothering Margaret at the office and Clint at the ranch. Hell, they'll be bothering everyone in town, trying to find out something scandalous about me. Scandal seems to be all that interests the public nowadays."

Janine scowled as she rubbed her arm, a habit she found irritating but couldn't break. "You're right about them going after your people. You'd better call and warn them so they'll know how to act. I hope to God they won't tell any secrets."

"Margaret and Clint? They don't know any secrets. Hell, I don't even know any secrets. But if reporters chase around long enough, they can certainly find someone to say something about me that sounds bad. I've represented a lot of people in my legal career. Some of them have been dissatisfied. And there are bound to be people who are mad at me over some vote in the legislature."

Ralph laughed as he looked at his friend. "No one gives a hoot about your senate votes. That's not the kind of thing that will make headlines. Have you stolen money from a client?"

"No, and I'm sure there isn't anyone who will say I did."

"Gotten any young girls pregnant lately?"

It was Bobby's turn to laugh. "Ralph, look at me. Am I someone that a young girl would be interested in?"

Janine did look at him and thought that a young girl might not be interested but any mature woman longing for a companion certainly would.

Bobby, unaware of her scrutiny, turned a sober face to

Ralph. "I see what you're getting at. And, no, there's isn't any sex scandal hanging over my head."

Janine asked the next question. "How about drugs?"

"Never did drugs, not even when I was young. Can't tell you why. I just didn't. Unless you're talking about booze, like that stuff Ralph is swilling. I drank plenty of it at times in the past. But I don't now. I've developed an allergy to the stuff."

Ralph turned to Janine and nodded his head. "I can testify to that. Bobby is the only guy in the Montana legislature that doesn't drink the lobbyists' whiskey. They don't know what to do with him."

Janine didn't give it up. "Think about it, Bobby. What have you ever done that will make headlines if reporters find it? Or the bloggers? Some of them are even worse than reporters and may try to create something juicy, if they can't find it for real."

"I don't know of anything. But I'll think about it. If something comes to mind, I'll tell you." He looked around for a place to put his glass. "What difference does it make anyway? In a couple of days the election will be over, and Governor Weldon will either win or lose. If he loses, the problem takes care of itself. If he wins, he's going to pick someone for vice president, and it ain't going to be me."

Bobby glanced around the room. "Where's Lance?"

"He's in his room talking on the phone to his wife. When they aren't talking, he's texting her."

"He doesn't look old enough to be married."

Janine grinned as she told him, "Not only is he married, but they're expecting a baby anytime. He's been beside himself with worry that the baby will come while he's with us, instead of at home in Denver."

"He should get himself back to Denver. A baby is more important than anything he can do here."

"Lance is like me. He put his heart and soul into Senator Blaine's campaign. He isn't going to leave us now."

Bobby thought about it, shook his head, and then turned to his senate friend. "Come on, Ralph, let's go eat. I'm hungry. I'm tired too. It was six o'clock in the morning when I left Miles City, and I expected to be home long before this."

Janine raised a hand. "You may as well get used to the idea that you can't just go to the dining room and have a meal. Or to any other public place for that matter. Like it or not, you're a celebrity now—at least for awhile. If you go to the dining room, you'll be swamped with people. We've ordered dinner from room service. It should be here anytime."

"That's right, Bobby. I ordered a filet for you. Done medium rare, the way you like it. And pumpkin pie with real whipped cream. How's that hit you?"

"That's good, partner. That's good."

Saturday, October 30, evening

NEW YORK CITY, NEW YORK

President Simpson rested in his hotel suite, a drink in his hand. "Who the hell is this Montana cowboy that Weldon has anointed as his running mate?"

"Damned if I know, sir. We're checking it out right now."

Tracy Wheat stood with his arms crossed. "The real question is what Weldon is trying to do with this announcement. Is the guy a red herring? Or is he somebody Weldon has known and now feels free to select?"

Wheat walked to the window and put his hands in his pockets. "One thing we know is that it has all of the media people chasing after the story. They aren't paying one damn bit of attention to us. Even the reporters assigned to us are speculating about our reaction to this guy, Hobaugh, instead of telling the world what you're saying." Wheat looked back at the President. "It's bad at this stage of the campaign. We need coverage. You can't get the message out without it."

"Hell, I know that. What do you have in mind to counteract it?"

"Sir, we just have to plow ahead and hope the whole goofy idea blows up in Weldon's face. The investigative reporters are sure to find out something bad about Hobaugh, even if we don't. When that happens, it'll be a different story."

"It better be. There isn't time. Why the hell did Blaine have to get killed right now?" Simpson took a big drink. "Well, I'll give 'em hell tomorrow and hope for the best." He looked at Wheat. "What's the latest tracking poll show?"

"No sense in lying about it. If the election is held right now, you're a loser by a wide margin. The last poll shows Weldon with fifty-one percent of the popular vote to thirty-nine for you, with only ten percent undecided."

5

Sunday, October 31, late morning

EN ROUTE TO LOS ANGELES, CALIFORNIA

Janine put the seat back and closed her eyes when the chartered Boeing 737 reached cruising altitude. The empty plane seemed cavernous without a herd of reporters and Secret Service agents filling the seats. It was another indication of the change in everything in her life since the death of the senator.

Exhausted, she let her mind wander. The last days of the campaign had been grueling. Even though the polls showed the Weldon-Blaine ticket had a comfortable lead over President Arthur Simpson and his running mate, Vice President Henry Larsen, she and the other campaign workers had continued to put in eighteen-hour days. The hard work and long hours had been worth it because she liked and respected Senator Blaine. She had also been sure he would eventually hold the presidency. He had all but promised her the position of his chief of staff after the election.

There was little chance of a position of any importance for her in a Weldon White House considering that she had even had to fight with Weldon's people for a greater role in the campaign. Too, Governor Weldon was an opportunist, without the principles of Senator Blaine. But she believed he was better for the country than the incumbent—an unprincipled scoundrel— in her estimation.

She opened her eyes and looked across the aisle at Bobby Hobaugh. She had learned from Ralph Phillips that he was fifty-one years old and a childless widower. Bobby lived alone in a large ranch house a short distance down the Yellowstone River from Miles City. He spent about half his time at his law office and the other half working at the ranch. Now, with glasses perched low on his nose, he was reading slowly through the morning edition of the Los Angeles Times.

The death of Senator Blaine was featured in the headlines of all the west coast daily newspapers, and the editorials generally paid tribute to the senator as a great American. Only the San Francisco Chronicle printed a brief report of the speech made by Bobby Hobaugh. Lance had reminded them that newspapers have deadlines to meet and couldn't adapt to breaking news as rapidly as the television and radio media, so the notion of Bobby Hobaugh as vice president wasn't prominent in print.

Ralph had used Janine's laptop to log on to the Internet and pull up his hometown paper, The Billings Gazette. The death of the senator and the investigation into the circumstances surrounding it filled that paper. It appeared that the Secret Service and local law enforcement were stumbling over one another in the process. The badly injured truck driver remained in a coma and was unresponsive to questions. The Highway Patrol officers responsible for stopping traffic at the top of the airport hill and those manning the campus intersection were being questioned extensively by the FBI. No one had been able to determine how the truck got through the security checkpoint. The lead editorial spoke of the possibility of foul play, perhaps a terrorist plot to disrupt the election. Ralph laughed out loud as he read that outlandish theory to the others. A story far back in the second section of the Gazette told of Bobby Hobaugh eulogizing Senator Blaine at a gathering of Republicans in Billings. Nothing was said about the vice presidency.

Janine watched Bobby grin at something in the comics. When he realized she was looking at him, he turned, put the paper down, and folded his glasses in his hand. His cheerful appearance emphasized the creases around his mouth and eyes. Smile lines, she thought, made a nice-looking man even more attractive.

"Do we go through the same exercise in Los Angeles?"

"Yes, we'll go to the hotel where you can change clothes again." Her eyes ran over his comfortable clothing as she added, "Change into the suit you wore in San Francisco." Her gaze returned to his face. "We have about three hours before the gathering of heavy hitters. That will be at Orville Roesener's house. Some of Weldon's biggest contributors and some Hollywood luminaries will be there. They'll all want to meet you before you speak. Can you handle some small talk with them?"

"Even in Montana we have to campaign. I'll schmooze 'em just like they were cow folks from Circle."

"Where?"

"You know, Circle. Big town. Two hundred people."

"Listen, I grew up in Detroit. To me a small town is Pontiac. I can't imagine a town with only two hundred people."

Bobby laughed his soft laugh. "Try Two Dot. It has less than thirty."

Janine laughed back. "Don't expect me to go to either one

of them." She glanced at her watch and added, "We should be landing at LAX in about thirty minutes. You'd better finish the paper so you'll know what the hot news is today. We'll catch CNN and Fox at the hotel for the latest. That way you won't appear to be uninformed when talking to the big contributors." The laugh left her face as she added, "Just remember, don't commit Weldon to anything while you're schmoozing."

Sunday, October 31, afternoon

LOS ANGELES, CALIFORNIA

The suite in the Westin Bonaventure Hotel was not much different from the one in San Francisco. Wallace Smith's old face was on the television again, talking about the deceased Senator Blaine.

> "All of the people who were important in the political world have said kind things about the senator. Even President Arthur Simpson said he was a remarkable man and a dedicated public servant." He paused for just a moment. "Since Senator Blaine's untimely death, a new name has come to our attention. Who is this mysterious Bobby Hobaugh? Louis Warden, a correspondent with our affiliate in Billings, Montana, has talked with people in the town of Miles City, where Bobby Hobaugh lives and has a law office. Louis, what have you learned about the man who may be vice president?"

The view changed to a windswept street, where a young reporter held a microphone.

> "Wallace, I visited with a number of people on the street. Almost universally they speak enthusi-

astically about him. He is described variously as honest, likeable, a good man, and a person who would be an excellent vice president or even president. I did speak to one Native American who complained that Hobaugh had represented white ranchers in a dispute with members of the Northern Cheyenne Indian Tribe. He said Hobaugh wasn't to be trusted. Later in the day, however, I talked with Margaret Lisa, Hobaugh's office manager. Ms. Lisa has worked with Mr. Hobaugh for ten years and has nothing but good things to say about him. She said, most emphatically, that he is not prejudiced against Native Americans or anyone else. His ranch manager also spoke highly of him. All in all, the people who know him best think Warren Weldon will do the right thing if he chooses Bobby Hobaugh as his vice president."

Janine marveled again at how soon the death of Forrest Blaine had become secondary news. It said something about the transitory nature of the public interest. Ralph Phillips, eyes on the television screen, apparently viewed the news only from the standpoint of his friend.

"See there, Bobby. It paid you to be nice to people all these years." He laughed. "When you get back home, you can thank 'em. You might even have to set 'em up at the local watering hole."

"I'll just be glad when this is over and I can go home. I'm tired of this game already. It ain't my line of work. Turning to Janine after rising from his chair, he said, "I'm going to need some clean clothes—socks, underwear." He gestured toward his Montana friend. "So does Ralph. Is there anyplace in this town where someone could find some on Sunday and purchase them for us?"

Janine laughed. "This isn't Circle, Montana. In the City

of Angels, the stores are always open—even on Sunday. "I'll call some of the local staffers. I'm sure they can find a good clothing store to accommodate us. She dug into her purse for a small tablet and handed it to Bobby. Write down the things you need and the proper sizes. We'll see what we can do."

Sunday, October 31, late morning

CHICAGO, ILLINOIS

"Mr. President, what do you have to say about Governor Weldon's choice for vice president?" The reporter's voice, coming from the back of the auditorium in a small community college, had a strident tone.

"If you are referring to the man called Bobby Hobaugh, I don't believe Governor Weldon has made a decision. Evidently Bobby Hobaugh is just one of several that he is considering. It would be foolhardy, it seems to me, for him to choose a man with absolutely no experience in national affairs. So if Hobaugh really is Weldon's choice, the voters should think carefully about putting him one step away from the presidency."

"What do you know about Bobby Hobaugh?"

"No more than anyone else." The president smiled at the reporter. "I'm sure that you people will be telling us more about him soon. No matter what we learn, I'm certain the people will decide that Henry Larsen is a better vice president than anyone Governor Weldon might choose.

Sunday, October 31, late morning

ATLANTA, GEORGIA

"What have you learned about Weldon's choices for vice president, Tucker?"

Tucker placed a sheaf of papers on the desk and stepped back. "That's the information on seven of them. There are only two or three on the list that Weldon will seriously consider." Tucker paused for a moment and then added, "I'm sure you've heard about Bobby Hobaugh, sir."

"Of course. Everyone who watches television has heard of him. Tell me what you know about Mr. Hobaugh."

"We've only learned the things that the news people tell us. He seems to be clean."

"Do you think Weldon is serious about him?"

"No. Our contact on Weldon's staff says that news release came from Blaine's press agent. Weldon didn't authorize it."

"What about others who Weldon might consider for vice president?"

"The chief contender, other than yourself, will be Allen Ward. You two made the best race against Weldon in the primaries. Weldon seemed to like Ward in spite of that rivalry."

"Ward is a bleeding liberal. I don't know what he's doing in the Republican Party. Who else?"

"There are several who are making noises. But it's impossible, sir, to know with certainty who Weldon will seriously consider until after the election. Right now, his only interest is in winning. And that seems to be taking all his energy."

"Continue to gather information about everyone who might be on Weldon's list. Look for anything we can use to eliminate each one, when the time comes." Jackson Tootell's cold, gray eyes focused on Tucker, who remained standing erect and unmoving in front of the desk. "I will be vice president, Tucker, and we will do what is necessary to achieve that goal."

"May I ask, sir, how you intend to persuade Weldon to choose you?"

Jackson Tootell stared at his employee for a long moment. "Tucker, you came to work for me about eight years ago, isn't that right?"

"Yes, sir."

"In that eight years I've made **Tootell Nationwide** the largest marketing organization in the world, haven't I?"

"Yes, sir. You have."

"In the process, it has been necessary to persuade some people to sell their companies to me, hasn't it?"

"Yes, sir."

"And I've always found a way to persuade? Found the one thing that was required in order to achieve my goal?"

"You have, sir."

"And you've always carried out my instructions so that the persuasion was effective, haven't you?"

"I believe I have, sir."

"You are being properly rewarded for your efforts, aren't you?"

"Yes, sir. I am very satisfied with our arrangement."

"Bear with me, then, Tucker. Weldon will be persuaded. I'll decide the means of persuasion. And when the time comes, you will carry out the plan, just as in the past."

As usual, Miss Lotus ignored Tucker as he walked through her small office on the way out. In passing, he noted again that her hair, neither brown nor gray, showed no evidence of an attempt at style and added years to her age. Her clothes, echoing that impression, were dark blue and rumpled. Her meek demeanor was at odds with the large desk and all of the accoutrements usual to the workstation of an executive assistant. Rumor had it that she lived alone in a small, comfortable townhouse. Evidently she had never married. Tucker wondered briefly about the relationship between such a mousy creature and Jackson Tootell. He only knew that she had worked for their mutual employer for at least twenty years.

6

Sunday, October 31, afternoon

LOS ANGELES, CALIFORNIA

The Hollywood house was palatial and more lavish than any building Bobby had ever been in. The approach over a long circular drive led to huge wooden double doors. The host, a heavy man in expensive clothes that failed to improve his gross appearance, greeted them when they stepped from the limousine. "So this is the mysterious fellow who will be our next vice president."

Bobby smiled as he shook the man's hand. "I've been called lots of things, but this is the first time I've been called 'mysterious.'"

"Well, you don't look mysterious, now that I've seen you in the flesh." Orville Roesener gestured for Bobby to precede him through the door. "We have lots of people here who think you're kind of a wraith, not real. Let's go meet them."

The large room was filled with people in designer clothes embellished with gold and silver. Each had a drink in hand and seemed more interested in scanning the crowd than in the conversation of the ones standing close by. Most of their eyes turned when Bobby and his entourage walked through the door. There was a slow rush in his direction as several in the gathering tried to be first to reach for his hand. His host and Janine stepped before him to act as an informal screening committee, mentioning names as they handed one and then another of the throng off to the object of their interest.

Bobby suffered through a couple hundred introductions, and his hand was beginning to hurt from all the handshakes. He heard everything from advice about how Weldon should finish the campaign to complaints about politicians' lack of respect for the voters. His eyes were burning from smoke as a stocky, heavily tanned man, whose name Bobby had already forgotten, held him by the arm. "This morning I listened to the things they said about you on the television. By God, if half of it's right, you're our man. We need people of integrity in public office. I'm sure Warren Weldon fits that description and so did Forest Blaine. We're going to win this election, and when we do, things will be different in Washington."

Janine rescued him. She smiled sweetly at Bobby's captor and called him by name, then turned and said, "Bobby, I'm sure you and Josh have lots to talk about, but you asked me to be certain you had time to refresh yourself before you face the multitude." She turned again to Josh and said, "You'll forgive me if I drag him away. After all, we want him to make his best appearance in front of those who haven't gotten to know him."

"Of course, of course. Give Simpson hell, Bobby. You've got my vote. Now go get the rest of 'em."

When they were out of Josh's hearing, Bobby turned to Janine with a quizzical look. "Got his vote? Hell, I ain't running for anything."

"It's just his way of saying he approves of you." She led him by the arm through more of the crowd who wanted a word with the new celebrity, saying to each, "Sorry, time for Bobby to get ready for his speech." Each of them smiled and waved. Many calls of "Good luck" and "Go get 'em, Bobby Hobaugh" followed them out of the room.

After a limo ride to the auditorium, Bobby waited to go onto the platform. He gazed at Janine who was talking to one of the local politicians, making that fellow feel important. She was tall and slender, with a figure that caught the eye of every male who passed by. Her dark hair was worn long and combed away from her face. Her business suit was perfectly tailored and, even though she had been traveling constantly for days, did not have a wrinkle. She had large, dark eyes with a narrow nose over a full mouth. Her physical appearance, together with her bearing, gave her a self-assured beauty.

Bobby decided she must be between thirty-five and forty years old. She wore no wedding ring, and he wondered absently if she had a boyfriend. His ruminations got no further before three of the local dignitaries surrounded him and escorted him to the podium. Walking away from Janine, he realized he didn't even know her last name.

When Roman Burke called Janine later that evening, his voice didn't have the usual imperious tone. "The Governor's exhausted. He's been hitting it hard the last week and is scheduled to appear tomorrow in both Ohio and North Carolina on his way home to Florida. Then, tomorrow evening, there's the final live television broadcast from Tallahassee. He needs rest and time to get ready. I've persuaded him to skip both Ohio and Carolina. Forget Phoenix. The governor of Arizona said he'd take over for us there and we'll win Arizona regardless."

He paused and Janine heard him clear his throat. "Fly to

Cleveland in the morning and have your guy follow Weldon's schedule there. Then get to Dallas for the afternoon appearance. That should help us hang onto votes in both Ohio and Texas. The polls show that Carolina is solid. And anyway, we can get someone else to fill in. One of the congressmen or the governor."

"My God, Burke. You're asking a lot of a man who's never been involved in a national political campaign. Are you sure Bobby's the one to handle both Ohio and Texas?"

"He's the hot number right now. I think we should stoke that fire some more, just to keep it in the news. We're putting out another press release saying that the Governor is very serious about Bobby Hobaugh as the vice presidential nominee. The web site will show the same thing. We'll ride that horse as far as it can run. "

Janine wondered how it was possible for a person to string so many clichés together. But her mind returned instantly to the conversation when Burke continued, "Weldon's worn out. He can't continue at this pace. This will give him some time to rest so he can be at his best for the final television appearance. Just keep your man, Bobby, going. He's generated a lot of press for us; so far all of it's good. But for God's sake, don't let him say anything foolish! Tell him Governor Weldon appreciates his efforts. Tell him to keep it up." Abruptly, the phone clicked off.

Scowling at the dead phone in her hand, Janine thought about Burke's remarks. Weldon too tired to finish the campaign? That was hard to comprehend. The man had always seemed inexhaustible.

Thank God, Bobby Hobaugh seemed to have interminable patience. She didn't think he would complain about flying from Los Angeles early in the morning for the long trip to

Cleveland. Ralph Phillips would revel in it. Ralph seemed to be having the time of his life. They both were, she decided, genuinely likeable men.

Bobby and his three handlers watched Headline News before retiring. The bleached blond woman on CNN seemed to be reading straight from the press release.

> "In a statement issued this afternoon, Governor Weldon claimed his victory is ensured. In addition, he said that he is strongly considering Bobby Hobaugh as his choice for vice president. The actual choice will, however, not be made until after the election. The governor stated that Hobaugh has the qualities that he wants in the man who is his vice president. Those qualities are integrity and character."

Saturday, October 31, afternoon

CAMBRIDGE, MASSACHUSETTS

Allen Ward flashed his handsome smile at Helene Williams, his secretary. "Governor Weldon will be choosing a vice president soon after the election. I have reason to believe he might find me acceptable."

"Why wouldn't he think you're acceptable? You gave him the closest race in the primaries until the lack of money forced you out. Obviously, many voters thought you should be president."

"Well, despite our differences, we like each other. That will be on his mind." Ward shifted in his chair. "Jackson Tootell will also be on Weldon's mind. What do we have on him? Anything that didn't come out in the primaries that would give us some leverage?"

"No, Allen. Nothing new has surfaced. And we can't conduct private investigations. We don't have Tootell's money to spend. We don't have any of his other resources either." She smiled, reached across the desk and patted his hand. "You'll just have to rely on your charm to get the job."

"What about this man Hobaugh we're hearing about? Any information on him?"

"None that didn't come from the television, the net, or the papers. He's an unknown."

"Well, then, perhaps my charm will have to do."

"Once Weldon's election is a certainty, you can put your charm to work. Call him to offer congratulations. That will remind him that you're available

"That's the logical thing to do." Ward seemed to stare into the distance. "Being Vice President wouldn't be so bad. After that, the presidency."

7

Monday, November 1, morning

DETROIT, MICHIGAN

President Simpson was putting on his tie when Tracy Wheat walked through the door to announce that Weldon had changed his schedule.

"What's going on, Tracy?"

"We don't know, sir. The rumor is that Weldon is exhausted. We'll find out pretty soon. The press is hot on it as a possible major story."

"Can we make anything of it? Some kind of flyer over the web?"

"Not until we know for sure what's happening. Maybe then there'll be a way to take advantage of it. But not yet." He looked at his watch. "In the meantime, sir, we need to keep to the schedule."

"I know and I'm ready. What's first on the agenda this morning?"

"Shaking hands and a short talk at another shopping center. Today's glad-handing is important, of course. But you should rest to be ready for the television appearance tonight. The election may be won or lost on that speech."

"You're right. I've got the speech ready, but I'll need to go over it several times to be sure I can give it the right touch." He finished with the tie and turned to Wheat. "How is the vice president doing? He's in Philadelphia, isn't he?"

"Yes, sir. He's been going hard and is really helping the campaign with his appearances. But he has the same problem you have. The reporters just keep asking him about Bobby Hobaugh."

"Well, we can't stop the reporters from asking their questions." He gave his tie one final jerk and started for the door. "Be certain that enough time is available toward the end of the day for me to rehearse the speech."

Monday, November 1, morning

LOS ANGELES, CALIFORNIA

Bobby had grumbled as he was hustled to the airport that Monday morning well before daylight. Ralph, sitting beside him in the limousine, made light of the change in plans. "Hell, Bobby, you've got that speech down to perfection. Another time or two won't kill you. Besides, Janine has ordered another suit for you that'll be ready when we get to Cleveland. She thinks the one from San Francisco is getting too much face time with the media. Don't want 'em to think you're a country bumpkin with only one suit of clothes."

"Ralph, I am a country bumpkin." He heaved a sigh, "You know, the only thing that keeps me going is the fact that we're finished tonight, no matter what. Tomorrow's Election Day. I want to be home in Miles City to vote. How're we going to get back to Montana from Dallas?"

Janine, seated on Bobby's other side, crossed her legs

as she turned toward them. "We don't need as large an airplane now as we did when Senator Blaine was alive, so Burke is sending a Cessna Citation to fly us to Cleveland and on to Dallas. I've arranged for the plane to take us back to Denver from Dallas and then fly on to Billings with you two. Don't worry about it. Just keep charming the voters through this evening. Then you're done." She paused and grinned, "Unless Weldon picks you for vice president."

Bobby didn't smile.

Monday, November 1, afternoon

DALLAS, TEXAS

The crowds had been large and enthusiastic in Cleveland and a sense of victory was in the air. Lance, who was in constant contact with members of the press, reported that the news people were already wondering about Weldon's sudden change in plans. Despite that concern, all four of them were at ease and cheerful during the flight to Dallas. Only a small group of reporters met the plane as it parked in the space reserved for private aircraft some distance from the main terminal, so Janine relaxed her vigilance. It was a mistake. Bobby stopped when one of them yelled, "Hey, Bobby Hobaugh, if you are chosen for VP, what's the first thing you'd do if Weldon is elected and, before his term ends, dies?"

Bobby turned to look at the questioner, thought for a moment and said, "I do not expect either of those things to happen, but I think that the first concern of anyone in that position would be to do the compassionate things for the deceased president's family, the things necessary to give them as much comfort as possible. Next, and most important, would be to give notice to the entire world that there would be no immediate change in our foreign policy. Any government or tyrant who tried to take some advantage of the period of transition would suffer the consequences. Finally, the citizens of the United States, especially those in the business community, would need assurance that there would be no abrupt change in domestic policy. It's important, at such a time, to eliminate any feelings of uncertainty about fiscal and economic matters."

Before he could say more, Janine, on one side, and Lance, on the other, dragged him to the waiting automobile. Ralph lagged behind long enough to say to the reporters, "We've been telling you Bobby's a thoughtful individual. That's why Weldon has him in mind for vice president."

Once they had Bobby in the automobile, Janine turned to him with a scowl and grumbled, "We told you not to talk to reporters."

Bobby's eyebrows went up. "Answering the question just seemed to be the polite thing to do."

The response seemed so innocent that Janine had to laugh. "Well, the answer shouldn't hurt Weldon's chances. But please don't scare me like that again."

Ralph grinned at her. "I told you Bobby could handle himself. His remarks, if they're reported, will just make Weldon's focus on him as vice president more understandable."

Instead of a large limousine, the vehicle waiting for them at the Dallas-Fort Worth airport was a standard four-door sedan. The driver apologized by telling them the limousine rented for the occasion broke down. Janine found herself squeezed in the seat between Ralph on her right and Bobby on her left. She had developed a feeling of fondness for Bobby in the short time since they met. Now, with their shoulders and thighs rubbing together each time the taxi swerved, she began to think about a relationship that might be more than friendship.

She glanced up at his profile and decided that he really was a good-looking man. As exhausted as he must be from the demands on him since they left Montana, he remained calm and patient. It had startled her the first time he held a chair for her. He was not only a gentleman but a courtly one at that. There was the slightest of chances that he might be vice president. If so, he would need a chief of staff. She would be the logical choice for the position, of course. Perhaps the professional relationship would lead to something more intimate. In Washington D. C., Bobby Hobaugh would need a wife. At that thought, she almost reached over and patted him on the thigh but stopped herself, and drew her hand back to her lap.

The reality of the situation—and her sanity—returned to her. Bobby Hobaugh would not be vice president. He would return to his ranch and law practice in Miles City, Montana. She had no desire to follow him to that cow-country wasteland. How could she even think of such a thing as marriage to Bobby Hobaugh? The only explanation was pure exhaustion from the rigors of the campaign. If her mind was so addled as to harbor thoughts of marriage, it was a good thing the election was tomorrow. The day after tomorrow, she could rest.

Bobby had the speech down pat. The crowd, wild with election fervor, whooped and hollered when he walked off the platform in Dallas at seven in the evening. Janine and Lance rushed him from the convention center, past the reporters to the automobile and then on to the hotel. They wanted no worrisome repeat of his impromptu performance at the airport.

Weldon's final television appearance was scheduled for eight o'clock, so they delayed the flight home and watched it in the hotel suite. Bobby was back in his brown pants and Ralph was wearing gray slacks and a black cardigan the staffers had found for him in Los Angeles.

Lance sat quietly in a tee shirt and chinos. Even Janine had changed to tailored slacks and a soft ivory blouse over which she wore a rose colored sweater. While relaxing and savoring the thought that the hard, tiring work of the campaign was over, they suffered through the usual collage of television preliminaries. The repetition of the blathering was numbing. At last, the upper torso of Warren Weldon filled the screen.

The candidate for President of the United States was seated before a bland wall that had only some bookshelves and a flag to break its monotony. While Weldon's posture was erect and his voice was strong, it was apparent to Janine that something about the man had changed. This was not the forceful individual who appeared on television so often during the campaign. His cheeks were shrunken, and his face appeared colorless despite the carefully applied makeup.

Janine inhaled and stared at the screen. In all the campaign sessions she'd attended, Weldon had been robust and forceful, tolerating no personal criticism nor any criticism of his ideas. Her first instinct was to wonder what caused the changed appearance. Then the effect it might have on the voters came crashing into her thoughts. Would voters, who didn't know the governor the way that she did, look at the man as he now appeared and wonder if voting for him was a wise thing to do, especially with the vice presidential matter unsettled.

Her distaste for Roman Burke led her first to blame him.

Why had he let Weldon appear at all? Any excuse should have been used to avoid it. Then she acknowledged it wasn't Burke's fault. He couldn't control the governor.

Janine looked across at Lance to assess his reaction. His face was a picture of astonishment.

She turned to Bobby and saw a quizzical look. Ralph was grim-faced and his grip on the arms of his chair was fierce. A possible disaster stared out at them from the television screen.

Their concerns were magnified after they watched Arthur Simpson, one hour later. He projected the image of a youthful, forceful, and confident leader. The president's speech contained just the right mix of self-congratulation for past accomplishments and promise of future achievements. The acknowledgment of his reputation as a conniver, who looked first to his own welfare before the needs of the nation, coupled with a promise that he would make that perception disappear if re-elected, was most effective.

When Simpson finished, Janine rose from her chair and turned off the television. Then she stood by the set, looking first at Lance, then at Bobby, finally at Ralph.

Ralph spoke for all of them when he said, "I don't know what's happened to our man but after what we just saw, this election isn't a sure thing any longer."

Monday, November 1, evening

ATLANTA, GEORGIA

Jackson Tootell sat alone in the den of his palatial home in Buckhead and stared at the huge television screen. When Governor Weldon finished speaking, he muttered, "Why in hell did you ever appear on the tube, you damn fool?"

When Tucker answered the telephone, Tootell growled, "Use all of our resources to get out the vote for Weldon."

Monday, November 1, evening

CAMBRIDGE, MASSACHUSETTS

Allen Ward, watching Weldon's speech with Helene Williams, noticed a difference in the presidential candidate, too. His observation was pragmatic. "Well, Weldon may not win, and then I won't need to think about the vice presidency."

Tuesday, November 2, morning

MILES CITY, MONTANA

After the long flight from Dallas to Billings, Bobby drove 135 miles through the night to Miles City. Near dawn on Election Day, he arrived at his ranch house. The old worn davenport in his den beckoned. Too tired to undress, he fell asleep in two minutes, still wearing the wrinkled brown clothing. Two hours later Bobby awoke. The bathroom mirror, revealing dark shadows under bloodshot eyes, told him how wearing the campaign tour had been. After a shower and shave, his bones still ached. Assured that he appeared presentable, he climbed into his car for the short drive back to town and to the law office.

Since the polls were open, he decided to cast his vote before beginning the day's labors. Comfortable in a different brown suit, he started the walk down the street toward the courthouse polling station. It took a long time for him to make the four-block journey because each person he met along the way wanted to visit. Most wanted to know if he was going to be vice president. At the courthouse he greeted the election judges and clerks and was handed a ballot. When he came out of the voting booth, he found a television crew from one of the Billings stations with a camera pointed his way. Bobby grinned, waved, and responded to the questions. "Yes, I voted for Warren Weldon for president. Yes, I expect Governor Weldon to win. No, I don't expect to be vice president."

The offices of Bobby Hobaugh, Attorney at Law, were in a two-story stone building that fronted on Main Street. Two small apartments were on the second floor. Bobby's office complex consisted of six rooms on the ground floor. In the front was a large open area furnished with chairs for clients, side tables holding magazines, and coffee table books to entertain the clients if they were required to wait to see a lawyer. A long counter faced the doorway. The receptionist sat at a secretarial work station behind the counter. To the back of the room was a wide opening into a lighted hallway that led to other offices and work areas. Bobby's private office was at the end of the hallway near the back of the building. It was a large room, furnished with a wide desk, credenza, and shelving along two walls holding the Pacific Reporter and Montana Reports. Charlie Russell prints graced the other two walls.

The same gauntlet of people wanting to talk about the vice presidency harried him on his return along the street. On entering the office door, he found the waiting room filled with people, all of whom were interested in the election and his future. One tiny, old woman, almost in tears because she was sure her dead husband's estate would never be settled, begged Bobby to finish it before he ran off to Washington. He sat down beside her, put his arm around her shoulder and said, "Now Eleanor, the estate is finished except for the judge's signature, and we'll get that next week. And Eleanor, I'm not going anyplace, anyway." He gave her a hug.

Margaret Lisa, his office manager, reached for his elbow and dragged him through the throng, past the receptionist who tried to ask if he would take incoming calls, and on to his office in the back of the building where he sank wearily into the large chair behind his desk. "Now," she demanded, hands on hips, "tell me what's been going on. What's all of this talk about you being vice president?"

Bobby looked across the desk at the woman with whom he had worked comfortably for more than ten years. At forty-six years of age, her round face remained smooth and unblemished with the appearance of a perfect summer tan. Gray was starting to show in her long, coal black hair, gathered gracefully at the nape of her neck. The small, classic figure she possessed ten years ago was thickening slightly at the waist. Now she required glasses for reading. Other than that, Bobby thought, she hadn't changed much since she first walked into his office to ask for help in divorcing her husband who was a chronic drunk. A year later, she returned to apply for a job as a receptionist.

Bobby soon realized her intelligence and ability were wasted answering a telephone. Over time, he had delegated more and more responsibility to her. Now she coordinated the activities of his associate, Russell Harrington, two paralegals, two word-processor operators, and a receptionist who also acted as billing clerk. In addition, Margaret worked closely with the ranch manager to ensure that Bobby's time was used efficiently at both the law office and the ranch.

"Margaret, I'm not going to be vice president. All of that is just talk. Once Warren Weldon is elected...," He paused, thinking of the television performance of the night before, and continued, "if he's elected..., he'll choose someone with credentials for the job." Bobby leaned back in the chair with his hands high above him in the air and stretched. "Ralph Phillips roped me into that escapade. It was an interesting experience but damn tiring."

"You shouldn't try to see any clients today, or even return any phone calls. Most people just want to talk about this vice president business anyway. There's nothing that can't wait 'til tomorrow."

"You're right. I think I'll sneak out the back way and go to the ranch for a nap. I have to be at the Miles City Club for the Republican victory party this evening. Unless I get some rest, I may fall asleep during the festivities." He sat forward and asked, "Would you like to go to the party with me? We can leave early if you don't enjoy what's going on." It was an impetuous invitation, spoken almost without thought.

Margaret crossed her arms and pondered for a moment. She often ate lunch with her employer and sometimes traveled with him for depositions but had always made certain that nobody thought of their association as anything but business. After a heartbeat or two, she decided that it would not appear as something personal if they arrived at a political function together.

"That might be interesting. I've never been to one of those affairs." She smiled and added, "I've always thought of myself as a Democrat. Will they let me in?"

"Sure, they'll let you in. Maybe we can change your politics."

Her laugh was quiet. "Not much chance of that." As she turned to leave, she asked over her shoulder, "Should I meet you there?"

"No, I'll pick you up." He raised his eyebrows and continued, "Would you like to have dinner first?"

Now, Margaret thought, it's beginning to sound like a

date, but she knew that Bobby didn't look at it that way. "That would be nice, but not at the Club. How about Gallaghers?"

"Any place you suggest is fine."

"What should I wear?"

"Anything you wear to the office will do. You always look nice. I especially like the light gray suit with the belt and red sweater that you were wearing the day I left on that crazy cross-country trip." He gazed at her for a moment before looking down at the clothes he had on. "I guess I'll just wear a brown suit, but one that hasn't traveled the whole country. That's what everyone expects of me."

Margaret walked to the door as Bobby rose from behind the desk. She turned to ask, "Will Weldon win?"

"I thought it was a sure thing until last night. But his appearance on television may change the minds of lots of voters. Maybe he shouldn't have appeared on television at all." He glanced back before he opened the door into the alley. "We'll find out tonight."

As he walked to his car, Bobby thought about her reluctance to be seen with him at places other than those involving legal matters. He wondered, could she still be concerned about acceptance in the white community?

The Republicans gathered on election night in the old Miles City Club. All of the local Republican candidates were there, as well as the precinct committeemen and women. People from town and the ranch community wandered in as the evening went along. One cattleman, a man of ancient age, approached Bobby to ask, "Aren't you runnin' for the state senate again? I looked for your name on the ballot, but it wasn't there."

"I'm a holdover, Jake. I don't have to run this time."

"Well, if you're gonna be vice president of the United States, you won't be spendin' time in Helena, that's for sure."

"I'm not going to be vice president, Jake. But if it ever happens, I'll invite you to Washington for the inauguration."

"Would you, Bobby? By God, that'd be nice. Don't you forget now." Jake cackled as he ambled off into the crowd.

As the local votes were tallied, poll watchers phoned in the earliest returns for races for county offices. The crowd heard scattered radio reports of early returns from around Montana on the race for Governor. But most of the interest was on the presidential election.

A large television set was perched high in a corner so the screen could be seen from any part of the room. It's volume was blasting. The initial exit polls from the eastern states were reported at about four o'clock in the afternoon, but the first tallies of actual results were not reported by CNN, Fox, and the other networks until after eight o'clock.

As expected, Simpson won Connecticut, New Hampshire, Rhode Island, and Massachusetts. Of the New England states, only Vermont went for Weldon. The huge block of electoral votes in New York went to Simpson. With the returns from those states, Simpson held a large lead in electoral votes as well as the popular vote. There were groans from some in the crowd, and the skeptics began to complain that the Democrats had won the presidency again.

Then reports from the southeastern states, the Carolinas, Georgia, and Weldon's home state of Florida, began to trickle in, and the electoral vote tally moved toward the challenger. A cheer went up when Weldon surged into the lead for the first time.

With the closing of the polls in the Midwest, the electoral vote count again approached a balance. Simpson won in Illinois, Iowa, Ohio, and Michigan while Weldon came out ahead in Missouri, Indiana, and Wisconsin. Bobby Hobaugh heaved a big sigh of relief and put his arm around Margaret's shoulder and gave her a hug when the Texas count showed Weldon the winner in that state.

Based upon exit polls, CNN and all the other networks continued to report that the total electoral vote remained in doubt long after the polls had closed on the West Coast. It was not until the early morning hours that the California votes were completely tallied. Weldon carried California. When Alaska's three were added to his total, Weldon had 283 electoral votes with only 270 needed to win. At about four o'clock in the morning, in a short televised address, President Simpson conceded the election to his opponent.

The tired, groggy crowd of Republicans in Miles City listened, cheered as wildly as their condition would allow, and then streamed out the door. Bobby drove Margaret to her apartment, stopped at the curb, and opened the car door for her. As she stepped out onto the curb, he said, "The night's gone. The office can get along without you, at least until this afternoon, so stay home and rest."

"Thanks for the suggestion, Bobby. But I'll be there at the usual hour." She patted his arm. "It was fun to watch the great American electoral process in action. And I'm glad your man won." With a tired giggle, she added, "When you're vice president, will you take me on a private tour of the White House?"

Wednesday, November 3, afternoon

DENVER, COLORADO

Services for Senator Blaine were held in the grand old St. John's Episcopal Cathedral, located in the Capitol Hill neighborhood of Denver. Janine thought the service was much like those she remembered from the Catholic Church of her youth, now all but forgotten. At the special request of the Senator's widow, Janine sat in the second row behind the members of the Blaine family. Across the aisle were members of the United States Senate, both Democrats and Republicans, as well as the Governor of Colorado and other dignitaries. She was surprised that President Simpson was there with the first lady at his side. President-elect Weldon was not in attendance. He had sent a short message of condolence to Mrs. Blaine, adding that the pressing business of transition prevented him from attending.

Janine, resting after the services in her small apartment, turned on the TV. The news organizations were focused on the failure of the president elect to make any public appearances since Election Day. To fill the void, Roman Burke made the rounds of the televisions news stations.

Burke was speaking on CNN to commentator Allen Thistead .

> "As you must surely understand, Allen, preparing for the transition is a serious and time-consuming activity. The President's schedule is fully taken up with that task. He believes that having the proper team is in place before the inauguration must take precedence over everything else."

> "That's understandable, of course." Allen answered. "Has Mr. Weldon decided upon a vice president? The whole country is waiting to hear who that person might be.

> "No, Allen, I can only report that several well qualified individuals are under consideration."

> "Is Bobby Hobaugh among them?"

> "Of course," he said smiling. "Also among those under consideration are three women."

> Allen raised his eyebrows. "Our viewers will surely want to know who they are. Can you give us their names, Sir?"

> "Not at this time."

> "Well, thanks, anyway, for taking the time to visit our studio, Mr. Burke.... We turn now to the weather."

Janine clicked the remote and stared for a moment at the blank screen. She muttered to herself, "A woman? Damn you, Burke, you could at least tell me what's going on." She stood and rubbed at her arm. "The bloggers will be in a frenzy of speculation." Another quick rub. "Well, none of it affects me anymore. Let that man Weldon make his own choice. He'll never get another with the fine qualities of Forrest Blaine."

Laws of the United States

The electors of President and Vice President of each State shall meet and give their votes on the first Monday after the second Wednesday in December next following their appointment at such place in each State as the legislature of such State shall direct.

10

Thursday, November 4, afternoon

BILLINGS, MONTANA

Ralph Phillips scanned a newspaper as he finished a solitary, late lunch in the restaurant on the ground floor of the building that held his office. From time to time he glanced at the television set high in one corner of the bar area, tuned to a rerun of a football game. He happened to be watching when the game disappeared from the screen and a somber-faced reporter appeared.

"We interrupt this broadcast for a special report. President-elect Warren Weldon is dead." The speaker paused. "We just received word that Warren Weldon died this morning of a massive heart attack. Weldon, Governor of Florida, was chosen only two days ago as president of the United States. It was reported that the governor was suffering from exhaustion toward the end of the campaign and that he had canceled several appearances as a consequence. Early this morning, he was rushed to a hospital in Tallahassee where he was pronounced dead on arrival. Again, President-elect Warren Weldon is dead. Stay tuned for more information as it becomes available."

Ralph remained quietly in his chair for a minute or two, digesting the news. Then he stood and pulled money from a clip to drop on the table as payment for his meal. He hurried to the elevator, head down in thought, and rode to his office on the fifth floor. In the small reception area, he said to his secretary, "I need to speak with Janine Paul in Denver as soon as possible. I don't know her phone number, either at home or at work. She's been on the staff of Senator Forest Blaine, so she may be wrapping things up at his headquarters. Try there first." As he turned toward his private office he added, "This is extremely important, so I don't want any phone calls or visitors until I speak with her."

While waiting for the call, he sat with his elbows on his desk and thought about the events of the past few days. Warren Weldon had pleaded exhaustion when he canceled campaign activities. During the final television speech his appearance was ghastly. The most peculiar thing, however, was his failure to appear again in public to acknowledge the victory. His staff issued a press release thanking the public for their confidence in him and stating he was considering cabinet appointments and was not available for interviews. His campaign manager, Roman Burke, had been busy responding to the cries of the press and covering for Weldon. That was it. Now the world knew that he had been dying at the very time the voters were electing him president.

Ralph let his mind wander back to his schoolboy study of the Constitution. On Election Day the voters of the country cast their ballots for president and vice president. At least that is what most of them think they are doing. In actuality they are voting for electors who then select a president and vice president. Each of the political parties in the various states chooses its own electors. Each state has the same number of electors as it has representatives in the House of Representatives plus its two senators. By law in Montana, and probably in most of the states, the electors are obligated to vote for the party nominee, so the position of elector is largely ceremonial. If the Republican candidate for president receives the largest number of popular votes in Montana, the Montana Republican electors then cast their ballots for him—or, if the nominee is a woman, for her. He, Ralph Phillips, is one of the state's three Republican electors. Warren Weldon had received the most votes in Montana.

He turned his back to the desk and stared out the window. Weldon was dead. Blaine was dead. Weldon had never formally chosen a running mate. Who was he, as a presidential elector, to vote for when it came time to cast his ballot?

He grabbed the phone on the first ring, but before he could speak, Janine said, "Ralph, what's going to happen now with both Weldon and Blaine dead?"

"I know what the constitution tells us is supposed to happen, but I don't know yet how it's really going to work. We'll have another election campaign, only this time there are just 283 voters, the 283 electors who were committed to vote for Warren Weldon. I'm one of 'em."

Janine thought about it for a moment. "With Weldon dead, can you vote for just anybody?"

"Yup, I believe I can." Before she could ask any more questions he said, "Listen, maybe you, Bobby, Lance, and I can do some more interesting things. Could you get the names and addresses of all of the presidential electors from the Republican National Headquarters?"

"I suppose they have that information. I don't know what you have in mind, but I'll call them and ask." Then after a pause, "What do you have in mind?"

"I have some calls to make. Then we need to get together. If I fly down there tomorrow or the next day, could you and Lance be available?"

"Of course we can. With Senator Blaine dead, neither one of us has a job at the moment, other than to finish up here in his office and clean it out. We still have some campaign funds left on hand. We have to figure out what to do with the money."

"Find out the names of the electors, if you will. I'll call you again to make the arrangements for us to get together. In the meantime, I'll make those other calls."

Ralph's next call was to Dallas, Texas.

"Mr. Saylor? This is Ralph Phillips from Montana. We've met in the past at oil and gas meetings in Denver."

"Hell, yes, Ralph. I know you. And my name's Dick, for God's sake, not Mr. Saylor. I saw you across the room when you were here last Monday with that man Bobby Hobaugh. I tried to catch you for a visit, but you got away."

"Sorry we missed each other." Ralph's voice turned serious. "I believe you're one of the Republican electors from Texas, aren't you?"

"Yes, I am. And isn't it hell about Weldon? It was bad enough when we lost Blaine."

"That's the reason for my call. I'm an elector here in Montana. We've got another election on our hands, and before this day is out, you and I and all the other electors will be besieged by telephone calls."

"That's a certainty. Everyone who ever thought of being president will want to give us a pitch."

"It seems to me it would be wise to have a position established when the calls come. We need to say that we have a man in mind for the job, someone kind of neutral. Then we can take our time in deciding who the next president will be.

We won't have to commit ourselves to anyone too soon."

The tone of Saylor's gravelly voice revealed his interest. "It certainly makes sense to avoid committing ourselves too early." Saylor paused and Ralph could almost hear him thinking. "I believe that two names will shake out as the likely choices—Allen Ward and Jackson Tootell. Ward is a Harvard liberal, in my view. And Tootell scares the hell out of me."

"Neither of those guys turns me on." Ralph swiveled in his chair. "Let me suggest we use Bobby Hobaugh as our stalking horse. We can just say we're leaning toward him. Then we won't be locked into anyone else, at least for a while. We'll have time to give careful consideration to the final choice."

"By God, I liked your man, Bobby. That speech he gave down here was a stem-winder. But what I liked best was the answer he gave to the reporter at the airport. You remember, the reporter asked what was the first thing he'd do if the president died. It's clear to me that he's thoughtful, not one to go off half-cocked. We could do worse than him for president." Ralph could hear Saylor's chair squeak as he moved around. "Your idea seems reasonable. I'll call the others here in Texas and tell them what we've cooked up. I know one of the electors in California, one that I think has influence with the others. I'll call him, too. Maybe we can get some of those California people in line."

"The only other elector I feel comfortable calling is a man in Indiana named Harley Smith. We went to grade school together a long time ago, but we've kept in touch. I'll try to reach him right now."

"Good, get on it. It's nice talking to you, Ralph. Keep me informed."

Ralph hung up, wondered for a moment if he should call Bobby and tell him what he had done, then thought better of it. He'd let Bobby know after more arrangements were made.

Instead he called Harley Smith in Terra Haute, Indiana. The conversation with Smith mirrored the one with Saylor. He, too, agreed to canvas the other electors in his state, and he agreed to call a friend in Missouri.

Then Ralph called Janine again.

"Janine, every one of the people who were candidates for the Republican nomination will be trying to grab the brass ring. You remember that Allen Ward and Jackson Tootell ran neck and neck and second to Weldon in the primaries. They're the ones most of the electors will remember and think about."

"Good Lord, Ralph. We don't want either one of them!"

"I certainly don't."

"What about some of the others, Tom Hansen, for example?"

Ralph grunted. "You know what ruined his chances? He's an alley cat. One affair with a teenager may not have been too much for the people to swallow, but there were seven women and none of them very savory. Do you remember that one of them called him 'Dimple Knees' in a television interview?"

Janine said, "Yuk!" Then added, "You're right about that. What do you have in mind? You didn't call me twice to pass the time of day."

"Okay, here it is. I think we should promote Bobby Hobaugh as a stalking horse, at least in the beginning. I've already talked to Dick Saylor from Texas and Harley Smith from Indiana. They're both electors, and they're both receptive. Saylor is going to call a friend of his in California to see if he can get some of the California electors in line. Harley Smith will call a friend in Missouri." He shifted the phone to his other ear. "Neither of them is very hot about Ward or Tootell. I suggested we just tell everyone that we're leaning toward Bobby Hobaugh. That way we won't commit to anyone right away."

Janine took a breath. "Okay, what do you want from me?"

"First, call Bobby and tell him he's going to be a candidate for president. If I do it, he'll just laugh. You have national connections so he's more likely to take you seriously. Besides, I think he really got to like you while we were traveling together."

"Oh, get off it! He'll just laugh at me too, or maybe just hang up."

"No, he won't. He's too polite to do that. Tell him what we have in mind and just keep talking. Answer his questions. It's mighty important, so do what it takes. We're talking about the choosing of the next president of the United States."

"All right, I'll call as soon as I hang up, but I expect he'll tell me we're crazy. What's his number?" Ralph gave it to her, and she said, "Be ready for a call from him. He'll know where this came from." She started to hang up the phone but asked instead, "What else can I do?"

"I don't know exactly. That's why we need to get together, tomorrow if possible. If I fly to Denver, can you and Lance meet me at the airport?"

"Just let us know the time."

"Your national connections will be important. We'll need Lance to handle press relations." A thought came to Ralph. "You must know Weldon's people pretty well. Could you call one of them to find out what they're thinking, now that Weldon's gone?"

"I guess I can call Roman Burke, Weldon's right hand man. He and I aren't the best of friends, but he knows the turf in Florida."

"That'll be great." Ralph moved the phone to his other hand so he could scribble the name on his desk pad. "See if he'll come to Denver tomorrow, will you? It would be nice if we could persuade him to join us in supporting Bobby."

"Roman Burke hates me. He's always rejected anything I've suggested. But I'll call him and ask if he'll join us." Then she chuckled into the phone. "It doesn't sound to me like you are thinking of Bobby as a stalking horse. You believe you might be a king maker—or president maker."

"Who knows what's going to happen? But I sure don't have anything to lose. Since Blaine's gone, you don't have anything to lose either. Let's give it a go. You may end up in the White House yet."

Janine had a melodious laugh. "Nice thought. I'll call your cowboy friend right now."

With the phone in its cradle, Ralph sat back in his chair, crossed his legs, and clasped his hands behind his head. He cast his gaze around the office, taking in the polished veneer wall finishing, the expensive drapes beside the windows, and the deep, plush carpeting. He reached down and ran his hand over the granite surface of his huge desk. One by one his eyes sought out the pieces of expensive and original western art-work, both oil paintings and sculpture, that graced the room. It was a long way from the shack at the foot of the Sweet Grass Hills in northern Montana. Ralph smiled and he thought, "I ain't done bad for a little guy."

Then his thoughts turned to his long association with Bobby Hobaugh. They had an effective working relationship in the Montana Senate. Ralph was the point man on legisla-tion that concerned them. He was usually first to recognize provisions in a bill that would, in his estimation, be injuri-ous to the state. He was generally the one who suggested the wording of an amendment to modify the bill and make it harmless. "Heal it up" was the term he used when explaining his thinking to Bobby. But it was always Bobby who talked to the sponsor of the bill and, using his soft voice and gentle manner, explained the wisdom of the amendment. It was always Bobby who sought out other senators who might need persuading and quietly secured their support. Finally, it was Bobby who rose during senate debate to defend the action they were proposing. With his easy, comfortable speaking style and the respect in which other senators held him, Bobby could, more often than not, convince a majority to vote for the amendment. Ralph chuckled at the remembrance of a quip by a senior lobbyist, "Senator Phillips is the conniver and Senator Hobaugh is the persuader—together they're unbeatable."

Ralph's thoughts returned to the present situation. Janine was right. He did want to be a president maker. The nearly inconceivable death of both Republican nominees made that a possibility. It wasn't likely that Bobby Hobaugh could be turned into a real candidate for president—even with his remarkable ability to charm the world—but with Bobby as a stalking horse, Ralph was sure he could influence, if not dictate, the ultimate choice. He was enjoying that thought when the phone rang.

Bobby's voice reflected his impatience. "Ralph, enough is enough. I went along with that vice president fiasco because I thought it might help Weldon and the party. But this business that Janine Paul just called about is insane."

"Calm down, friend. I've talked to some of the other electors, and we've decided that we need a stalking horse. They've all agreed you should be the one. It doesn't mean you have to go on a nationwide campaign or anything like that. Just agree to serve if you're chosen."

"I'm not going to be chosen and, damn it Ralph, if you talk me into this, it's going to take a lot of my time. There's too much to do here at the office and at the ranch, and I'm too far behind already because of that trip around the country. I can't be wasting any more time or effort on political foolishness."

"Bobby, just tell me you'll serve as a stalking horse. That's all I need." Ralph laughed into the phone. "Since you're sure you won't be chosen, it isn't much of a commitment."

Ralph waited for what seemed like ten minutes. Bobby finally breathed a deep sigh. "All right, Ralph. But don't let anything start that will require more of a commitment from me than that. The deal is that I'm only a stalking horse. Nothing more. Keep me informed of everything that happens."

"You bet, my friend. You won't be sorry."

Ralph sat and looked at the phone after he put it back in its cradle. He mumbled to himself, "I suppose you're right, Bobby. You won't be chosen. But if you were, you'd be a damn good president."

11

Thursday, November 4, afternoon

MILES CITY, MONTANA

Margaret sat quietly and listened, reading glasses down on the end of her nose, and hands clasped in her lap. "You know," Bobby said, "since I've been in the Montana Senate, Ralph has become my best friend. We have the same interests and enjoy the same things. I suppose the fact that we both lost our wives may have something to do with it." He leaned forward and propped his elbows on the desk. "But this election thing seems to have become an obsession with him. I wouldn't mind if it didn't involve me."

"He said it wouldn't take much of your time, didn't he?"

"Yes, but I know different. If Ralph and the others are to pretend that I'm a legitimate candidate, they'll want me to act like one. That will take time."

"Do you think the ultimate choice will be better if you do what Ralph asks?"

"Probably. The worst thing that could happen, it seems to me, would be for the electors to be stampeded by either Allen Ward or Jackson Tootell. Or by anyone else, for that matter. They need to take their time in deciding who the next president should be. It's as serious a responsibility as anyone can have."

"Then maybe you should do as Ralph asks. Do the things a candidate would do."

Bobby waved his arm. "What about everything that needs to be done here? I can't just forget about my clients. I can't abandon the ranch either."

"Bobby, Russell Harrington can handle most of the legal matters that will come up in the next month or so. And Clint knows all there is to know about the ranch. Think of it this way. You might die tomorrow. If you did, the ranch wouldn't just gather up its skirts and run over the hill and hide. And if you died, your clients would either be satisfied with Russell or go to someone else."

He smiled and reached across the desk toward her. "You're right—as usual."

Margaret paused only briefly, then reached out and patted his hand. "Bobby Hobaugh, you're a good man. The United States should be lucky enough to get you for president."

Thursday, November 4, afternoon

CAMBRIDGE, MASSACHUSETTS

Alan Ward posed the question to the lady seated across the table. "Helene, the situation has certainly changed, hasn't it? With both Weldon and Blaine gone, there's a possibility that I can still be president of the United States."

"There is indeed, Alan, and you should act upon it without delay. Here's a list of the Republican electors with the telephone number, email and snail mail address for each. Wouldn't it be wise to make contact with them—one by one—

right away? Call each one of them on the phone? Or, at least, send a personal email post?"

Helene was intent and it showed on her face. "All the others who want to be vice president will be after them." She paused. "Especially Jackson Tootell."

Ward flashed the winning smile. "What would I ever do without you?" He scanned the list. "I'll begin by calling Daniels in Wisconsin. He was one of my most loyal supporters during the primary campaign. I'm certain he'll give me his vote when it comes time for the electors to cast their ballots. Perhaps he'll even help to line up electors from other states."

Helene stood and returned his smile. "The sooner you get on it, the better. Use your famous charm. Put it to work right now."

Ward rose and stood, hands on hips. "That I can do." The smile widened. " I think my chances are as good as those of anyone else."

Thursday, November 4, evening

WASHINGTON, D.C.

President Simpson listened as Tracy Wheat talked about the electoral process and finally interrupted, "I know all about the electors. Weldon got 283 electoral votes. I got 257. The electors holding those 257 votes will cast their ballots for me no matter what. With Weldon dead, the Republican electors can vote for anyone they choose. They won't vote for me, so why are we talking about it?"

"Mr. President, if fourteen of those Republican electors vote for you, you'll serve another term."

"No Republican is going to vote for me."

"Probably not. But as president you can make some very interesting offers, can't you?"

"You mean try to buy some of those electoral votes?" Simpson steepled his hands under his chin as he thought. He shook his head, "No. That won't work. It would be too obvious. Any Republican elector who voted for me would face too much trouble—and so would I."

"Well, most people have skeletons in the closet. How about if we do a little digging? Maybe some things will turn up to convince fourteen electors that the country will be better off with you in that chair than either Ward or Tootell."

"Good Lord, the thought of either one of them as president makes me sick to my stomach. Especially the thought of Jackson Tootell."

"Then we'd better see if we can prevent either of them from getting the job."

"No. I won't have any part of that. I lost. That's all there is to it. There's no sense in trying to undo the election."

Outside the Oval Office, Tracy Wheat scowled, shook his head, and muttered, "Damn the man and his belief in the legitimacy of the election process." When Simpson was no longer president, he was out of the job he loved, the job that gave him public stature and power. After some more thought, he muttered again, "Well, there's nothing to prevent me from scouting those electors. Who knows what might turn up?"

12

Friday, November 5, afternoon

DENVER, COLORADO

The conference table in Senator Blaine's office suite had a battered look. When they were seated near one end, Ralph looked around at Janine, Lance, and Roman Burke. "We need to think about the people who will be voting in this next election, who they are and what their beliefs are."

Janine held up some pages with a list. "The Republican headquarters sent the names, addresses, and phone numbers of the electors. But that doesn't tell us anything about them."

Ralph reached for the list. "It seems to me we can assume that the electors will be old party stalwarts. The position of elector is usually given as a reward for service. If I'm correct, they'll be much more conservative than the general population, more pragmatic, and little interested in the kind of empty promises that political candidates generally make."

"If that's the case, we'll probably have Jackson Tootell for president." Janine, head tilted, wore a solemn look.

"Not necessarily. There are bound to be some, maybe more than we think, who see Tootell as extreme and dangerous. Those electors would probably support Ward. What I'm afraid of is that the supporters of each of them will take a hard position and refuse to budge. If that happens, we could have a deadlock, with neither of them getting all the Republican votes."

Lance gasped, "My God! Could we wind up with Simpson again after all?"

"Not unless some of the Republican electors decide to vote for him and that isn't likely. It takes a majority of the votes of the electors to choose a president. Even if the Republicans split their votes between two or more people, Simpson won't get a majority."

"But neither will any Republican. What happens then?"

"Let's not think about what happens then. Let's assume that the Republican electors will agree on a candidate and then vote for him. They could, of course, decide to choose a third person, someone other than Ward or Tootell," Ralph answered.

Lance ran his hands over his blond hair and shook his head. "This is hard to believe. We didn't have the real election on November second. The vote of those people on Janine's list is going to be the only one that counts."

Ralph nodded. "That's right. And it's our job to figure out how to persuade them to vote the way they should."

Janine pointed her finger. "Ralph Phillips, you really are trying to play kingmaker." She laughed, "Well, it sounds like fun, so I guess I'll go along. How about you, Lance?"

"Why not?" Lance turned to Ralph. "Okay. What do we do next?"

"Let's think about the things that will concern the electors. First of all, I don't believe they'll give a hoot about candidates' television talk. They're going to want to hear it in person. If I'm right, there's no sense in trying to get Bobby on the tube. We probably couldn't get him to do it anyway."

Lance picked up on the idea. "We need to start sending information about Bobby to each elector and keep it up till the votes are counted. I'll start by faxing or emailing each one of them a copy of Governor Weldon's last press release. You know, the one where he gave the reasons to choose Bobby for vice president." He paused. "And we need a web site. We can use the site to put out new information about Bobby each day. Keep it fresh. I'll get to work on it right away."

"Good. That's the kind of thing that will get the electors' attention." Ralph leaned back in his chair and turned to face Roman Burke. "Mr. Burke, is that all right with you?"

Roman Burke was carefully dressed, tall with an athletically trim build, and swarthy complexion. A hint of beard showed on his firm jaw. He had listened without speaking until Ralph asked the question. He nodded at Ralph and said, "Call me Roman, please." His face remained impassive as he continued, "I think you should know that the Florida electors won't vote for Tootell under any circumstances. A majority of them won't vote for Ward either. That's the reason I'm here. We're looking at a split among the Republican electors, unless another candidate surfaces."

"Why won't they vote for Tootell?" Lance asked.

"You probably remember the things Tootell and his people said about Governor Weldon during the primary campaign, horrible things that had no basis in truth. That was bad enough, but then they spread the story that the Governor's wife was unfaithful. Tootell denied any responsibility for it, but it infuriated the Governor. The people in Florida, where Weldon was extremely popular, haven't forgotten. And they won't forget either."

"Do you share that feeling?"

"You're damn right I do. Tootell is an unscrupulous bastard as far as I'm concerned."

"Will you support Hobaugh as a stalking horse by reminding all of the electors that Weldon was focusing on him as vice president?"

"Yes. I agree, and I will do that. You send out the faxes and emails, and I'll go back to Florida and spread the word among the electors there."

"You can do more than that. Will you lend your name to our communications with all the electors? They know you as Weldon's right-hand man. They'll assume you speak for him, since he obviously can no longer speak for himself."

"You've got it." Burke paused for a moment and then said, "You realize that Florida has twenty-nine electoral votes. Without them, Tootell won't have the 257 votes needed to win, even if he gets every other Republican electoral vote."

"That's true," Ralph said, "but we should still get as many as we can who will support Bobby, and from as many states as possible. The more we have, the greater the likelihood that Tootell—and Allen Ward too—will agree to some compromise candidate."

Janine leaned toward Burke. "I agree. Let's get as many electoral votes in our corner as we can. It will give us more leverage when negotiations begin."

Roman Burke smiled for the first time. "Agreed. I only mentioned the Florida vote count to point out that Tootell isn't going to get the electoral votes needed to win. Frankly, I doubt that Ward can do it either."

Janine favored him with a smile in return. "Florida seems to have a penchant for controlling elections. If I remember my history correctly, Florida cut a deal so that Rutherford B. Hayes became president in 1876 instead of Samuel Tilden."

She smiled again as she added, "And then there was the Bush and Gore fiasco in 2000."

"I guess those of us who live in Florida just have a knack for doing the right thing at election time."

Ralph laughed at Roman's remark. He got up from his chair and stretched. "That plane ride made these old bones stiff, and I have to catch the four o'clock flight back to Billings. Lance, I'll fax Bobby's biographical information to you so you can spread it around among the electors. Send 'em anything else you think will make him look good. Make sure that Janine, Roman, and I get copies, so we know what's going on."

Turning to Burke, he said, "It's nice to meet you and have you on board. I think we'll get along." At the door, he stopped and said, "We'll all be talking on the telephone several times a day, won't we?"

When all heads nodded in agreement, he smiled and added, "Who ever thought we'd be doing this? Four people, deciding who should be the president of the United States."

13

Sunday, November 7, morning

BILLINGS, MONTANA

Seated in the kitchen of his gracious home, Ralph pushed his solitary breakfast dishes to the corner of the table. He watched the television out of the corner of his eye as he opened the newspapers. All the talk shows focused on the "electoral crisis," as the commentators characterized it. Media-savvy lawyers and law professors pontificated about the electoral system, ostensibly as a means of educating the public but really for their own gratification. Political pundits speculated about the ones who might receive Warren Weldon's electoral votes. Most speculation focused on Allen Ward and Jackson Tootell. Despite Lance Caldwell's efforts, the media still didn't take Bobby seriously.

Allen Ward appeared on three of the Sunday talk shows. He preached the same message and made the same promises he made during the primary campaigns. Several others who aspired to be president made noises about their availability. But it appeared, at least to the media, that the electors would choose either Ward or Tootell.

Ralph spread the New York Times and the Washington

Post before him on the table. He found articles featuring the two principal contenders for the presidency. One told of Jackson Tootell's rise from son of a dirt-poor farmer to business tycoon and compared that with the patrician background of Allen Ward. Neither paper mentioned Bobby Hobaugh. "Give us time," Ralph mumbled to himself. "Give us time and you'll both be writing about the man from Montana."

Sunday, November 7, afternoon

ATLANTA, GEORGIA

Tucker listened, posture rigid, to Jackson Tootell, seated at his large desk in the Tootell Tower. "First of all, we must send a brochure, preferably by fax or email, to each elector. The brochure should portray me as the logical choice."

"The brochure is being prepared right now, sir. It will go out this afternoon."

"And the web site. Is it current?"

"Yes, sir. I reviewed it just before I came here."

"Facebook and Twitter?"

"We'll keep current information on each site."

"Good work. Keep our people spreading information about the good things I can do for the country as president. And of course with positive information about me personally." He paused. "Next we need to find out everything there is to know about every one of the Republican electors. Please have that to me as soon as possible."

"I've already started the process, sir. We have much of that information in our computers, left over from the primary campaign. The rest can be gathered from sources such as the records of the Republican National Committee and from local courthouses. After we have that much, we will begin discreet local inquiries about each of them."

"We want information that we can use to persuade, not just general information."

"Yes, sir. We will seek critical information of the kind to which you refer."

"Time is vital. By acting quickly, we can make it appear that my election is inevitable."

"Yes, sir. I understand. The information will be available promptly."

"The other thing we must know is the way each elector is inclined to vote. There's no sense wasting time trying to persuade someone who will vote for me anyway."

"The press will help with that, sir. The media is already hounding the electors, asking about their preferences."

"Tucker, let's not rely on the press. Have our own people do a canvass. That will be our working base from this time on." Tootell's gaze was hard again. "This is the most important thing I've ever undertaken. Let there be no slip-ups."

"I understand, sir."

"One thing more. Even though the general public will have no voice in this next election, it is important that they remember who I am. Arrange for a couple of public appearances—not talk shows—where I can be the main speaker."

"Some trade associations have their annual meetings this time of the year. Perhaps one or more of them?"

"Yes. Something like the Association of Independent Businesses. If I speak at a gathering like that, the press will pick it up. Excerpts will be on the evening news. That's the kind of thing I have in mind." Tootell focused his cold gray eyes on Tucker again. "See what you can do."

As he passed Miss Lotus on his way out, Tucker noticed the odor of alcohol. It wasn't the first time.

14

Monday, November 8, morning

BILLINGS, MONTANA

The call came early, before Ralph left home for his office. "This is Dick Saylor again. I've talked to most of the thirty-nine Texas electors, and they're willing to consider your guy Bobby Hobaugh as a stalking horse. Most of them don't like either Ward or Tootell. But before they commit to anything, they want to talk to Hobaugh. We'd better have him fly down here in the next day or two. If you'll arrange it with Bobby, I'll get most, if not all of our people, to come to Dallas to meet him."

"Bobby made me promise we wouldn't demand too much of his time, but I believe he'll go." Ralph thought for a moment, then said, "But the trip's going to cost money, and we can't expect him to pay for it."

"No, of course not. I'll send our company jet up to get him. We'll put him up in a good hotel." Saylor thought for a minute. "You'd better come too. Is there anyone else who should be with Bobby?"

"Yes. Two people from Blaine's campaign organization,

Janine Paul and Lance Caldwell. They have good national connections. Bobby and I are both country bumpkins and need
that kind of help. They're in Denver so you can pick them up
on the way."

"Sounds good to me." The tone of his voice changed. "You
know, when it comes to politics, California is kind of like two
different states. The electors in L.A. don't think like the folks
in San Francisco. The ones I talked to in Southern California seemed to think our idea for a place-holder alternative to
Ward and Tootell is a good one. Evidently the folks up north
aren't so sure. Anyway, they want to meet Bobby too. Maybe
y'all could fly over there after the Dallas meeting."

Ralph began to worry about his promise to Bobby. "Well,
help from at least some of the California electors would be
nice. I'll talk to Bobby and call you back. It may be tomorrow."

"Tomorrow will be fine." Saylor laughed a hearty laugh.
"By God, Ralph, this sure is fun. I never thought I'd be in a
position to decide who's going to be president of the United
States. A guy could begin to think he's important."

"The electors are important. That's the way the Constitution envisions it. A few people with good judgment are to
choose the country's leader. Let's just hope we do the right
thing and live up to the constitutional requirement.

Monday, November 8, afternoon

TALLAHASSEE, FLORIDA

Throughout the weekend, the body of Governor Weldon had
lain in state in the Florida capitol building. At seven o'clock

Sunday evening, friends and long time associates of the governor gathered in the state senate chamber to share remembrances. Funeral services were held Monday afternoon at the resplendent United Lutheran Church. Roman Burke, who for years had been Weldon's reliable executive assistant, was given a prominent seat directly behind the governor's wife. He was amazed to discover that the president was not in attendance. He'd sent the secretary of state in his place. Nor were there many members of Congress or other prominent Washington figures seated in the long pews. It was a startling contrast to services recently held for Senator Blaine where all of those who were prominent in the political world came to honor him. The widow had, of course, received offerings of condolences from hundreds. Among them were those from the president and from some members of Congress. Still, Roman thought, the showing at the funeral was strange.

When asked by a reporter about the absence of the president from the funeral service, Roman Burke shook his head. "I can't explain it." After a moment he continued, "I just wish they'd shown more respect for Mrs. Weldon."

15

Tuesday, November 9, morning

BILLINGS, MONTANA

While he ate his lonely breakfast, Ralph read through the lead article on the front page of the Billings Gazette in which he and the other two Montana electors were named. He grinned at the description of eighty-year-old Emily Proctor as "a venerable Republican workhorse." The editor would be getting an earful as soon as Emily, who did not think of herself as old, could reach him. Tom Horan was described as "a Gallatin County farmer with little to speak for him other than years of attendance at Republican conventions." Ralph laughed out loud as he read that he was "a senator most noted for his ability to derail legislation proposed by a Democrat."

When he finished reading the article, he called Saylor. "Dick, you should read what they're saying about me in the Billings paper this morning. I just found out I'm both a scoundrel and a conniver."

"I'm not surprised. Our papers discovered us a couple of days ago, and they haven't had a good thing to say about any of us. The editorial made it appear that we're all incompetents, if not crooks, and the only reason we're electors is because we contributed lots of money to the Republican Party."

"Don't feel too proud. The Billings paper just implied the same things about those of us up here."

"What surprises me is how long it took the newspapers to understand that we so-called incompetents are going to choose a president."

Ralph nodded his head as though Saylor could see him. "Let 'em write. They can't hurt us." After only a second, he continued, "If you're still with me, we'll make certain the country gets the best man. To hell with the news folks."

"I'm with you, Ralph. We'll work on that in Dallas."

Wednesday, November 10, morning

BILLINGS, MONTANA

Dick Saylor sounded harried when he spoke. "Ralph, we're catching hell from some of the electors who support Ward and Tootell. They think we're trying to run a whizbang by meeting with Hobaugh and not with them. They want it to be an open forum where all three of them can appear. I think we'd better back off on our plans for a while."

"I had a hard time persuading Bobby to do it anyway. What do you have in mind instead?"

"Ward is running around the country campaigning like this was the general election. I guess he thinks that, by drumming up support among the people, he can influence the electors. You and I both know that isn't the way it works. In any small group of people, a few always lead the others."

"What's Tootell up to?"

"That's a worry. I'm sure you've gotten all of the stuff

he's been sending out. Other than that, he's been quiet."

"He's probably discovered what we have in mind but isn't bothering us yet. I imagine he's working on any electors who aren't already committed to him."

"That makes sense. It's important that we get to the opinion leaders as soon as possible."

"I agree with that." Ralph's mind raced. He was determined to be one of those opinion leaders. "I suggest we gather one or two electors from your state and one or two from California, Florida, Indiana, and Colorado and have a strategy session. We could do it in Denver. Janine Paul can find a place to meet that's out of the way. That way we can keep it quiet."

Saylor hesitated only a second. "You're right. Let's plan on meeting a week from today. You call Harley in Terra Haute and have Janine get the folks from Florida and Colorado in line. I'll bring some Texans and get a couple from California. Let me know the time and place so I can tell the others."

16

Thursday, November 11, morning

ATLANTA, GEORGIA

"What the hell are Weldon's people doing, Tucker?"

"A small group of people, including Roman Burke, who was Weldon's campaign manager, have decided to use Bobby Hobaugh as a stalking horse so they can remain uncommitted. They want to prevent either you or Ward from stampeding the electors, sir."

"Get something on Hobaugh. We need to shut that business down right now."

"We've tried, sir. Strange as it seems, Bobby Hobaugh doesn't have any skeletons that we can find." Tucker never relaxed his rigid posture. "I don't think he's seriously interested in being president. He's just playing the game that others have laid out for him. He'll probably get tired of the charade and drop by the wayside."

"Probably isn't good enough. I want him out of the picture—soon. Figure out a way to get that done."

Tucker nodded, turned on his heel and walked toward

the door. Jackson Tootell stopped him by asking, "Who's really behind Hobaugh?"

"His friend from the Montana senate, Ralph Phillips." Tucker turned again to face his employer. "He's one of that state's three electors."

"What does he do for a living?"

"He has a petroleum exploration and production company."

"If we can get to Phillips, we can be rid of Hobaugh. Can he be bought?"

"I've already investigated that possibility, sir. It doesn't appear he needs money. He's never been involved in anything questionable that we've been able to find. Phillips seems to be as clean as Hobaugh."

There was silence in the room as Tootell stared across the desk at Tucker. Finally he said, "We need to turn Mr. Phillips' attention to something other than this election. Is there a way that can be done?"

"Yes, sir. I've made some inquiries and have a plan in mind."

"Is it something that can be carried out discreetly?"

"Just as you have always required, sir."

"Very well. Move on it." Again Tootell's stare bored into Tucker. "Don't delegate the job to someone else, Tucker. Handle it personally. Let nothing happen that will interfere with my plans."

Miss Lotus smiled a crooked smile and her eyes seemed dreamy as Tucker passed her desk. The odor of alcohol was strong.

Sunday, November 14, night

SALT LAKE CITY, UTAH

"It's done."

"Where are you calling from, Tucker?"

"The phone kiosk at the airport at Salt Lake City. I'll be in Atlanta tomorrow morning and will report in person."

"I'll meet you at the airport so we can discuss it."

Monday, November 15, morning

CUT BANK, MONTANA

Ralph put a finger in his left ear in order to hear Janine on his cell phone. "Ralph, there's a short news item in today's paper about a gas plant that exploded in Montana. Did that have anything to do with you?"

"Yes, it did, Janine. One of my production company's natural gas compressors was sabotaged day before yesterday. One of my men was killed in the blast."

"My God, Ralph, that's terrible. Who caused it?"

"We're not sure yet. I've been here at the site near Cut Bank since last night, meeting with my superintendent and some of my other people. The superintendent is a good man and can handle the cleanup and repair. The local sheriff is looking into the matter. It was obviously deliberate, and there's a murder charge hanging over the one who did it."

"Why would anyone want to do that? It couldn't be linked to the election, could it?"

"I don't see how. Blowing up a gas compressor in Montana isn't going to influence any of the electors."

"I don't suppose so. But it scares me anyway." Before he could put in a word, Ralph heard her take a breath and say, "What if someone just wants to keep you away from Bobby's campaign? If you have to deal with repairs to your distribution system and sabotage, you won't have time to even think about the election."

"My mind hasn't been on the election since I got here." Ralph took a second to contemplate what had happened. "I've met with the dead man's wife. She knows that she and her children will be taken care of. There are workman's comp death benefits, of course, and he had some life insurance. But I'll create a trust fund to supplement those. I want to ensure that the family is comfortable." Ralph stopped, shook his head, and then continued. "God, it's tough. He was really a good worker, a comer, someone who would have accomplished things in his life. She's an intelligent, attractive young woman. Their three children are small." He paused. "Well, I can't bring him back. We just have to hope the authorities catch whoever did it."

Thinking Janine might be right about the tragedy keeping him from the election, he continued. "My superintendent will handle the repairs. If the sheriff needs to talk to me about any criminal activity, he'll call. I don't want to seem crass or unfeeling, Janine, but the election still remains my principal interest. I can't stand the possibility of Jackson Tootell as president. I'm certain the only way to prevent either him or Ward from winning is to work as hard as we can for Bobby."

"That's comforting to hear, Ralph. I feel the same way." After a moment, she added, "If this were an attempt to derail your efforts to defeat Tootell and Ward, it seems to have had the opposite effect."

"You're damn right! I'm going to call Dick Saylor to tell him the same thing."

Saylor's gravelly voice boomed over the phone. "Ralph, do you suppose it was one of those monkey wrench gangs that did it? You know, the crazy eco-green outfits that go around spiking trees and wrecking anything having to do with lumber, ranching, or petroleum?"

"Could have been, I suppose. But they usually do their dirty work near population centers to get the most publicity. Blowing up a gas compressor in Cut Bank, Montana, won't even make the regional news, much less the national news."

"Well, you need any help with things up there, let me know. We oil men have to stick together."

"Thanks, Dick. The support is appreciated, but my people can handle the repairs and get the gas flowing in short order." Ralph shifted the cell phone to his other ear and continued. "The reason for my call is to tell you I'm not slowing down on the election campaign. I still think we have to keep working to get as much support for Bobby as possible."

"That's good to hear. I plan to talk to the electors from California again this morning about the gathering in Denver."

"Keep me informed, will you, Dick?"

"You bet, partner. Hang in there."

17

Tuesday, November 16, morning

CHARLESTON, SOUTH CAROLINA

The face on the television screen was livid with anger. "Ten years ago I was accused of stealing money from the company where I worked. I didn't do it. No charges were ever filed, and no warrant was issued for my arrest. Day before yesterday I got a call from someone telling me I'd better vote for Jackson Tootell. He intimated that if I didn't, the world would be told that I'm a crook."

The talk show host interrupted to ask, "Did he say who he was?"

"No, and he didn't say who he worked for either, but it's pretty plain isn't it? He had to be one of Tootell's henchmen."

"That's a pretty serious allegation. Do you really believe Jackson Tootell would authorize something like that?"

"It happened. You tell me who stands to gain by it."

Tuesday, November 16, morning

ATLANTA, GEORGIA

Tucker stood rigid before his huge desk. Tootell's anger was apparent in his voice. "No excuses or beating around the bush, God damn it. How did it happen?"

"I have no idea who made the call to that elector, sir. I'm confident that none of our people did it. They're all too knowledgeable and have never failed us in the past."

"Well then, who the hell did?"

"I don't know, sir, but we'll know before long. It's possible it was one of Ward's supporters, trying to put you in a bad light."

"What's being done to control the damage?"

"A denial of any involvement was sent out right away. I suggest, sir, that you go on television tonight and deny any knowledge of the matter. Your personal appearance will be more persuasive than anything else."

"Get me on CNN. And be sure it's during prime time." Tootell's look was hard and cold as he added, "Tucker, this kind of thing must never happen again. Do you understand what I'm saying?"

"Yes, sir."

"Then continue to gather information on the Republican electors and provide it to me. I'm the one who'll decide how to use the information, not some flunky."

"I understand, sir."

"And, Tucker, when you find out who made that damn phone call, be certain he suffers the consequences."

Yes, sir. He will have a very real reason to regret that he made the call."

Tuesday, November 16, afternoon

BILLINGS, MONTANA

Ralph arranged the conference call. On the line were Bobby, Janine, Roman Burke, Dick Saylor, and Harley Smith. "It's agreed then? We'll get together Thursday in Denver. Janine will reserve conference space at a hotel near the Denver airport. Janine, you'd better reserve rooms for each of us, too."

"All the reservations are made. If you or any of the others can't make it, please let me know."

Harley broke in. "How many are coming anyway?"

Saylor answered. "We have one from Texas besides me, and three from California. How many from Florida, Mr. Burke?"

"I'll have two electors with me. They're the ones the others will listen to."

Harley spoke again, "I'll bring a woman with me. She's probably the best political operative in Indiana."

Ralph went over the plan one final time. "Bobby won't make any speech. That's right isn't it, Bobby?"

"Yes. I'll just answer questions, but only about the presidency. If we're going to do this, let's keep it focused."

Saylor answered. "We can't control everyone who'll be there, but we'll make your wishes known. I don't think you'll have a problem."

Ralph broke in to ask, "Any questions?"

When no one answered, he said, "Folks, you're going to like Bobby. After this meeting, you'll be able to tell your people they can't go wrong with him."

Bobby's call to Ralph came only a minute after the conference call ended. "Ralph, you told me this wouldn't take any of my time. Now you've got me going to Denver to campaign."

"Well, this shouldn't take more than a couple of days." Ralph laughed and went on, "At least we haven't arranged for you to go to New York to appear on all the talk shows like your competitors are doing."

"Damn it Ralph, those guys aren't competitors of mine. I'm not a candidate, I'm just a stalking horse, remember?"

"Let's get the Denver gathering under our belts. Who knows, you might enjoy it. Janine will be there. She's easy to look at and sure is interested in you."

"She's a good kid, Ralph, but that's it. Don't try to make any more of it." There was a pause. "Unless you're interested in her yourself."

"Don't be a fool, Bobby. She's a head taller than I am. She could carry me around like a pocket watch."

The mental picture of Ralph as a pocket watch made Bobby laugh. "Well, I'll go to Denver, but don't count on anything else from me. After that I'm staying home and tending to business."

"We'll see, Bobby. We'll see." Ralph started to hang up but stopped and spoke again. "What do you think of the guy who said Tootell threatened him?"

"Who knows? I've never met Tootell. What do you think?"

"I think Tootell is capable of anything, but I don't think he's dumb enough for that."

"Or dumb enough to blow up one of your compressors?"

"No. That would really be dumb. No matter how smart he thinks he is, there's always a chance something like that might get out. He wouldn't risk it."

"Probably not, Ralph." The tone of Bobby's voice changed when he asked, "Have you learned any more about who might have caused the explosion?"

"Nothing yet. The state attorney general has his investigators on the job, and he asked the feds to look into it. We'll just have to wait and see what they find."

"It's a hell of a note to have something like that happen in Montana." Bobby sighed. "Well, I'll meet you at the Billings airport Thursday morning."

Ralph's phone rang again almost as soon as he put it down. He answered it to hear Janine say, "I forgot to tell you. Lance's wife had a baby boy last night. That's why he wasn't on the conference call."

"Are his wife and boy all right?"

"They're doing fine. Lance is the one who's exhausted. You'd think he's the one who did it all."

"Congratulate him for me. And tell him I'll expect a cigar next time we see each other."

18

Thursday, November 18, afternoon

DENVER, COLORADO

The room was small and seemed to be filled with people when Bobby and Ralph walked in. Janine grasped Bobby's hand and then introduced him to the ten electors, one after another. Dick Saylor's voice could be heard throughout the room when he and Bobby shook hands. "I heard you talk in Dallas, and I sure liked the things you said. It's good to finally meet you in person."

Bobby smiled up at the man who towered six inches over him. "It's nice to meet you too, sir."

"Now don't give me any of that 'sir' stuff. My name's Dick, and you're to call me that. I expect every person in this room feels the same way. No formalities."

There were nods of assent from the others as Ralph, taking charge, moved to the head of the large conference table and called out, "Let's get on with it."

After everyone was seated, with Bobby at the foot of the table next to Janine, Ralph continued, "You've all met Bobby Hobaugh. He's here to answer questions. If you don't mind,

I'll ask the first one." Gazing at his friend out of hooded eyes, he asked, "Bobby, what's your philosophy of government?"

Bobby sat for a moment, looking back at Ralph, before he spoke. "Government should do for people only those things that individuals can't do for themselves. Things they must join together to do. Such common actions should be at the lowest level of government that is possible."

The large, gray-headed woman from Indiana was quick to ask, "What do you mean by that?"

"Simply that local school boards should run our schools and the national government should take care of foreign policy."

"What about such things as Medicare?"

"That program exists. People depend on it and expect it to continue. The obligation of government is to keep it solvent."

"How does government keep it solvent?"

"Some changes were made in the original program to achieve that purpose. Now, it seems to me, government must avoid any more haphazard additions to the benefits. Some additional changes in the program may be required."

Dick Saylor's loud voice was next. "You said the federal government should handle foreign policy. When would you commit American troops to combat?"

"Only when it is absolutely clear that the interests of the country require it." Bobby leaned forward, arms on the table. "I don't believe we should try to patrol the world, nor can we ensure, with our armed forces, that every person in every country has the same kind of government we have."

"How should we decide when the interests of the country require the commitment of our armed forces in a place where combat may occur?"

"If the situation is grave enough that we must involve our military, then it is grave enough that the rest of us must be willing to sacrifice, at least to some degree. We have no business asking our young men and women to risk their lives while the rest of us go along with no sacrifice at all. We've tried the 'business as usual at home' approach before, and the results weren't good."

"You're referring to Vietnam? Or Iraq? Afghanistan?"

"Yes. They're all good examples of what I'm saying."

A man from California asked, "But what could Lyndon Johnson and George Bush—and even Barack Obama have done? The number of troops just grew as time went along and as the need appeared."

"An even greater reason to measure the ultimate commitment, and with it the sacrifices that the general public should be asked to make, before any initial commitment of troops is made."

"What about the World Trade Center disaster? After that occurred, we committed troops to fight terrorism without asking for the slightest sacrifice from the civilian population."

"That's true. And I believe it was a mistake for the president to lead us into wars in the Middle East without asking the general public to sacrifice along with the troops." He paused in thought. "Well, all of us did sacrifice to a minor degree after the twin towers were destroyed. We put up with travel restrictions, with searches of our belongings, with limitations of some activities at critical locations. But the sacrifices were nothing like those made by the public during the Second World War. The civilian population knew at that time that there was a war going on and were willing to do the things that were asked of them."

"President Bush didn't ask for civilian sacrifices during the war in Iraq, did he?"

"No, he didn't. And neither did Obama in Afghanistan. In my opinion, they should have. Most of the people originally supported President Bush in his desire to create democracies in the Middle East, despite the efforts of some who disagreed with him. I believe the people would have been willing to sacrifice in some way had they been asked." Bobby paused, shook his head, and then concluded, "I just believe this country shouldn't engage in extended military action without a commitment from the entire population."

A man from Florida jumped in. "That guy, Ward, thinks we should give financial aid to every country on earth. What do you think of that?"

"Foreign aid should be given only when the clear and direct interests of the United States require it. The Middle East is an example. We will continue to give aid to Israel because we need the stability of that country. Israel is our staunchest ally in the part of the world that holds a majority of the world's energy reserves. We have also given substantial aid to other countries because we see them as stabilizing influences in the same area."

"What about our domestic petroleum industry?" Dick Saylor, always the oilman, asked. "Would you do anything to protect that industry so we can produce petroleum when the overseas supplies are interrupted or when the cost of those supplies gets too high?"

Bobby smiled and pointed to Ralph. "That man and I argue about strong governmental protection for domestic oil producers all the time. He thinks we should have it. I don't." Looking at Saylor, he went on, "You have to remember that the public wants cheap gasoline. The price we pay goes up and down, but so far the foreign producers are providing enough petroleum so that the fluctuation has been tolerable. If an embargo comes along or there is some other disruption in supply, the price of petroleum will go up and domestic producers will have the incentive to explore domestically. They'll be able to sell their product at a price to justify the exploration and, despite environmental concerns, they'll be allowed to explore in places that were prohibited until now."

Bobby looked around the table and added, "In the meantime, we as a nation can't allow any hostile foreign power to gain control over such a large share of the world's oil that it can wreak havoc with the economies of the industrial nations. That was the reason for the first Gulf War. It was also a factor in the action to overthrow Saddam Hussein, although the threat of his weapons of mass destruction was the principal reason the world community decided he had to go. We found that Hussein had no such weapons but, as we all now know, that was after the fact."

The man from California spoke again. "What about the environment? If you are president, what'll you do to ensure us clean air and water? And what about climate change?"

Bobby turned to speak directly to the questioner, a smile warming his face. "I won't do anything because I won't be president. I'm just a stalking horse, remember?" He turned to include the others as he continued. "We all have an interest in a clean environment and effective steps have been taken to clean up after some of the mistakes of the past." Bobby returned his gaze to the Californian. "You know that most people of the world must spend all their time and energy just to have food and shelter. Environmental protection is beyond their comprehension or concern. We're able to do things to improve our situation only because we have the wealth to do so. It's critically important that we protect our ability to generate that wealth. Without it we won't be worried about the environment. We'll be just like other people, struggling to survive. That's why we must weigh any well-intended action of government carefully to be certain it doesn't impede our ability to create wealth. That even includes government actions intended to influence climate change."

He paused as though finished with his answer to the question, then took a breath and continued, "The good work of the original environmentalists resulted in such successes as the clean up of the Love Canal and, in my state, the clean up of the residue left by a century of copper mining and smelting activity. The pronouncements and the activities of some of the most extreme of those who claim to be concerned about the environment tend to alienate many people whose interest in a clean environment is sincere and who are in a position to do something about it."

"Like who?"

Bobby looked at the man and smiled. "Those who live on the land and must be at peace with nature. I'm one of 'em."

The Californian didn't smile in return.

The questioning went on for about two hours before Ralph spoke up from the head of the table. "You've all had a chance to listen to Mr. Hobaugh's answers and to observe the way he handles himself. It's time to take a break for fifteen minutes. Then I suggest we electors gather again, by ourselves, to discuss how we go forward from here." He turned to Bobby and said, "I'm sure the others join me in thanking you for coming to Denver and for the forthright way you answered our questions. We'll let you know about any decisions we make with regard to the election."

Bobby shook hands all around and then left the room with Janine, Lance, and Roman Burke. In the hallway, Burke reached for Bobby's hand. "Mr. Hobaugh, I'm impressed.

Frankly, I didn't expect much from someone without national political experience."

Bobby smiled in response. "Thank you, Mr. Burke. That's a nice compliment. But I'm just a country boy who reads the newspapers. Most anyone could do as well."

Burke shook his head. "Not so." Turning to Janine he said, "Now I know why you were so insistent that this man carry on when Forrest Blaine got killed." With a look from one to the other, he added, "Let's go get a cup of coffee while we visit some more."

When the waitress finished pouring coffee for each of them, Burke took up the conversation again. "I've thought the notion of Bobby Hobaugh as a candidate for president was foolishness. I felt that even the stalking horse idea was nonsense, but I agreed to go along with it because it was the only idea around to stop Jackson Tootell. After listening this morning, I've changed my mind. The way it stands, Allen Ward and Jackson Tootell seem to be the ones that the electors consider to be the real candidates. I don't believe either one of them is right for the country." Turning to Bobby, Burke added, "With your permission, I'll start calling the members of the Republican National Committee to suggest they throw their support to you. They can influence the electors more than anyone else."

"Look, Mr. Burke, I don't want to be president. I'm just a guy who is a parking place for votes until the real decision is made. That's all I agreed to do."

"I know that. But after listening to you, I've decided the country could do worse than have a real citizen president for a change." With a smile he added, "And there's no need to call me Mr. Burke. My name's Roman."

"Bobby, Roman's a pro. He knows politics better than

anyone in the country. If he says you should go for the brass ring, do it." Janine's hand was on Bobby's arm as she spoke.

Lance chimed in. "You're a public relations dream. A cattle rancher evokes visions of the old west and rugged individualism. A country lawyer is viewed as a good guy who saves widows and orphans, not as a villain like those big city trial lawyers. You seem to be squeaky clean—no scandals. We've been promoting that image, both with the electors and with the public. We can make you irresistible." Lance swept the group with his eyes. "The responses to our web site have been interesting. We get messages from many who hate Tootell. We get messages from some who worry that Ward will be chosen and the socialists will take over. And, believe it or not, we're getting contributions of money from some who just seem to like what they're learning about Bobby."

Bobby shook his head. "Before you all go off half-cocked, you'd better wait to hear what the people in that meeting room decide. They may have already agreed to support either Ward or Tootell. Or maybe they'll come up with someone else."

Half an hour later, Dick Saylor strode up to the table where Bobby, Janine, Roman, and Lance were sitting. All he said was, "Come on. We'll tell you what we've decided."

When they were seated around the conference table once again, Saylor took the lead. "Bobby Hobaugh, we liked what we heard from you. None of us agreed with everything you said. I don't agree with you on petroleum matters. Fred, here," he nodded in the direction of the elector from California, "thinks you're plumb wrong on the environment." Saylor smiled a small smile. "Frankly, some of us think you're a little naive in believing the whole population of the United States should be put on a war footing just because we have to send some troops to a small country to protect our interests there."

His face turned sober again. "But we're in agreement that we can vote for you, if the other choices aren't acceptable." He put his elbow on the table, pointing his hand at Bobby. "Let me make it clear. Some of us can vote for Ward and some can vote for Tootell, but we can't unanimously agree to support either one of them. We still think that a person with national experience, someone we all can support, will come to the fore. If that doesn't happen, you may be the one who gets some, if not all, of our votes."

Ralph spoke again from the head of the table. "Bobby, I'm afraid the Republican electors will split between Ward and Tootell. If that occurs, neither of them would get a majority of the votes. We shouldn't let that happen. We need an alternative, one that both camps can agree on. We think you might be that alternative."

Janine watched with amazement as the heads of all the electors, even the one from California, nodded in agreement. Incredible! Ralph was going to pull it off. He was going to be the kingmaker. It might not be Bobby, but Ralph would be one of two or three who dictated the ultimate choice.

Bobby listened to Saylor and to Ralph without interruption. When Ralph finished and no one else spoke, he took a deep breath, then looked around at each of those in the room. "If you and the other electors can't agree on Ward or Tootell, find someone besides me. There are lots of good men and women who would like to be president. It's not a job I want, and it's not a job I feel I can handle. It would be too great a risk to the country to elect someone to that high office who has no national experience."

After a long pause, he said, "Be careful what you do."

Friday, November 19, morning

ATLANTA, GEORGIA

"Tucker, it appears that Ralph Phillips hasn't been deterred. He's still devoting his time to the foolish notion of Bobby Hobaugh as a candidate for president."

"Yes, sir, that's correct." Tucker stood silent for a moment and then said, "I could arrange to have something happen to Mr. Phillips personally. Something that would keep him out of your way until after the electors cast their ballots—or longer." He looked at his employer for a moment and then added, "Or perhaps something should happen to Bobby Hobaugh."

Jackson Tootell almost smiled. "No. I've decided it isn't necessary—at least for now. As long as Hobaugh is the only one mentioned as an alternative to Ward and me, it's possible that no truly serious candidate will surface. When December 13 rolls around, Ward and I will be the only ones the electors will really consider. By that time, I'll have enough of them committed that the ones supporting Ward will see the inevitable." Jackson Tootell's voice then took on a frigid tone. "Maybe at a later time I'll repay both Phillips and Hobaugh for the difficulty they've caused."

Miss Lotus kept her eyes on the computer as Tucker passed by. He wondered what her voice sounded like.

19

Monday, November 22, afternoon

BILLINGS, MONTANA

"Janine, you can't believe the kinds of letters, faxes, and emails I'm getting. Every organization in the world wants to tell me how to vote." Ralph picked up a letter, and then spoke into the phone again. "Here's one from the Sierra Club demanding that I vote for Allen Ward. They say he's the only one who will save the environment." He dropped that sheet and looked at another. "And here's one from the National Organization for Women. They say Allen Ward is the only one who will preserve a woman's right to choose."

Ralph shuffled some more papers. "OK. Here's one from the NAACP that would lead you to believe that the election of Tootell will result in the re-imposition of slavery." Before Janine could interject, he snorted and said, "Not one of those outfits would support a Republican candidate. Now they want to dictate which Republican we'll choose."

"Well, that's politics, Ralph. What about organizations supporting Tootell?"

"Oh yeah, we've got'em too. The Chamber of Commerce,

the National Farm Bureau, the National Rifle Association. Here's one from a Right to Life group and one from an outfit that wants the federal government to turn all the public lands over to the states. They all claim the world will end if Tootell isn't the man."

"You can't say that life is boring, can you, Ralph? It sounds like you're really enjoying yourself."

"To tell the truth, I am."

"What about support for Bobby?"

"Not a word. He's flying under the radar screen. Not one of those organizations seems to know he exists."

"How does that affect what we're trying to do?"

"I don't think it hurts. It may help. The electors may come to see that neither Ward nor Tootell will satisfy very many people."

"I hope you're right." Janine's voice sounded tired. "Thanks for the call, Ralph."

Before Janine could hang up, Ralph asked, "What's the Republican Party doing? No one from the national office has contacted me."

"As near as I can tell, neutrality is the word. The party is going to stay out of the fray, despite Roman Burke's efforts to persuade them to speak out for Bobby. The chairman of the Republican National Committee, and others like him, don't want to risk alienating the eventual winner."

"Please ask Lance to keep feeding them information about our guy anyway. At some time, they may decide a split between Ward and Tootell isn't in the party's interest."

"Don't worry, Ralph. Lance keeps the web page updated and emails material to each elector pointing out Bobby's virtues. Roman and I have never stopped working the phones." She paused. "It's interesting. None of the electors I've talked to is adamantly opposed to the idea of Bobby Hobaugh as a candidate. They all seem interested in him and want to know more about him, even those who are obvious supporters of either Ward or Tootell. That tells me there really is a possibility he'll end up being the compromise choice."

"That possibility is always on my mind."

Janine's melodious laugh came over the line. "Oh yes, Ralph, I know. The kingmaker never rests."

Thursday, November 25, morning

BILLINGS, MONTANA

"Ralph, this is Dick Saylor. I suppose you've been getting the same emails and faxes and calls that I have. So you know that McDougal, an elector from Georgia, has taken the lead in support of Tootell."

"Yup, and Daniels in Wisconsin is leading the charge for Ward."

"That's right. No one, other than Ward and Tootell, has generated any support, except the support we've created for Bobby Hobaugh."

"How do you see the votes splitting right now?"

"If we had to vote today, I think Tootell would get the most votes, about 170. Ward would get about eighty, and Bobby would get about fifty. Bobby would get about twenty-nine votes from Texas. The rest are moving toward Tootell. Tootell's doing something to persuade people to go for him. I don't know what, but it's working."

There was silence on the phone for a beat or two, then Saylor went on, "Some just think he'll eventually be the winner, and they want to be on the right side. One or two just can't stand Ward and are unsure about Bobby. I worry that a few are being pressured to support Tootell. Damn it, Ralph, I don't trust that man."

"None of us trusts him." Ralph leaned back in his chair. "That split is a dangerous thing, though. What more should you and I do since we can't vote for Ward and don't trust Tootell?"

"I've been thinking of calling McDougal and Daniels to suggest all of the electors meet, listen to the three candidates, then thrash it out and decide on the one we can all vote for."

"Sounds good to me. We'd better get it done soon, though. We're about to run out of time. Election Day is just over two weeks away. That's when we have to cast our ballots."

"You're right. I'll call those two and tell 'em what we've got in mind. Then I'll let you know their reaction."

Thursday, November 25, afternoon

CAMBRIDGE, MASSACHUSETTS

Allen Ward added the column of figures, frowned, and leaned back in his chair to ponder. By his reckoning, Tootell had about a hundred votes, he had about the same, and the rest were uncommitted. While the numbers didn't look bad, they were not as good as his first estimate indicated. Tootell was gaining votes slowly but steadily. Perhaps that fellow in Carolina, the one who told of being threatened, was right. Tootell wasn't above such tactics.

Ward rose and paced his study. Without the kind of money that Tootell could spend, it was impossible to meet personally with every elector, even though that contact would help win their votes. Maybe a gathering of all electors, with the candidates present, could be arranged. Then Ward's ability to charm and persuade could be used to its greatest advantage. He reached for the phone to call Daniels.

Thursday, November 25, evening

DENVER, COLORADO

Janine switched to Fox News while resting comfortably in an easy chair in her apartment. Finished with the day's labors, she relaxed in pajamas and a robe. The usual evening news program consisting of Franklin Gary as moderator and two panelists, Fred Harrington and Molly James, appeared on the screen. One of the panelists, Fred Harrington—elderly, gray-headed, garrulous, and an editor of a conservative magazine—was speaking.

> "All the talk about Bobby Hobaugh as president is just that—talk. In the end the electors will choose Jackson Tootell."

> "Well," Franklin Gary said, "the latest Fox poll of the electors certainly seems to indicate that you are correct. Let's look at the numbers."

A graphic appeared on the television screen, and the man seemed to read from it.

> "President Arthur Simpson has 255 votes. Those are locked in and won't change. The poll has Jackson Tootell with 171 votes. Allen Ward has 52 votes. Bobby Hobaugh, 21 votes. Susan Washington and Thomas Lowell have one vote each."

The graphic disappeared and the moderator's face reappeared.

"What's most interesting is that 36 electors are either undecided or refused to commit themselves."

Molly James, young, blonde, and attractive, spoke. "Don't put too much stock in those numbers. It's my guess that the electors will soon coalesce around either Tootell or Ward. They aren't going to let the day arrive when they actually vote without agreeing on one or the other."

"Molly, How will they manage to come to such an agreement?"

"If necessary, they'll gather together somewhere, listen to the things that Tootell and Ward have to say, and make the choice."

"Well, time will tell," Gary said, "We'll be back after a two-minute break."

Janine poked the button, making the smiling face of the moderator disappear. She sat in the silence, considering the large number of electors who refused to disclose their preference. Were they still undecided? Or just reluctant to tell a pollster? After pondering that question, her thoughts focused on the showing of Lowell and Washington. No one seemed to be making any effort on their behalf, and she wondered how it was that their names appeared in the poll. Her mind turned to Bobby Hobaugh's showing in the polls. If Ralph Phillips was going to be kingmaker, he had lots of work to do!

Thursday, November 25, evening

ATLANTA, GEORGIA

"Mr. Tootell, the Hobaugh people are trying to arrange a gathering of all of the electors. If they pull it off, you, Allen Ward, and Bobby Hobaugh would be expected to attend."

"Where and when will this gathering be held, Tucker?"

"They want it to be in Denver. They've been informed that you might not even consider attending such a gathering. And that if you did consider it, the meeting would have to be in Atlanta. They're planning on December 3 as the date."

"I'll attend. I think I can be persuasive, don't you?"

"Yes, sir. You certainly can be persuasive. You can probably gather all of the votes at that meeting."

"Keep it in Atlanta if you can, but if necessary, I'll go to Denver."

As Tucker turned to leave, the big man spoke again. "I believe in covering every contingency. There's always a remote possibility that I won't get the two hundred electoral votes needed to win the presidency. To cover that remote possibility, I've reviewed the Constitutional provisions for the selection of the vice president. We need to convince the electors to cast their ballots for me for vice president as well as for president."

"Can they do that, sir?"

"There seems to be nothing to prevent them from doing so."

"Will you settle for the vice presidency?'

Tootell leaned forward, elbows on the desktop. "We've discussed that question before, Tucker. The vice presidency would just be a first step."

"I'll make certain that our people understand the need to secure the most votes for both offices."

Friday, November 26, night

BILLINGS, MONTANA

Ralph picked up the phone by his bedside and heard Saylor's voice. "Sorry to call this time of night. I talked to Daniels yesterday afternoon, and he was all for a get-together. McDougal didn't return my call until an hour ago, and I've been arguing with him since. He thinks his man is ahead and will win. All he sees in such a meeting is risk for Tootell."

"Did you talk him into it?"

"Finally. I told him we needed to reach unanimous agreement before December 13, and the best way to do that was to get everyone in the same room at the same time. I think he decided he could run the show and ramrod his man through. Maybe he can."

"Perhaps Tootell can. If he does, we won't have to worry about a split vote." Ralph shifted the phone to his other hand as he turned over in the bed. "When are we going to meet?"

"I suggested we meet in Denver on the 3rd of December. That's a week from today. It will give everyone time to make travel arrangements. Both of them agreed on the date but neither one of them liked the idea of Denver. McDougal wants to meet in Atlanta, and Daniels wants to meet in Chicago."

"How about Saint Louis? That's kind of neutral."

"I tried that. Neither one would budge." Saylor's voice carried his exasperation. "God damn it, Ralph, neither one has a reasonable bone in his body. I'll tell you what I think. I think we should tell 'em it'll be Denver or nowhere."

"Do it. They'll go for it. Most of the electors won't care where we get together. They'll all have to travel no matter where it is. McDougal and Daniels might not like it, but I'll bet Tootell and Ward show up."

"OK. Let's contact all the others as soon as possible, tell them a meeting is scheduled in Denver on the 3rd of December, and see what happens."

"That'll either get 'em all to Denver or not. If it does, we might get something done. If it doesn't, we're going to have a split vote and may as well face that fact."

"Get Janine and Lance busy spreading the word."

"I'll do it."

Monday, November 29, morning

BILLINGS, MONTANA

Saylor called early. "They went for it, Ralph. Denver on the third. I'm not sure all the electors will be there. Janine told me some of the Florida electors refuse to be in the same room with Tootell. They're still mad over the things he said about Weldon's wife during the primaries. But Roman Burke will be there with the rest of the Florida delegation. They still look at him as a spokesman for Weldon, even though Weldon's dead. They'll all probably do whatever he suggests."

Ralph nodded as though Saylor could see him. "Some of the others may not make it either. It's pretty short notice. But if those of us who are there can agree, the rest will probably go along."

Saylor cleared his throat. "How are we going to handle this? Who will run the meeting?"

"Let's keep it neutral. Harry Jones is an eighty-year-old elector from Colorado. Janine tells me he's still sharp and has a way with people. Colorado is the host state, so it would seem logical for him to chair the meeting."

"That sounds good. What about a format?"

"Let's seat the candidates at a table in the front where everyone can see them as they talk. I suggest we just let the electors fire questions at them. No long speeches to begin, just answers to the questions. It seems to me that would be the best use of time."

"Can Janine line that old guy up, give him the agenda, and get him ready?"

"You've learned by now that Janine is a wonder woman. She'll get it done."

Saylor grunted approval. "See you in Denver, buddy. I hope we can all agree on the next president of the United States."

Ralph punched the off button on his cell phone and put it on the table next to his morning breakfast of soft boiled eggs and toast. His choice of words to describe Janine wasn't an exaggeration. She would have the gathering of the electors in Denver properly organized, with every detail carefully thought out and correctly addressed. From the time he first made her acquaintance, when Senator Blaine was killed, Ralph had watched her work organizational wonders. She was quick to analyze any problem and suggest the solution. Once the others accepted her suggestion, she would do the things necessary to put it into effect.

It was her pleasant personality that allowed her to be so effective. She was efficient without being brusque. She was seldom irritable and, if so, only briefly. Her smile, Ralph thought, brightened the darkest room. And she shared with him his interest in the mechanics of politics and the electoral process. She could tease him about wanting to be a kingmaker, but he knew she shared that ambition. Ralph drank slowly from his coffee cup, put it back on the saucer, stared thoughtfully at the wall, remembering the fragrance of her perfume— and wished he could add six inches to his height and take ten years off his age.

21

Tuesday, November 30, morning

MILES CITY, MONTANA

Bobby looked across his desk at Margaret, heaved a great sigh, and rubbed his forehead. "Why did I ever let myself get into this mess?" The question was directed more to himself than to her.

"Because you thought you were doing the right thing." Margaret smiled at her employer. "And you *are* doing the right thing. You're giving the electors an alternative to two bad choices. At least that's what your friend, Ralph, keeps saying."

"In the end, my participation won't make a bit of difference. The electors are going to choose either Ward or Tootell. Some may not like the choice, but they'll go along just to get a Republican president in office."

"Ralph sees it differently. He is certain there are some who won't vote for Ward no matter what, and some who won't vote for Tootell."

Margaret moved her hands to the desktop and leaned forward. "If Ralph is right, the only possible unanimous vote will be for a third person. You're that third person."

"It just won't happen. The electors know that I have nothing to offer. I've no experience in national affairs. They'll be wondering what I'd do in the event of a nuclear crisis. Or how I would handle myself at a meeting of the leaders of the industrialized nations. It's crazy to even think of it."

"Crazy it may be, but it's a possibility." Her smile was warm and reassuring. "You're in it now and you'll have to carry it through."

Bobby put his elbow on the desk and leaned his chin on one hand. "Yes, I know. But I hate the thought of appearing with those other two at the meeting in Denver. They'll make me look like the ignorant country bumpkin that I really am."

Margaret reached across for his hand and patted it. "Maybe, Bobby. Maybe not. I think not." Then she sat back, crossed her legs, and asked in a serious voice, "What is it about Allen Ward that your Republican friends don't like?"

Bobby thought for a moment before answering. "Allen Ward was a very liberal governor of Wisconsin, and now he's a professor at Harvard University. Most Republicans, at least those in the western states, see him as the closest thing to a left-wing Democrat. In addition to that, he divorced his wife to marry one of his students who was twenty-five years his junior. They've since divorced. Now he is too often seen with some other young woman on his arm. Republican electors are often older and tend to be very conservative. His liberal tendencies and lifestyle are a political liability in this contest."

"While they're not inclined to support Allen Ward, they seem to positively distrust Jackson Tootell. Why is that?"

Bobby thought for another moment and then sat back. "I'm sure you've read in the national magazines how Tootell started out in Georgia without anything—no money, no education, nothing. Then he created a very successful regional business—mining, gathering, and distributing decorative rock used in house construction for things like fireplaces, planters, and wall facing. When the electronic revolution came along, he realized that e-commerce was where the action would be and started selling the decorative rock on the Net." Bobby smiled and said, "It didn't work very well because rock is too heavy to ship long distances.

"To be successful, Tootell had to have quarries and trucking facilities in too many locations. Rather than give up, he started marketing things that are used with the rock, such as decorative grills and trellises, things that could be delivered easily and cheaply. That led him into the sale and distribution of items found in hardware stores and home centers. But he wasn't satisfied. He wanted to expand into other lines and decided it would be easier to take over existing businesses rather than create new ones."

"He did that, didn't he?"

"He sure did. Before very long, **Tootell Nationwide** became a giant e-commerce retail organization, selling everything you can imagine. He just gobbled up most of his competitors."

"How did he do it?"

"Rumor would have us believe that he did it any way he could. Some of his methods were thought to be less than ethical. He's said to have used threats, intimidation, and bribery, in addition to the usual methods of acquiring another business."

"Didn't the government take him to court?"

"The Justice Department filed suit against him, not for any supposed criminal activity, but on an anti-trust basis. The suit alleged that he had created a retail monopoly."

"If I remember right, that went to trial."

"It did, and the first judge obviously believed the government's case had merit. At least that's what the popular newspapers and magazines reported." Bobby rubbed the back of his neck, then continued. "Midway through the trial, that judge was killed in an auto accident. The police report said he was drunk at the time and hit a tree. That was more than strange. His family and friends all said he was a teetotaler who never touched alcohol."

"What happened to the trial?"

"A new judge was assigned to handle it. He heard a small amount of additional testimony and then ruled that the government's case was without merit and dismissed it."

"Did the government appeal that ruling?"

"No. And everyone in both the legal and business world wondered why." Bobby shook his head. "The consensus was that Tootell had gotten to the higher-ups in the Justice Department, and they called off the dogs."

"You're telling me that you believe Jackson Tootell is a crook."

"I'm telling you what was reported in the newspapers and magazines. I don't have any personal knowledge of it."

"Neither do any of your friends, but they seem to believe the man can't be trusted."

"That's true."

"Tell me, if all of this is public knowledge, how is he a serious candidate for president?"

"During the primary campaign, Tootell successfully parroted the conservative Republican line. He was anti-abortion, for school vouchers, for protection of domestic businesses from foreign competition, for a strong military, against gun control. With that line, and a huge amount of his own money, he was able to come in second to Governor Weldon in the Iowa caucuses, third behind Weldon and Ward in New Hampshire, and second to Weldon in the remainder of the primaries. He never dropped out of the race, even when it was certain he couldn't win the nomination. And then, toward the end, he attacked the Governor and his wife in a personal way."

"None of that should make him a front runner in the race to get the votes of the electors."

"Tootell put on a strong public relations campaign at the time of the trial. He characterized it as a vendetta by the Simpson administration simply because he was successful in business. He made it appear that a bunch of government people were out to get anyone who made money. Those who support him now do so because they think that was true and because of his strong conservative positions. They choose not to believe the bad things that were said about him. And, perhaps the rest of us should forget them too. After all, nothing contained in the rumors has ever been proven."

"I guess Ralph and the others don't think he passes the smell test."

Bobby smiled at the cliché. "That's a good way to put it." He leaned forward again to say, "None of that changes the situation Ralph has put me in."

"No, it doesn't. You have to go to Denver."

Bobby paused, then reached across the desk and grasped her hand. "Margaret, will you go to Denver with me? I need someone there for company. Otherwise I'll be surrounded by people who just see me as a tool, something to use to further their ambitions."

Margaret's eyes went down to her small hand held in Bobby's larger one. Then she looked back up at his face and said quietly, "Ralph will be there. He's your friend."

"It's true that Ralph is my friend and will always be my

friend. But right now he's caught up in this presidential business, and it's affected the way he looks at things." He shook his head. "No, I need you there with me. You don't have to do anything other than keep me company—then I'm not at the mercy of all those politicians."

She didn't respond for a moment; then withdrew her hand, and finally said, "I don't think that's a good idea."

Her look of concern finally registered. "Oh! Lord! I don't have anything like that in mind. We'll get a two-bedroom suite with a sitting room in the middle. No hanky-panky."

Margaret smiled at the childhood term. "I'm sure you don't have hanky-panky in mind, Bobby. But, if I travel to Denver with you it will cause lots of talk, both among the people there and the people here. Like it or not, you're a national figure now and you have your reputation to consider." She rose from her chair, sober-faced, and looked down at him for a long minute. "I'm a member of the Northern Cheyenne tribe. To some people, an Indian is the worst thing a human being can be."

"My goodness, Margaret. I'm proud to be seen with you. We've traveled together before, to depositions and trials." Bobby paused and blinked as a thought came to mind. "I'm sorry. I should be concerned about your reputation."

Margaret's eyebrows went up, and then she laughed and sat back down in her chair. "Perhaps we're both worried too much about reputations. All right, Bobby, I'll go with you to Denver. Maybe I can be of some help." She rose again, turned for the door, then looked over her shoulder with a twinkle in her eye. "Remember, separate rooms."

It was Bobby's turn to laugh. "You make the reservations at the Brown Palace yourself. Then you can be certain."

22

Thursday, December 2, afternoon

DENVER, COLORADO

"Who is that woman?" Janine asked.

Across the hotel lobby, Bobby was at the registration desk. Margaret stood at a discreet distance, near the door. Ralph responded, "That's Bobby's office manager, Margaret Lisa. You've heard us speak of her. She practically runs Bobby as well as his office."

"She must have come with him. I wonder why."

"I suppose he wants her here. After all, they've worked together for ten years."

Janine looked toward Margaret for a moment and then said, "I need to meet her." With that, she started across the room to introduce herself.

Ralph watched Janine walk away, admiring her trim figure and purposeful stride. Once again he mentally bemoaned his short stature, wondered if she might become interested in him despite his height and age, and decided there was not a chance. Then his thoughts turned to Janine's reason to seek out Margaret. A quick smile tugged at his lips. Bobby Hobaugh was certain to be the subject of that conversation.

Janine approached Margaret with a smile on her face and her hand extended. "I'm Janine Paul, and I believe you are Margaret Lisa. Bobby Hobaugh speaks of you often. So does Ralph Phillips."

"I'm pleased to meet you. Bobby has told me how he came to make the campaign trip. He's impressed by your ability."

"I understand you've worked for Bobby for a long time. Is he always a gentleman? Holding coats and doors for ladies?"

"That's Bobby. He wouldn't know how to be anything but a gentleman. It's just his nature."

"You're lucky to work for such a man." Janine turned and moved an elbow toward Ralph. "I'm curious about Bobby's friend, Ralph Phillips. What kind of person is he?"

"Ralph?" Margaret stared in Ralph's direction for a moment. "Ralph is a nice man. He's a widower. That's why he and Bobby got to be such good friends. They lost their wives about the same time."

"Tell me more about him. I know he's in the oil business and he surely is interested in politics. What else?"

"He has one son who is a physician in Seattle." Margaret looked closely at Janine, then added, "Why are you so interested?"

Janine stood for a moment, looked directly at Margaret, and said, "Well, if you must know, I think he's kind of cute." She laughed and walked away.

Friday, December 3, afternoon

DENVER, COLORADO

The room seemed almost cavernous, and the noise of the

crowd reverberated from one wall to another. The television and radio network people were responsible for most of the noise as they pursued electors and stuck microphones in their faces in an attempt to catch an unwary elector muttering an embarrassing sound bite that could be used on the evening broadcast. A few reporters from Colorado newspapers were also visible, wandering amongst the mob. The electors began to drift toward chairs in front of an elevated platform.

From the back of the room, Janine looked over the heads of the seated electors toward the platform where Harry Jones, Allen Ward, and Jackson Tootell sat in a cluster, behind the middle of a long table. The chair provided for Bobby Hobaugh placed him a slight, but discernable distance to the side of Allen Ward. Whoever made the arrangement must have thought his presence was of little consequence. It seemed strange to her that neither Thomas Lowell nor Susan Washington had shown any interest in attending the gathering of electors.

Allen Ward's tall, lean stature was evident even while he sat behind the table. He wore an elegant dark blue suit, accented by a starched white shirt and crimson tie. His silver hair was carefully coifed to highlight his handsome face. He had an appearance of relaxed self-confidence. The differences between Ward and Jackson Tootell seemed magnified by their appearance.

Tootell, even taller than Ward, was so muscular as to appear burly. His large, bald head reflected the overhead lights. His suit was cut from expensive cloth but it rumpled somewhat around his bulky shoulders. Hunched over, leaning his arms on the table, his unblinking gaze shifted from those on one side of the room to those on the other.

Lance Caldwell and Roman Burke sat on either side of Janine in the back of the room. She was surprised to find that Burke was positively friendly and conversational. It was a dramatic change from his attitude toward her during the campaign. A few people Janine didn't know, aligned with one or the other of the candidates, were also seated along the back wall. They had all been told they could observe but were directed not to participate in the proceedings in any way.

Margaret Lisa sat quietly on the far side of Lance. After a short time, she turned to him and introduced herself. When Lance responded with a gracious smile, she said, "Bobby told me you and your wife have a new baby. Is all well?"

"Yes, Heather and little Lance are doing fine. It's strange being a father but I'm enjoying it—when I'm not busy with election business."

"Enjoy your family while your child is young. In a few years you won't even remember why you thought this meeting was important."

"That's what everyone tells me. and I know it's true. But I have a lot invested in this election. Still, it's hard to concentrate on political matters when your first child is waiting at home."

"This gathering shouldn't last long. Then you can be on your way to your wife and child. When you get there, give the little one a hug for me."

Janine, hearing the conversation, silently thanked the woman from Montana for her consideration. The burden of fatherhood was wearing on Lance's nerves.

The electors agreed to close the meeting to the press. They unanimously believed the candidates would express themselves more freely if they didn't have to worry about misquotes. One newsman, with a lawyer in tow, threatened to file a suit and get a court order requiring that the meeting be open to the press.

Saylor, using western vernacular, said, "Go ahead. Turn loose your wolf," and then walked away without giving the reporter or his lawyer a chance to respond. Other reporters, less worried about legal matters, were busy interviewing as many electors as possible before the doors were closed to them.

Janine assumed that some enterprising journalists would succeed in concealing their occupation and remain seated along the rear wall. They only had to act like guests of one of the candidates. The news always came out, especially when an attempt was made to prevent the world from hearing it. Events that took place in private seemed more tantalizing than others.

At two o'clock, Harry Jones leaned toward the microphone in front of him and began the proceedings. "The members of the press know that this meeting will be closed to everyone but the electors and guests invited by the electors. For that reason we ask that all the media people leave the room." He stood quietly while there was a general exodus by reporters and cameramen." Will someone please close the doors so that we may conduct this matter in some privacy?"

Lance moved to the double doors and closed them with a bang. Jones continued, "Let me welcome those of you who made the long trip to Denver. It's my understanding that we have 242 of the 283 Republican electors here today. Some of the missing simply couldn't get here. They sent their regrets. A few declined to come, as is their privilege." He paused, looked right to Tootell and then left to Ward, and then back out at the crowd. "We are here to listen to the principal candidates for president of the United States. After hearing them, the electors will meet together for the purpose of choosing one for whom we all may vote. Is everyone agreed?"

When no one said anything, he continued. "There will

be no opening statements from the candidates. Each will just respond to questions from electors. I ask that you raise your hand if you wish to direct a question to a candidate. I'll recognize you, one at a time. You are asked not to interrupt one another and not to interrupt a candidate when he is speaking. Ask one question, and only one question, when I call upon you. It's my intention to maintain strict order." He paused. "Are there any questions about the procedure?" There was some shuffling of feet and squirming in chairs by the electors, but no one asked a question.

Jones turned his face toward Ward and then toward Tootell, then back to the crowd. "I'm sure you know all about these gentlemen, but I'll introduce them anyway. On my left is Allen Ward. Mr. Ward is a former governor of Wisconsin. He is presently a visiting professor of public policy at Harvard University. Mr. Ward did well in the early primaries, especially in New Hampshire."

Jones then gestured to his right. "On my right is Jackson Tootell. He is the creator of **Tootell Nationwide**, an on-line marketing company that has become one of the retail giants of the world. He, too, showed well in the early primaries and continued his campaign through to the Republican convention." Jones looked down at his notes and then up at the electors and asked, "Is there anything else I should say before we begin the questioning?"

Before anyone could speak, Jones realized his omission, looked down at his notes to be certain of the name, and turned toward Bobby for a moment, as though inspecting him. He faced the electors and said, "On my far left is Bobby Hobaugh. Mr. Hobaugh is a state senator from Montana." Then he repeated. "Is there anything else?" In a blink of an eye, he went on, "Let's begin the questioning. First question."

He pointed to an elector seated in the second row, one of many with his hand in the air.

The man rose to his feet and said, "I'm Stanley Stotts from Wyoming. Mr. Ward, you've said we have an obligation to ensure that no one lives in poverty. If we are to provide everyone with money at the taxpayers' expense, why not just put up a sign that says, 'Don't work. Live off the government'?"

Allen Ward leaned forward, then paused for a moment as though thinking about the question. When he answered, he looked directly at the questioner. "I've said before that we live in an enormously rich country and that we should not rest until each of our citizens is able to earn an income above the poverty level. That will not happen overnight. Until it does happen, we have an obligation, as compassionate people, to provide public funds to those in need." Ward looked from the electors on his left to the electors on his right, while smiling as though confident that his answer would satisfy them all.

Stanley Stotts' headshake as he sat down made it clear that the answer didn't satisfy him and, furthermore, that he disliked Allen Ward.

Harry Jones then pointed to a man so overweight that his chair appeared on the verge of collapse. He remained seated to ask, "Mr. Tootell, you've said we have no business sending troops to quell disturbances in foreign countries. You've also said you would warn any dictator who crossed our path that we would use our military force to destroy him. You can't have it both ways, sir. Which is it? Will we hunker down behind our borders and ignore the rest of the world, or will we send troops to overthrow every dictator that we don't like?"

Tootell's face remained passive as he leaned over the table and pointed at the questioner. "We've been sending men and equipment to every scuffle in every dinky little country in the world, trying to make people love one another. Some in this room think that's proper. At the same time, we've allowed the leaders of other countries to thumb their noses at us and wreak havoc with our ability to do business in those countries. I've been successful in business because I wouldn't put up with threats or blackmail. When I'm president, every leader of every other country will know that to interfere with the interests of the United States will result in immediate retaliation and in the harshest form." When he leaned back in his chair, his mouth widened in a pleasant smile—a smile that gave him an amiable appearance. It was the face the electors were accustomed to seeing in campaign commercials during the primaries.

A woman jumped up and yelled at Ward even before Jones could point to another questioner. "Mr. Ward, you're one of those who said we have an obligation to quell internal squabbles such as those that seem to occur interminably in the Balkans. Isn't Mr. Tootell right? Shouldn't we mind our own business and not try to run the lives of other people?"

Ward flushed but answered in the same calm manner as before. "There are many things about which Mr. Tootell and I disagree. This is one of them. I believe we have an obligation as the leading democracy to help the people of other countries in their attempts to establish democratic self-government. It is to our credit that we've been doing that. When I'm president, we will continue to provide help when evidence suggests that help will achieve the desired result."

A Ward supporter shouted, "Tootell, China and India have two of the world's largest economies, and both of them have snubbed their noses at us over trade issues. You're talking about them, aren't you, when you talk about harsh measures? What you're proposing would have us in a war with one of them before you were president for ten days!"

Tootell's voice was flat but his expression did not change. "You're damn right, they're the ones I'm talking about. They've played Arthur Simpson like a fiddle." Jerking his head toward Ward, he added, "And this guy sitting up here with me would be just as bad as Simpson or worse."

A rumbling was heard from some of Ward's supporters but quieted as Ward put his hand in the air, palm out. "It's that kind of intemperate remark that scared the voters in the primaries. The only reason Jackson Tootell got any votes at all was because he spent more money than Warren Weldon and I combined."

In an instant the calm in the room dissipated. The supporters of each candidate began to cast caustic comments to the supporters of the other. Soon shouts and insults were being hurled across the room, creating bedlam. Janine, watching and listening, quickly realized that the supporters of Tootell were making far more noise than Ward's supporters. She tried to decide if it was because they were the greater number or if they were just more vocal.

Harry Jones, without a gavel, slapped the table repeatedly with a tablet until the noise quieted. "Ladies and gentlemen, let's be calm and do as I asked at the beginning. If you have a question, raise your hand, and don't speak until I recognize you."

Ralph Phillips was first on his feet, his hand in the air. Jones pointed at him and said, "Mr. Phillips, I believe it is."

"Thank you, sir. You're correct, I'm Ralph Phillips from Montana." Turning to Bobby he asked, "Mr. Hobaugh, what do you think of all this?"

Bobby stared at him for a moment, looked over at Ward and Tootell, then finally faced the group, now again quiet.

"Two hundred eighty-three people have the ability—and the obligation—to choose the next president of the United States. This is not the way to make the decision. The electors should closet themselves here in the room and discuss the choices in a reasonable manner, remembering all the while that they must keep the interests of the country in mind, not the interests of any individual." Turning to Harry Jones, he said, "Mr. Jones, I think you should dismiss the candidates and observers so that the electors, you included, can talk in a rational way about your responsibility to the rest of us."

Ralph had remained standing. Before anyone else could speak, he asked, "Mr. Hobaugh, how will you act if you are chosen as president?"

Bobby's usually smiling face was a solemn mask. "I've not asked to be president, and I don't expect to be chosen. But, if it should happen, I will do my best to protect the interests of this country, both in foreign and domestic matters. I can't tell you more than that."

The room remained quiet until Jones nodded his head and muttered softly, "Mr. Hobaugh, you may be right." Then he looked out at the crowd and spoke in a voice loud enough to ensure that he was heard in case the bedlam arose again. "Everyone other than the electors please leave the room." Pointing his finger at Roman Burke, he said, "I'm appointing you to keep everyone who isn't an elector out of here. Get yourself a chair and sit outside the door. Pick some others to help, but be sure they're trustworthy." Looking out at the electors, he added with determination, "We're going to choose a president."

23

Friday, December 3, minutes later

BROWN PALACE HOTEL, DENVER

Bobby and Margaret found themselves alone in the corridor outside the meeting room. Allen Ward strode by with his entourage and with a group of reporters traipsing along behind. Margaret could see Jackson Tootell and his followers hurrying in the opposite direction with an even larger band of reporters in tow. None of them paid any attention to the man from Montana. Bobby didn't seem to notice, or, if he did, he gave no indication that he felt slighted. Margaret, on the other hand, was offended. After all, Bobby was one of the candidates and had been on the platform right along with those two men who seemed to think they were more important than her employer.

Bobby took her arm and walked her to the elevator. Their suite in the venerable Brown Palace Hotel seemed very much like the ones from his campaign excursion: too richly furnished to make a Montana rancher feel at home. He escorted her to the most comfortable chair and held the back of it as she sat down. When he asked if she would like some refreshment, Margaret declined. Bobby removed his suit coat and sank wearily into another chair. "Margaret, the electors, even those who supported Weldon during the primaries, have chosen sides—some for Ward, some for Tootell. Now they seem to be more interested in reigniting the primary fight than they are in choosing the right person for president. It's mighty discouraging to see that kind of behavior when the stakes are so high."

"Maybe they'll come to their senses and choose you."

"I keep telling you that isn't going to happen. No one even knew I was on that platform until Ralph asked me a question."

"And you answered it exactly right. Maybe they can discuss the decision reasonably if the candidates aren't in the room. Then they won't have to worry about offending either Mr. Ward or Mr. Tootell."

"What do you think about them? Which one would you choose?"

"Mr. Ward is smooth but seemed insincere. Mr. Tootell is much too arrogant. Maybe the rumors about him are true. I guess if I had to select one it would be Mr. Ward." She smiled and leaned forward, "But, Bobby, I think you would be better than either one of them."

"That's nice to hear, especially from someone who knows all of my faults and weaknesses."

"We all have faults and weaknesses. Yours are few and not serious." Her smile was gone. "I really hope they can't agree on either Ward or Tootell and turn to you. It would be good for the country to have a real citizen in the White House. As long as I've lived, every president has thought the whole universe was centered in Washington D.C. None of them had any knowledge of the problems ordinary people face every

day. You spend your days listening to ordinary people. The
people you listen to aren't campaign slogans. They're real."

Bobby smiled, blew a long breath and said, "Well, we'll
know what the electors decide soon enough." He combed at
his thinning hair with his fingers. "Thank you for coming here
with me. I really need someone to visit with, someone who
isn't caught up in this ruckus the way Ralph and Janine are."
Then he brightened and added, "I'm hungry. Let's go down to
the coffee shop and get a piece of pie."

"Do we dare? The reporters will be after you as soon as
you step off the elevator."

"We'll take a chance. Maybe they're all standing outside
the doors to Ward's and Tootell's suites. If so, we can find a
table out of sight so we won't be bothered."

Outside the conference room, Roman Burke turned to Lance
and said, "Will you watch the door for a few minutes, please?
Janine and I need to visit." Lance nodded, pulled a chair from
the room, and leaned it against the wall. He watched with interest as Burke turned to Janine and asked, "How about the
coffee shop across the street?"

Janine was puzzled, but merely smiled as she turned
toward the door. She would find out what Burke had on his
mind soon enough. For now it was enough that they could
speak civilly to one another.

Roman Burke chose a booth in the rear, even though an
odor of something burning seeped from the kitchen. It was
out of the sight of any stray reporter who might wander in.
After they had ordered coffee and a sweet roll, he leaned forward. "Okay," he said, "we've had our differences, and most
of the problems were my creation. But you and I have something in common now." He broke a piece from the roll, put it

in his mouth, chewed quickly, and swallowed. "The majority of the electors favor Tootell. That's apparent. Even Ward's own supporters must realize he can't get the votes to win the presidency."

"You're right. Ward won't win. So all of the electors will probably agree to cast their ballots for Tootell."

"That's almost surely what Tootell is thinking right this minute. But I can tell you, the Florida electors will never vote for him. It just won't happen. Weldon was our governor—our guy—well-liked and respected in Florida. We didn't appreciate the accusations made by Tootell at the time he made them and our feelings haven't changed. They still stick in our throats."

"My God, Roman, Florida has twenty-nine electoral votes. As you said, even if all the remaining electors vote for Tootell, he won't have the 270 he needs for a majority."

"That's right. Besides, I'm certain there are others who won't vote for him, no matter what. He didn't help himself with his remark about Ward a few minutes ago."

Burke looked solemnly at Janine. "Do you agree that Ward doesn't have the votes to win either?"

"I've believed that since the day Senator Blaine died."

"So Jackson Tootell isn't going to be president of the United States and neither is Allen Ward."

They sat looking at one another for a long time. Then Burke surprised her again by asking, "What do you have in mind for your boy, Bobby Hobaugh?"

She thought a moment before answering. "I've wondered if he might not end up being a compromise choice for vice president." She looked down at her hands, folded on the tabletop. "It really does seem unlikely, though, that he could be selected for president." She looked up and continued, "I like the man. There's nothing phony about him. And believe me,

I've been around lots of phonies, including one I married."

She held Burke's gaze as she spoke. "When I listened to Bobby Hobaugh say he would do his best for the country if he were president, I knew he wasn't just blowing smoke like all politicians do. He meant it." She smiled a wry smile. "It's too bad someone like him can't be elected. Someone who isn't tainted by the political maneuvering and compromising that you and I know so well." Then Janine stopped and her face took on a practical look. "Well, if neither Ward nor Tootell can get the necessary 270 votes, who can?"

"There isn't any other person in the world of politics whose name jumps out, is there?"

"No, there isn't. Thomas Lowell and Susan Washington show up in the polls, but neither one has generated any support. So what do you have in mind? You didn't ask me over here just because you like me."

"As a matter of fact, I do like you. The truth is, I've been hoping we could spend some time together. You're a very attractive lady, one I'd like to know much better. We have a lot in common." The look on her face stopped him. "But you're right—that's only one reason I wanted to visit with you." He nodded his head in the direction of the hotel across the street. "The other is the election. I believe we should go to Ward and suggest that he ask his supporters to vote for Bobby Hobaugh and then let the other electors know what they intend to do. When it becomes clear to Tootell that he can't win, he may be willing to accept some compromise candidate."

"And who will that be?"

"Who knows? It may be your man, Bobby. It may be Lowell or Washington. But whoever it is, we need to get those two out of the way because neither of them can get it done."

"All right, you go tell him."

"I need you to go with me. We can speak as the ones closest to Governor Weldon and Senator Blaine when they were alive. That should give us an appearance of authority."

"When do we do it?"

"How about right now?"

Ralph found Bobby and Margaret sitting alone in a back corner of the hotel coffee shop. Lance followed and joined them. Ralph asked, "Could you hear all the yelling and shouting?"

Bobby grinned at his friend. "Did you yell and shout?"

"I didn't, but it seemed that everyone else did." Ralph shook his head. "Those people will never reach an agreement on either Tootell or Ward. When Dick Saylor and I tried to suggest that we consider some alternative candidates, they shouted us down. It was worse than anything you or I ever saw in the Montana legislature."

"That bad, huh?" When Ralph just nodded his head, Bobby asked, "What happens now? Did you take a break to cool down?"

"Nope. Ward's supporters could see they were outnumbered and just got up and left. About two thirds of the electors support Tootell, so they think Ward's people will change their minds between now and December 13. That's only ten days away. They seem certain that Ward's electors will, in the end, hold their noses and vote for Tootell."

"What if they don't?"

"Then we've got a problem, a real problem." Ralph turned to Lance and said, "You're the one who knows how to handle the news people. Impress on them their obligation to report that Bobby Hobaugh was the only candidate who acted in a responsible manner today."

Lance raised his eyebrows and rose from the table, "I'll get on it."

The reporters were waiting when the meeting adjourned in disarray. They surrounded any elector willing to talk. Most who talked were supporters of Tootell. They criticized Ward for not throwing his support to Tootell right away. They also stated, as a fact, that Tootell would get all 283 Republican electoral votes on December 13. Ward's supporters, on the other hand, told reporters with equal certainty that Tootell would never get a majority of the electoral votes. Some hinted at a willingness to consider a compromise candidate. When asked who that candidate might be, some mentioned Bobby Hobaugh; others couldn't suggest any name. In minutes, all of this spread across the nation on the Internet and television.

The television talking heads took up the discussion. They ran through a list of men and women who might be acceptable to the supporters of both Tootell and Ward and then promptly told the viewing audience why each wouldn't be acceptable. Bobby Hobaugh was among the ones mentioned, but, despite Lance's efforts, little time was spent on his chances. They were deemed to be slight, if not nonexistent. The political bloggers went wild with speculation, but they didn't include a single instance in which Hobaugh was named as a credible possibility.

Friday, December 3, evening

DENVER, COLORADO

Bobby, Margaret, Ralph, and Lance were watching the news on CNN when Janine and Roman Burke banged on the door to the suite. They each wore an excited look as they barged into the room after Lance opened the door. Janine started talking as she strode across the room to an empty chair. "Ward will go on national television in a few minutes to concede that he hasn't the votes to be elected president." She sat back in the chair, crossed her legs and glanced around the room. "He'll state that he can't support Tootell, and he'll ask his supporters to vote for Bobby Hobaugh. Then Ward will ask Tootell to recognize that he, Tootell, can't get the required 270 either and suggest that Tootell come up with the name of someone, other than Bobby, that they both find acceptable. If Tootell does it, Ward will ask his supporters to vote for that person. Otherwise, he wants them to be firm and cast their votes for you, Bobby."

Ralph rushed to the television and turned to the Fox News channel. The newscaster glanced sideways, apparently at a laptop near at hand, blinked, and then turned back to face the camera. In solemn tones he said, "We'll step aside for a late breaking political announcement."

Allen Ward, appearing somewhat haggard, stood before a small group of supporters and looked directly toward the camera. He spoke without notes.

> We are facing a critical moment in the history of our country, a time when those of us in the political arena must put our own ambitions aside for the benefit of all. It is apparent that neither Jackson Tootell nor I have sufficient electoral votes to succeed to the presidency. For that reason and so that an orderly choice may be made, I'm directing those electors who support me to cast their votes for Bobby Hobaugh....Unless Jackson Tootell and I can agree on some other candidate that we both can support. I've informed Mr. Tootell that I will

select three possible candidates and make them known to him within the next twenty-four hours. I'm asking him to do the same and send his list to me. It is my hope we can find one among the six that we may mutually recommend to the electors. If not, my support—and the support of those who would prefer me to Tootell—will remain with Bobby Hobaugh.

The eyes of every person in the room were on Bobby. He didn't speak or move for what seemed a long time. When he did speak, it was to Margaret. "All of a sudden, Miles City, Montana, seems a long way away."

In his suite in the same hotel, Jackson Tootell turned the television set off and walked to the window. Tucker spoke to his back. "The votes aren't there, sir. Twenty-eight from the Florida delegation will vote in a block for Hobaugh. We turned one woman by reminding her of the illegitimate child she had thirty years ago. We handled it in the manner you directed. She'll vote the right way."

"What about the ones from the other states that we've discussed?"

"We've had success with several." Tucker reached into the inside pocket of his suit coat and brought out a long, narrow sheet of paper. "If the vote were held right now, you would get about 213 votes. After Allen Ward's request that his supporters go for Hobaugh, Hobaugh would get about sixty. Ward would still get about ten." He looked at the sheet again and added, "Right now, you're short about fifty-seven votes."

With his back to Tucker and still looking out the window, Tootell muttered, "It was a mistake to agree to this gathering. When they got together, Ward's people were able to lend support to one another. We were better off when we could work on them individually." Tootell turned from the window with a strange smile. "I'm the one responsible for this fiasco. I was the one who agreed to come here."

"We have ten days, sir. Shall we continue to work on electors who haven't yet agreed to vote for you?"

"Of course. I never give up."

"With your permission, sir, I'll start right now. Some of those in this hotel are susceptible to pressure."

"Very good." Tootell turned again to the window. "I'll think about it on the way back to Atlanta, Tucker. We may have to devise another strategy." The large man was silent for another moment before turning back to say, "And, Tucker, at some time it may be in our interest for something to happen to Bobby Hobaugh. He's become too much of a nuisance."

24

Saturday, December 4, evening

MILES CITY, MONTANA

Bobby walked Margaret up the steps to her apartment. After she unlocked the door and turned to tell him good bye, he reached out to place his hand gently on her upper arm and said, "I can't thank you enough for making that long, tiring trip to Denver. I don't know how I would have survived if you hadn't been there."

"You'd have survived, Bobby, but it's nice of you to flatter me."

"It isn't flattery. It's the truth." He gave her arm a squeeze and added, "Get some rest, Margaret. That's what I intend to do." He started down the walk toward his car and then looked back to say with a smile, "I'll see you at the office Monday morning?"

"I'll be there—as always."

Later, as he sat in his easy chair in the old house at the ranch, Bobby's thoughts remained on the lady with whom he spent his working days. He could no longer think of Margaret only as his office manager. She had become much more than that, even though he didn't dare tell her so. He found that she crowded into his first thoughts of the day and into his last thoughts at night. He valued her judgment and always asked for her advice, often merely to have the chance to spend quiet time with her, away from the others who populated the law office. Quiet times in her presence gave him the most satisfaction. Conversation between them was always comfortable.

Margaret was interested in many things, from sporting events, to historical happenings, to classical music and literature. Once she had asked him if he had read the works of Dickens. When he admitted that he had not, she told him, with some pride, that she had read them all. Her use of language was excellent. Some would say it was surprising, considering her limited formal education. It spoke of her intense desire to overcome the limitations of her early years and to improve herself in every way. The closeness that he felt to her during the trip to Denver made him wish she were with him now. Instead, he was alone in an empty room, feeling sorry for himself.

Margaret's thoughts were on her employer. She had liked Bobby Hobaugh from the first time she met him, when he made her difficult divorce as painless as possible. Later, merely because he was a nice man, she went to his office to ask for employment without any real expectation that she would be hired. It was a pleasant surprise to find herself working as a receptionist the very next day. From the beginning, he always took time to answer questions and give guidance. Bobby provided opportunities to learn, and always seemed to take personal pride in the things that she accomplished.

If Bobby had a case to try, and his efforts were a success, he would give credit to her good work in preparing and managing the exhibits. The next morning, flowers, with a thank you note, would appear on her desk. If the result wasn't as good as Bobby had hoped, he took the blame—and still sent the flowers.

Over time, her admiration for him grew. Now, as she relaxed at her small kitchen table with a cup of hot chocolate in hand, she admitted to herself for the first time that she was in love with her employer. She could not help feeling sad because the sentiment was futile. Bobby Hobaugh was a respected man in the community and the state. There wasn't a place in his life for someone with her background. But, in the quiet of her room, and since no one would ever know of her feelings, she could continue to dream the dream of a romantic tryst that would never occur.

Sunday, December 5, morning

DENVER, COLORADO

Janine, wearing a long robe over her pajamas, drank coffee as she watched the morning news programs. Allen Thistead on CNN was interviewing two Washington insiders, Timothy Johns, a former congressman, and Roger Doyle, a former presidential advisor. Timothy Johns was speaking:

> "No, Allen Ward's attempt to force Jackson Tootell to compromise just won't work. Tootell knows that he has the votes of a majority of the electors. Why would he give up now?"

> "Roger, would you like to answer that question?"

> "Certainly. Because, by asking his supporters to

vote for Bobby Hobaugh, Ward has changed the equation. Hobaugh seems to be somewhere in the middle ground—between the hard-core conservatism of Tootell and the liberalism of Ward. The supporters of both may tire of the standoff between the two front runners and turn to Hobaugh."

"Hobaugh's an almost complete unknown. What we do know about him is that he has absolutely no national experience." Thistead turned to Doyle again. "Do you really believe that any elector would seriously consider voting for him?"

"With the things that have happened so far in this election, nothing will surprise me."

Janine smiled to herself as she poked the remote to change channels. Doyle just might be right, and Bobby Hobaugh could be in the White House. Then her smile turned to a self-embarrassed chuckle. It would never happen—no matter what Ralph Phillips might come up with next.

The Fox News moderator, Roberta Kelly, was questioning two members of Congress, Joseph Slingsby, a Democrat, and Bill Pasha, a Republican, about their views of the electoral system.

"Congressman Slingsby, what changes would you make in the system we use to elect presidents?"

"Roberta, we need a constitutional amendment to abolish the system of electors, and we need it immediately. The manner in which the Republicans have conducted themselves since Governor Weldon died makes that as clear as can be."

"How, then, would a president be chosen, if a situation like the one we have now were to occur again?"

Slingsby answered, "We must provide for a second election, one in which the voters will select a replacement for the dead nominee."

"Would the election be open to both parties? Or could only the members of the party of the dead nominee participate?"

"Oh, the election would only be to elect a nominee for the party that lost its man. It wouldn't be fair to give the other party a second chance—even if it was my party that needed it."

"But how would you ensure that only the members of the dead nominee's party vote in the election? Couldn't members of the other party try to sneak one of their own onto the ballot?"

"I suppose we would have to require that every voter declare his party affiliation at the time he registered to vote."

"Congressman Pasha, the electors from your party are the ones who seem to be having difficulty at the moment. Do you agree with your colleague that we should change the system?"

"Not at all. Let me explain why. Suppose the nominee died the 10th of December. Remember, the president takes office the 20th of January. There would be about one month in which to hold that election. Who would have the advantage? Someone with national name recognition or someone with unlimited money to spend, that's who. Those who might be legitimate candidates, if there was time for them to campaign, but who were without unlimited resources at their immediate disposal, would be at an insurmountable disadvantage.

You can't raise money fast enough to conduct a creditable campaign in one month."

"But," Roberta asked, "what would you do about the system that seems to have your Republican electors tied in knots?"

"I say, leave the system as it is, but require that the ballots in every state reveal the names of the electors alongside the names of the candidates for president. Let the people know the names of those who will be choosing a president, should we ever find ourselves in this situation again. If the names of the electors were on the ballots, the parties would be certain to choose responsible people for the job. If a party doesn't do so, it would run the risk of having its candidate lose votes because of a bad choice of electors. Some states have this system now. If all states did, we would be certain to have trustworthy electors, people we could rely on to make an intelligent choice."

"Congressman Pasha, are you implying that the electors we have now can't make an intelligent choice?

"No, of course not. I'm only saying that they were generally unknown until Governor Weldon died."

"Congressman Slingsby, do you agree that having the names of electors on the ballot would solve the problem?"

"With all due respect to my colleague, Congressman Pasha, I think that's foolishness. We would still have a very small number of people choosing a president for the rest of us. That may have been satisfactory for the founding fathers, but it just isn't the way it should be done in this day and age. Nowadays, everyone expects to participate in the choice of elected officials. We must recognize that's what the public wants."

"Gentlemen, it seems to me that there is no more agreement between you two than there seems to be among the Republican electors who are supposed to choose a president in eight days. But thank you both for appearing with me today."

Janine pushed the remote to turn off the television, swallowed the last bit of coffee, and muttered to herself, "There will be a hundred different bills in the next Congress to change the system. It will surprise me if any of them ever get out of committee."

Her thoughts turned to Ralph Phillips, as they were inclined to do in recent days. She could hardly believe she was developing feelings for an older man who wasn't tall, especially a man who was portly. She refused to think of him as fat. In fact, he didn't have a paunch. His body was just shaped like a small barrel. Besides, it was their mutual zeal for the mechanics of politics, rather than his physical appearance, that drew her to him. They both liked to make things happen. Ralph, at times, acted like a man moving pieces on a chessboard. And he was good at selecting the moves. She enjoyed moving the pieces once the selection was made. This had been their mode since the day Senator Blaine died.

It was just plain fun to be with Ralph and watch him in action. He was a nice, courteous gentleman, different from Bobby Hobaugh, but extremely likable in his own way. Her hand went to her arm as the old habit dictated. Why not arrange to spend time alone with Ralph, she wondered, and see what might happen?

Monday, December 6, morning

DENVER, COLORADO

Lance Caldwell, home at his comfortable suburban town-house, was like Janine, Ralph Phillips, and Roman Burke—he couldn't stay away from the television. Who knew what might happen regarding how the electors cast their votes? Seated in an easy chair with his newborn child in his arms, he half watched and half listened as the CNN anchorman blathered on about the split between those who supported Tootell and those who supported Ward. His attention focused sharply, however, when the image changed. Large letters flashed "News Alert" at the bottom of the screen, and a different face popped into view. A dark-haired woman, seated at a wide desk, dropped her eyes slightly as though reading from material on a computer screen.

"Federal authorities have just released a preliminary report of the investigation into the death of Senator Forrest Blaine. According to a synopsis of the report, the truck that crashed into the senator's limousine was an older-model farm truck that had been converted to haul gravel. Its ownership had passed through several hands and no maintenance records for the vehicle were kept by any of them. The truck's brake lines were determined to be old, brittle, and seriously deteriorated. A break in the lines—perhaps merely the result of vibration—apparently occurred about the time that the driver put the vehicle into gear and began the descent down the steep grade that led to the crash site.

"The investigation disclosed no evidence of deliberate wrongdoing by any person. The owner of the truck, however, has been interrogated about his knowledge of the condition of the faulty lines. A question still remains about the communication, or lack thereof, between the officers manning the road block at the top of the hill and those at the intersection where the crash occurred."

The report ends with a cautionary note that it is preliminary and may be changed if new information surfaces.

In less than a minute the telephone, resting on the side table at Lance's elbow, rang. He put the receiver to his ear to hear Janine ask, "Did you hear the news?"

"Yes. Just now." He paused. "I guess that puts any ideas of terrorist activity to rest."

"You're right." Janine breathed out a long sigh. "God, what a tragic and unnecessary loss. What a waste of a man who had so much to offer the country."

"And what a sad loss for his family," Lance added.

25

Tuesday, December 7, morning

MILES CITY, MONTANA

Reporters from the Billings newspaper and from regional television stations called from time to time in an attempt to discuss the presidential contest with Bobby, but Margaret politely turned them away. They might have been more persistent if they believed that Bobby could be elected. He was a curiosity, more than anything else.

The editor of the Miles City Star, however, was an old friend. On Pearl Harbor Day, he found Bobby on the street and dragged him into a nearby coffee shop. The editor began by talking about the Japanese attack on the island of Oahu and then turned the conversation to the notion of patriotism. At last, he asked Bobby how he felt, being a candidate for president of the United States. Bobby responded out of habit. "I'm not a candidate." After a slight pause he added, "At least I didn't want to be, and I won't be chosen."

"What do you think of the other two who are the likely choices?"

"Both have national reputations. Either of them would, I'm convinced, try to do what is best for the country."

"C'mon, Bobby, we're old friends. You can do better than that. You've actually met the guys, and I haven't. What are they really like?"

"They're human, just like all the rest of us."

The editor smiled as he said, "Not going to talk, huh?'

"I'll talk about anything but the presidential election. That's out of bounds."

"Well, friend, I'm going to run a story about you anyway. I'll try to make it interesting. It'll go out over the wire." He got up from his chair, dropped change on the table for the coffee, and said, "It would be nice if you would give me something juicy so my circulation would increase."

"Juicy, I'm not."

The article went to print in the Sunday edition. It described Bobby's childhood on the ranch that had been in his family for more than a hundred years. He was the second of two sons and, since the older of the two was expected to be the rancher, Bobby went to law school and launched a practice in Miles City. Events occasionally changed his life's plans. On a flight to Denver, the light airplane in which Bobby's parents and brother were flying caught fire and crashed, killing all three. Bobby suddenly found himself with both a ranch and a law practice, each of which required his attention and energy.

Not long thereafter, Bobby married the neighbor's daughter, a beautiful, talented, and charming young lady. Cynthia's attributes complemented Bobby's personality and ambitions. They were a gracious and handsome couple, liked and admired by most in the community, envied by a few.

Bobby was active in local affairs, both those in the town

of Miles City itself and in the ranching community that surrounded it. When he ran for the state senate, he won in a landslide. Four years later he was re-elected without opposition. For the article, the editor interviewed several prominent Montana politicians, both Republicans and Democrats. Even some of the Democrats stated that they had expected Bobby to be governor one day, but hadn't thought of him as a candidate for national office.

The death of Cynthia Hobaugh was told in a sympathetic manner. On a pleasure trip to Calgary, Alberta, she began to suffer bouts of fatigue. Upon returning to Miles City, she was diagnosed with pancreatic cancer and died within two months.

Apparently the editor, as well as the whole community, was aware of Bobby's devastation at the loss of his wife. The article indicated it took him six months from the time of her death to begin to function as he had in the past. After about a year, his sorrow no longer was evident to acquaintances. The editor intimated that only his office manager, of all those who knew him, understood how much he continued to suffer from his loss. Finally, the article opined that the country would do well to choose the Miles City native for its president.

Much to the chagrin of the editor of the Miles City Star, not a single national media outlet picked up the article.

26

Thursday, December 9, evening

BILLINGS, MONTANA

Ralph read the feature article in Time magazine with interest. He was surprised at the accuracy with which the meeting of the electors in Denver was reported. The remarks attributed to both Ward and Tootell and those of their supporters were exactly as Ralph remembered them. It led him to believe a reporter managed to remain in the room after the media people were asked to leave. Or maybe a reporter had placed a recorder somewhere in the room and retrieved it afterward. The news hounds always seemed to find a way. The report concluded by telling how the statements of Ward and Tootell caused the meeting to degenerate into bedlam.

He read the US News and World Report analysis of the electoral system carefully. The authors cited the Federalist Papers and other such writings, and from those drew some conclusions regarding the manner in which the Founding Fathers intended the system to work. In the beginning there were no political parties, and apparently the writers of the Constitution didn't contemplate any would come into existence. The use of electors to choose a president had resulted in only one serious controversy since the strong two-party system came into existence. That, the article said, occurred in 1872.

The election of 1872 was described briefly in a side bar. It told how the selection of the electors from the state of Florida was challenged in Congress and, as a result, the selection of the president was left to the House of Representatives. The article recited the allegation that Rutherford B. Hayes defeated Samuel Tilden only because he agreed to withdraw federal troops—troops that had occupied the southern states since the end of the Civil War—from all of those states. Ralph smiled as he read, thinking of the parallel between that election and the current one.

Ralph's interest really picked up when US News and World Report reported on the current electors. The article didn't set forth a complete list of the names of all of them. It emphasized their general anonymity. Only Herman McDougal and Arnold Daniels were quoted extensively. McDougal praised Tootell as an entrepreneur who raised himself from poverty to immense wealth, "the very epitome of American free enterprise."

Daniels countered that Ward was a moderate overwhelmed in the primaries by Tootell's unparalleled spending. While he did not speak directly of the questions about Tootell's business practices, he alluded to them as a dark shadow hovering over the man. He characterized Ward as "a temperate individual who represented the beliefs of all Americans and who would bring dignity to the office of president."

The authors of the article had interviewed Ralph on the telephone when preparing the piece. But the long interview had been reduced to a brief statement that read, "Phillips states emphatically that neither Tootell nor Ward is acceptable to a majority of the electors and that an alternative is needed. That alternative, according to Phillips, is Bobby Hobaugh."

The article, Ralph concluded, was intended to bring the burden now borne by the electors to the attention of the public and to enlighten them about the struggle for the votes of those electors. In that regard, it was a public service. He was disappointed, however, that Hobaugh was given so little mention. And, to be truthful, irritated that McDougal and Daniels received more coverage than he did. After all, it was because of his initiative that the meeting in Denver took place.

Putting the magazine aside, he considered calling Bobby to talk about it, but decided his friend probably wanted nothing more than respite from the whole election discussion. He would have a chance to share thoughts with Janine before too many days went by. She was the one who seemed to delight in the strategical maneuvering of politics.

Friday, December 10, afternoon

WASHINGTON, D. C.

Arthur Simpson rose from his desk in the Oval Office to greet the vice president. "Well, Henry, we lost the election in November and, despite the disarray in the ranks of the Republican Party, it appears that they'll elect someone other than us when the presidential electors cast their ballots."

"That's right. I've wondered if there is a way to sway some of the Republican electors to vote for you."

"There isn't. No matter what was offered, any Republican who voted for us would be known and ostracized by his party. And it wouldn't be hard to figure out who voted for us, if any did, once the ballots were made public. If they voted in secret, it might be another matter."

"So, what are your plans, Arthur? Will you just go back to Ohio and sit in a rocking chair?"

"It's not my plans I want to talk about." Simpson walked around to sit behind the desk again. Henry Larsen took a chair on the other side. "You once said you'd like to be a federal judge. I obviously can't appoint you to the Supreme Court because there aren't any vacancies, but one of the judges on the D.C. Circuit is suffering from terminal cancer. He plans to resign, effective immediately. Are you still interested?"

The vice president stared at Simpson, then smiled. "Sure, I'm interested. You know about my background in the law. I would serve the country well on the bench."

"We'll both be out of here in January. I can give you an interim appointment now, while Congress isn't in session. That way you'll be on the job when Congress reconvenes. The Republicans retained control of both the House and Senate and they may not want to approve a former vice president, a Democrat, to the judiciary. But you served in the Senate. Your former colleagues seem to abide by the old boy code. They'll probably suggest the new president affirm the appointment. Then they can confirm it when they reconvene. What do you think?"

"The Republican leadership will remain the same. Timothy Welch will be Speaker, and Paul Wheeler will be senate majority leader. Paul and I have always gotten along." Larsen thought for a moment. "I'd have to resign the vice presidency. That would be unusual, to say the least. I don't want to be remembered as another Spiro Agnew."

"This whole election has been unusual. Everything that

has happened has been improbable. Hell, it's worse than that, it's bizarre." Simpson spread his arms wide. "Who would have thought a cowboy from Montana, a man no one had ever heard of a month ago, would be a serious candidate for president?" Simpson shook his head. "No matter how good a man he is, how would he even begin to act as president? We had two months before the inauguration to prepare, and we still had trouble getting people in place to begin our administration. If this guy, Hobaugh, should by some chance win, he'll have to take the office in a little over a month. He has no real organization to help him and no knowledgeable advisors with national experience."

"The possibility is bizarre, all right. But Hobaugh won't make it. In the end, the Republicans will vote for Tootell. He's got most of them now and the rest will fall in line before the electors vote."

The president's face contorted into a grimace. "God, how I hate the thought of that man sitting in this chair. He's an unscrupulous bastard, without any redeeming qualities. You were privy to all the information that was gathered by the Justice Department, so you know he's as crooked as a dog's hind leg."

Larsen nodded. "I still don't understand what happened in the anti-trust suit."

"The attorney general told me that two key witnesses changed their stories at the crucial time. He had suspicions about the reason, but his people couldn't secure proof of any illegal activity by Tootell, or by anyone on his behalf, that could be used in court."

Larsen grinned. "At least we agree that he's an unscrupulous bastard, but we're Democrats. That may influence our judgment."

"Well, what will be will be, as the old song says." The

president rose again from the desk and walked around to shake the hand of his friend. "Prepare your resignation. As soon as I have it in hand, I'll appoint you to the bench."

Larsen started for the door, then stopped and turned to look back at the president. "What if some other bizarre thing happens and we're elected?"

Simpson threw his head back and laughed. It was a pose that was often seen in pictures. "Well, if that happens, you'll just have to decide if you want to be a judge or vice president of the United States."

27

Sunday, December 12, morning

BILLINGS, MONTANA

"We're losing votes, Ralph. Five of the electors here in Texas have decided to vote for Tootell." Worry was reflected in Dick Saylor's voice. "I don't know what he's doing but it's been effective. He may get elected yet."

Ralph switched the phone to his other hand so he could make notes. "I know what he's doing. He's trying to buy votes. One of the Indiana electors told Harley Smith about a call he received. Some guy told the elector a job in the Interior Department would be his if he voted for Tootell and if Tootell won. Smith said the man would like to have the job. Of course, we can't trace the actual offer to Tootell. He's too smart to let that happen. Harley said that particular elector will stand hitched and vote for Bobby, but he is concerned about others who may get an offer that's too good to refuse."

"How about your Montana people?"

"We're all Bobby's friends. Tootell knows we'll stick with our man. He won't try anything in this state."

"What have you heard from Burke about Florida?"

"Not a thing. He seemed certain that none of his people would change their minds, but I'll call him for an update."

"Let me know what you learn."

Roman Burke sounded tired. "I would've sworn that none of the Florida electors would ever vote for Jackson Tootell, but at least two are going to do it. Although one of them hasn't said what made him change his mind, I've heard he's been threatened with exposure to a charge of pedophilia. True or not, doesn't matter. He won't risk his reputation, so Tootell gets his vote. The other is a woman, and she's so scared she won't even talk to me." Ralph heard Burke swallow and take a deep breath before he spoke again. "There may be more."

"Well, none of us expected Tootell to sit on his dollar watch and let the election slip away. I still think enough electors will vote for Bobby so that no one gets a majority."

"Tomorrow's the day when you and the other electors will cast your ballots. All we can do is wait until those votes are counted."

Ralph's phone rang almost as soon as he ended his conversation with Burke. Janine said, "Ralph, we've lost some votes here in Colorado. I thought you'd want to know."

"'We're losing them everywhere. Tootell's been busy."

"Will Bobby get enough votes to stop him?"

"I still think so."

"How's Bobby? I'm reluctant to call him to ask."

"Bobby just wishes it would all go away. When I talked with him last night, he said he hopes Tootell wins."

"Is he angry at you and me? Does he still think it's our fault that he's a candidate for president?"

"Of course he thinks it's our fault, and it is." Ralph took

a deep breath. "Janine, do you still believe Tootell would be wrong for the country?"

"I surely do."

"So do I. If we're correct, and I'm certain we are, then what we've done is right."

"Maybe so. But neither you nor I is in Bobby's position. He's a great guy. It's too bad he's not more ambitious—not more anxious to be a great man."

"That's not Bobby. That's why he is a great guy. I just keep hoping that some way he ends up in the White House."

Janine was silent for a second, then said, "Ralph, we should talk, face to face. Could you fly here to Denver tomorrow after you cast your ballot? Or maybe the next day?"

It was Ralph's turn to pause. "I can't get a flight out of Helena tomorrow. That's where I have to go to vote. But I can be on a flight from here in Billings day after tomorrow. It gets in there at three o'clock in the afternoon." After another pause, he went on, "What do you have in mind?"

"We need to talk about the results of the voting by the electors." Janine paused again, took a breath, and then said in a rush, "Ralph, I'd just like to get to know you better. Spend some time without all the political furor. Do you realize we've never said a word to each other that wasn't about the election?"

"That would be nice, it really would. I'll plan on staying over. Can we have dinner together?"

"Yes, we can. I'll make reservations at a place you'll like." Her laugh was soft in her throat. "Fly safely, Ralph. I'm anxious to see you."

Ralph held the phone for a long time before returning it to its cradle. Then, with his eyebrows raised in amazement, he muttered to the empty room, "Well, I'll be hornswoggled!"

Sunday, December 12, evening

CAMBRIDGE, MASSACHUSETTS

Allen Ward sent an email to those presidential electors who were not publicly committed to Jackson Tootell. The email read:

It is evident that Jackson Tootell will receive the majority of the electoral votes tomorrow. My attempt to use Bobby Hobaugh as a means of persuading Tootell to agree to some compromise candidate has not been successful. Therefore, I'm asking you to cast your ballot for me rather than for Bobby Hobaugh. We may still be able to stop Tootell.

Monday, December 13, morning

HELENA, MONTANA

The reporters were standing outside the secretary of state's office when Ralph and the other two emerged. Ralph stepped up to the nearest microphone and smiled toward the camera with the corner of his eyes crinkling. "We've all three voted for a great Montanan. We expect, when the votes are counted, that Bobby Hobaugh will be the president of the United States." Then he led the others down the hall of the capitol building and out to their waiting automobiles.

The Secretary of State, aided by his administrative assistant, bundled the ballots and the election certificate in a sturdy envelope addressed to the President of the United States Senate. Then the Secretary personally carried the envelope to the capitol post office and handed it to the chief postal clerk with directions to ensure that it reached its destination.

Laws of the United States

Congress shall be in session on the sixth day of January succeeding every meeting of the electors. The Senate and House of Representatives shall meet in the Hall of the House of Representatives at the hour of 1 o'clock in the afternoon on that day, and the president of the Senate shall be their presiding officer. Two tellers shall be previously appointed on the part of the Senate and two on the part of the House of Representatives, to whom shall be handed, as they are opened by the president of the Senate...all the certificates of the electoral vote...

...said tellers...shall make a list of the votes as they shall appear from the said certificates...the result of the same shall be delivered to the President of the Senate, who shall thereupon announce the state of the vote, which announcement shall be deemed a sufficient declaration of the persons, if any, elected President and Vice President of the United States...

28

Tuesday, December 14, evening

DENVER, COLORADO

The French restaurant was small and out of the way. Ralph and Janine were seated at a table toward the rear, away from the noise of the large crowd near the bar. During the initial pleasantries, the wine steward came by and handed the list to Ralph. His hesitation told Janine that he wasn't a connoisseur. Ralph's smile was shy as he confessed, "Bobby Hobaugh isn't the only country boy from Montana." He passed the wine list to Janine.

"That's your charm. Neither of you tries to be anything other than what you are." She perused the list, then asked the steward to bring a California wine, the name of which was unknown to Ralph.

Ralph picked up the menu to discover that it was in English, but described the offerings in such a pretentious fashion that made it difficult to know if he was ordering halibut or chicken. Again he looked at Janine, eyebrows raised, to ask, "What do you suggest?"

She leaned forward and pointed to an item on his menu. "If I remember correctly, you like beef. Try the Boeuf Bourguignon, it's great."

When the waiter returned, Ralph simply gestured with his hand toward Janine. She looked at him for a second, smiled graciously across the table, and then ordered for both of them.

To cover his embarrassment, Ralph turned the conversation in Janine's direction. "What about you? Are you really the sophisticate you pretend?"

"No. I'm just another woman trying to make it in a man's world."

"Tell me about yourself. How did you get involved in politics?"

"It's a long story, but I'll give you the short version." She sipped her wine, looked at Ralph over the rim of the glass, set it down, and continued. "After college, I married a guy who had ambitions to be a congressman. He believed it would improve his chances for election if he had Washington experience. So he got a job with one of the representatives from Michigan, and we moved to the capital. It was natural for me to seek a job with another member of Congress. After some false starts, I got on with Senator Blaine. It was great. He was such a fine man and, with all the excitement of Washington, I was in heaven—until I found out that my husband was spending more time with the female staffers on the hill than he was at his job. The divorce was excruciatingly painful, and I wanted to get as far away as I could. The senator was good enough to give me the job in his Denver office."

"And then Governor Weldon chose the senator as his vice presidential running mate."

"That's right. Senator Blaine needed a staff person to

coordinate the campaign activities, and he chose me. Almost immediately, I found myself quarreling with Roman Burke about the senator's role in the campaign. The Weldon people wanted to limit him to minor appearances. I insisted that he had the stature and public appeal to bring in major blocks of votes. In the end, I got my way to some degree but not altogether."

"You did well for him."

"He's gone now. I still miss him. He became sort of a father figure to me." She took a breath. "But thanks to you, I've had another campaign on my hands. Only this time, the candidate is mighty reluctant."

"Yes. Bobby's reluctant, all right." Before Ralph could comment further about politics, the meal arrived.

Janine savored the fragrance. "Let's enjoy this good food. Then we'll visit about anything other than campaigns, politicians, or government."

"I promised you that, didn't I?"

Janine allowed him to eat without interruption until desert and coffee were served. Then she started the conversation again. "I've told you about me. What about you? We've spent a lot of time together, and I hardly know you."

"There's not much to know. I'm a native Montanan, grew up on a farm near Shelby. That's oil country in Montana. I went to work as a roughneck in the oil fields out of high school. After a time, I gathered enough money to pick up an oil lease or two and contract a drilling rig. Luck was with me. The first hole I drilled proved to be very productive. I've just gone on from there."

Janine looked across the rim of her coffee cup at him. "For a guy that had only a high school education, you certainly speak well."

Ralph laughed quietly before answering. "That's a nice compliment. Especially nice from someone who holds a college degree." He looked down at the table and then back up before he spoke again. "It didn't take long, when I was roughnecking, to figure out that the ones in charge of the operation, the owners and superintendents, didn't use the same language as the roughnecks. They seldom used profanity. Their use of grammar was always just the way Miss Olson tried to teach me in the eighth grade. And they used big words." Ralph chuckled again at the memory. "I knew I wanted to be more than a oil patch laborer, and so it seemed wise to emulate the guys who used their brains rather than those who used their backs. I borrowed some old school books and really studied the way the English language was supposed to be spoken. And then I made a determined effort to speak correctly, all of the time." One more laugh before he continued. "I took a lot of ribbing from some of the others on the rigs, but later, when they were working for me, the ribbing stopped."

"That's remarkable. But how about your good manners? Did you learn those from a book too?"

"If my manners are good, I can thank my mother." Ralph's face reddened slightly as he recalled his embarrassment. "As you can see, I don't know how to order the wine."

Janine shook her head. "Don't sell yourself short, Ralph. You do better than many of the pseudo-sophisticates I encountered in Washington." She sipped again from the cup and then changed the direction of the conversation. "What about the explosion that killed your man. Did they ever find out who was responsible?"

"No." Ralph shook his head. "Apparently someone attached a plastic explosive to the compressor pump. When it blew, the gas coming from the intake line ignited and created a tremendous fire. My people cut off the gas that was flowing to the compressor, and that stopped the flames." Ralph shook his head. "The man who was killed just happened to be there for routine maintenance. He got caught in the blast and the flames that followed." He looked across the table at Janine as he added, "At least it was a quick death."

"Who would want to do such a thing?"

"The authorities first thought it was one of the eco-terrorist groups. Those outfits like to claim credit for the havoc they wreak, but no such claim has been made about the damage to the compressor. Investigators from the state attorney general's office and the FBI thought it might be someone out to cause trouble for me, but I can't think of anyone I've offended that badly. They also wondered if someone might be angry at one of my employees. Who knows?"

Ralph stopped, looked at his empty cup, and asked, "Would you like more coffee?"

"That would be nice."

He signaled to the waiter and then continued, "Whoever did it was an expert. The investigators haven't been able to figure out how the perpetrator got there to place the explosive. No unusual tracks were found. No strange fingerprints were detected. Most of all, they're puzzled by the manner in which the explosion was triggered. They found no timing device, so they concluded that it had to be done by remote control. If so, the one who touched it off may have seen the worker and chose to detonate the explosive even though it would kill him. Maybe the death was intended."

"Cold-blooded murder?"

"Maybe." Ralph shifted in his chair. "The thing is, Janine, it has taken the pleasure out of my life's work. When I've had opportunities to sell the business in the past, I had no inclination to do so. But the other day, the president of one of the major independent oil companies made an offer, and I think I'll take it. The money from the sale will leave me comfortably situated and give me the freedom to do other things that I enjoy."

Janine smiled as she said, "Like play kingmaker?"

"Well, I have to admit that working with you and the others on this election has been fun."

Janine ran her finger slowly around the rim of her cup. "I understand you have a son who is a doctor in Seattle."

"That's right. He got the education that I missed and has done very well. I'm really proud of him."

Janine looked at him closely as she said, "Margaret told me you're a widower."

"Yes. I lost my wife five years ago to cancer. That's a terrible disease. She suffered horribly toward the end. It was really a blessing when she went."

Janine's eyes dropped again to her cup and said softly, "I'm sorry." She looked up at her dinner companion. "You're an attractive man. If things in Montana's capital city are like they are in our nation's capital, I'm sure you've had women chasing after you."

Ralph shook his head and chuckled. "I'm a short, chubby, old man. No woman could find me interesting."

There was a long pause, and then Janine leaned forward, arms on the table. "Tall, thin, and young aren't the only things that attract women. You are an interesting guy. And we have a lot in common. I've enjoyed the time I've spent with you." Then she laughed a throaty laugh, leaned back in the chair, and said, "But I won't embarrass you any more with all that." Before he could respond, she went on, "You and the other electors voted yesterday. The networks conducted exit polls and report that Tootell got a big majority of the votes."

Ralph was glad to discuss something less personal. "I expect they have it pretty close. We in Montana announced how we voted right after we cast the ballots." He drank the last of the coffee, pushed the chair back, and crossed his legs. "I'm surprised how many electors refused to disclose how they voted. We won't know the final count until the tally is taken by Congress."

"What about Alan Ward's change of heart? Will he get the votes that we'd hoped would go to Bobby?"

"Who knows? His email was late in the game. My guess is that it will have little effect."

"We know that Bobby got enough to keep Tootell from being elected."

"We do know that."

"How is Bobby taking it?"

"I don't know. After I voted yesterday, I drove to Billings. It was late when I arrived home. This morning, I took care of some things at the office before I caught the flight down here." His face showed some embarrassment when he added, "My mind wasn't on Bobby. I was anxious to see you, I guess."

"That's nice to hear, because I was anxious to see you too."

Janine stopped the car at the entrance to the hotel. Ralph opened the passenger door a crack, and then turned to her to say, "It is the custom, I believe, for the man to deliver the lady to her abode, not the other way around."

"It's a new age, Ralph."

"Thank you for a delightful evening, Janine. You really are pleasant company."

She reached over and patted him on the knee. "Do you know that this is the first time in years that my date hasn't suggested we spend the night together?"

"Gracious lady, that's an enchanting thought. But I know better than to ruin things by making such a suggestion. I want to remain friends. Maybe we can have an evening like this again sometime."

"If I have my way, we will."

29

Thursday, December 16, morning

TALLAHASSEE, FLORIDA

Roman Burke wondered why he suffered from anxiety as he waited for Janine to pick up the phone. She was just one of many women he had found to be attractive over the years. When she answered, he used the same light voice that women always seemed to find appealing. "This is Roman, Janine. I've been wondering how you count the electoral votes?"

"Hello, Roman." Then after a brief pause, "I only know what's reported. Tootell has most of the Republicans, but not a majority, according to the news reports."

"Maybe we should discuss strategy. Would you be able to meet me if I flew to Denver tomorrow?"

"Why, I suppose so. What exactly do you have in mind?"

"I'll be at your office tomorrow at two o'clock. We'll talk about it then." When she didn't respond immediately, he added, "Or could we have dinner tomorrow evening? I owe you, because of my behavior during the campaign."

"We can have dinner, Roman, but remember, its just business."

Friday, December 17, evening

DENVER, COLORADO

At seven o'clock in the evening, Janine appeared at the door of the hotel dining room. She saw Roman Burke rise from his chair and hurry in her direction. He greeted her with a firm handshake and a smile. At the table, he held the chair for her, and then took a seat on the other side. "Thank you for joining me. I thought we could visit privately about the Electoral College vote." His handsome face had an earnest look. "And I'd like to make up to you for the way I behaved during the campaign."

Janine returned his gaze steadily before answering. "Roman, you were an ass during the campaign."

"I know. All I could think about was electing Governor Weldon. That's an explanation, but not an excuse, for the way I acted." His eyes dropped to the table and then returned to her again. "You, on the other hand, never lost your cool. I admire you for that."

"Listen, buddy. You have a reputation for having your way with women. You may as well know right now that sweet talk isn't going to work with me. I've been around the block, and I've heard it all." Her gaze didn't waver. "Now, if you want to talk about the voting by the electors, I'm willing."

"Fair enough. We'll talk politics." Roman laughed quietly. "But you really are an attractive woman. And my reputation as a man who ravishes women is overblown. I'm really just a shy, lonesome boy."

"Yes, and I'm Miss Piggy." Janine picked up the menu. "Let's order. Then we'll discuss Bobby Hobaugh's chances."

There was a momentary pause in the conversation after

the waiter took their orders. Janine crossed her arms on the table and looked over at her companion. "Tell me, Roman, you must have known that Governor Weldon was critically ill in the days right before the election. Didn't it bother you to keep that information from the voting public?"

Burke straightened in the chair. "Of course it bothered me. But what was I supposed to do? Tell the world not to vote for the governor? Then what? We'd have had Simpson for another term." He mimicked Janine by dropping his arms to the table and leaning forward. "You have no idea what it was like in those last few days. I watched as Weldon's fatigue progressed from mild to extreme. I'm not a doctor so there was no way for me to know the cause of fatigue. He'd always been such a vigorous man." Roman Burke shook his head. "My suggestion that he should have a medical exam was met with a profane rebuff."

"When did you realize just how bad it was?"

"The evening when I told you to have your cowboy friend take Weldon's place in Cleveland. We were in Milwaukee, and the governor was so weak that he could barely climb the stairway onto the plane for the trip back to Tallahassee."

Janine frowned. "Did you try to stop him from making that final television address?"

"The whole staff did. The man wasn't just sick and exhausted, but he'd become even more obstinate than usual."

"At that time, did you consider the consequences if Weldon won and then died? That some unknown presidential electors would be making the new choice? Did the quandary we're caught up in right now ever cross your mind?"

"No. If it came to my mind at all, I just hoped that those unknown electors would use good judgment when making their choice."

"It appears your hope will go unrealized. Jackson Tootell may be their choice."

"I haven't given up hope. That's why I've gone along on the Bobby Hobaugh ride." Burke leaned forward with a quizzical smile. "How in the world did that man come to fill in for Senator Blaine after he was killed in that accident? Whose idea was it?"

"You remember how you barked at me on the phone to deal with the consequences of the senator's death? 'Don't lose any California votes!' I was stuck in Billings, Montana, for God's sake, and we needed someone to speak for Blaine in that burg. Bobby was the one who took the stage and did a great job of stirring up the crowd. Ralph Phillips suggested we take him to San Francisco." She paused. "He also suggested we make him a 'somebody' by putting out a press release saying Hobaugh might be the choice for vice president." She looked hard at her companion. "You remember that you gave me hell for that, don't you?"

"I do remember, and I did speak too harshly. My excuse, if any, is the strain caused by Weldon's condition."

Janine nodded, sat back, and smiled. "Well, here we are—hoping that Bobby Hobaugh can stop Jackson Tootell from becoming president."

They made trivial conversation while they ate. When the dessert was finished and they were enjoying the last cup of coffee, Roman said, "We know from reading the newspapers that Tootell has a majority of the Republican electoral votes. But he doesn't have a majority of all the electoral votes—the 270 votes needed to get the presidency."

"You're right, of course." She leaned her elbows on the table, hands folded under her chin. "Nonetheless, it seems that we will lose, and Tootell will win in the end."

"I hate Tootell so much that it's hard for me to be rational. The thought of him as president makes me sick to my stomach." Roman sat straight in his chair, hands folded in front of him on the table. "Can you think of any way to stop him?"

"If no one gets a majority of the electoral votes, then Congress makes the pick. The Republicans control both houses, but in the House of Representatives it's a whole new ball game." She stopped, leaned forward again, and spoke with some excitement in her voice. "We haven't seriously thought of trying for Simpson's votes. Is there any chance that some Democratic congressmen might go for Bobby?"

"Oh hell, Janine, you know politics. You couldn't get a Democrat to vote for a Republican, no matter what was offered. Every politician knows the rule that House Speaker Sam Rayburn laid down more than half a century ago—go along to get along. No Democrat will vote for a Republican and give up any opportunity for power, if and when the Democrats are in control again."

"I suppose you're right." When Roman remained silent, she asked, "Well, what should we do? Just give up and sit around until the matter is decided?"

"Let's see if we can get Bobby to travel to Washington when Congress convenes. Why don't you call him? Frankly, Janine, I think he has a thing for you."

"Bobby Hobaugh has never been anything but gentlemanly toward me. If he has a thing for anyone, it's probably the woman who works for him. You remember Margaret?"

"Maybe you should call her and tell her how important it is. Perhaps she can persuade Bobby to come to Washington."

"I don't think she trusts me. She may think I have designs on her boss." After a heartbeat, she went on, "No. I shouldn't call her. Maybe Ralph Phillips could persuade her to talk to Bobby about it. I'll ask Ralph to do it. At least a conversation with her may give us a better idea of Bobby's thinking."

"Good. Get in touch with Phillips right away." Roman reached across the table for her hand. "I'm really not a bad person, Ms. Paul. And I would like to know you better. How about giving me the benefit of the doubt?"

She let his hand linger on hers for only a moment, before drawing hers away. "You haven't given me a reason to do that, Mr. Burke."

30

Saturday, December 18, morning

DENVER, COLORADO

"Ralph, this is Janine."

"Janine! How nice to hear your voice."

"The last time we visited, you came to Denver. We need to visit again. How about I come to see you?"

"Gee, Janine, that would be great. When can you be here?"

"Would tomorrow do?"

"Tell me the time, and I'll meet the plane. Should I make a hotel reservation for you?'

"I was rather hoping you would invite me to stay at your house."

Ralph hesitated only a moment. "I'll have the guest room cleaned and ready."

Sunday, December 19, evening

BILLINGS, MONTANA

Ralph, dressed in a soft shirt and sweater rather than the usual coat and tie, gave Janine his comfortable chair to watch the late news while he sat on the davenport. There was still speculation about the outcome of the vote of the Electoral College, although it seemed to be commonly accepted that Jackson Tootell had the most Republican votes and would eventually be elected. After the final comment by the newscaster, Ralph reached for the remote and turned the set off. "I've taken up your whole day and you must be bored by it all."

"Not so, Ralph. It's been a wonderful and interesting day. I enjoyed seeing your city. Except the place where Senator Blaine was killed." She shook her head silently, looking down toward her lap. Then, after a moment, she looked up with a smile. "And your home is lovely."

"After my wife passed away it was too difficult to live in the old house, so I bought this. An interior decorator chose the furnishings."

"The decorator did well." Janine crossed her legs as she changed the subject. "I'm sorry, Ralph, that you weren't able to persuade Bobby to go to Washington."

"Well, we tried." He stretched. "It's past my bedtime and probably past yours, too. Do you need anything that isn't in your room?"

Instead of answering, Janine stepped across to sit beside him on the davenport. "How old are you, Ralph?"

Ralph's brows raised in surprise. "Why, I'm fifty-four."

"So you're not too old to be interested in women, are you?"

"No, of course not."

"I'm a woman. Or hadn't you noticed?"

"Believe me, Janine, every time I see you, I notice."

She cuddled up next to him, put her arm around his shoulder, lips close to his ear, and said, "Let's really get to know each other."

Tuesday, December 21, evening

TALLAHASEE, FLORIDA

Roman Burked dialed Janine Paul's home in Denver. "Janine, this is Roman."

"Good evening, Roman. How are you?"

"Christmas is coming soon. I wondered if you would join me in a water jaunt through the Florida Keys over the holiday. We could rent a cabin cruiser out of Tampa."

"It's nice of you to ask, Roman, but I've already agreed to spend Christmas in Montana."

"I thought you said Bobby Hobaugh wasn't interested in you."

"Bobby isn't, but Ralph Phillips is."

"You're spending the Christmas holiday with him?" The fact that he found the notion incredible came through in his voice.

"That's right. I'm looking forward to it."

"Well." Roman paused, and then attempted to put the best face on his disappointment. "I hope you both have a nice holiday." He started to put the phone down, then added, "I'm sure we'll be talking again—about the election, of course." He punched the off button on the phone and stood holding it as he gazed out the window.

"I'll be damned. She's gone for that little fat man."

31

Thursday, December 23, afternoon

ATLANTA, GEORGIA

"The electors have voted, and I'm certain that I didn't get the 270 votes needed to win."

Tucker was in his usual stance before the desk. "No, sir. Our tally shows that to be true."

"Start gathering information on Republican congressmen from the states controlled by that party."

"I've already begun the process, sir."

"Very good. And, Tucker, we must give thought to the nuisance that Bobby Hobaugh has become. Is there something that might be done to distract him—to cause him to forget any ideas he might have about the presidency."

"I have given it thought, sir."

"Can you tell me what that is, without disclosing more than I should know?"

"Sir, if we act directly against Hobaugh personally, it could attract a great deal of media attention and perhaps more attention from law enforcement than is desirable. If something were to happen to his assistant, however, the likelihood of such attention is remote."

"His assistant?"

"Hobaugh depends upon Margaret Lisa in the management of his law office. I have reason to believe he's become enamored of her as well."

Tootell pondered for a moment, then leaned forward with his arms on the desktop to ask, "Complete deniability on my part, of course."

"As always, sir."

"Don't act on this immediately, Tucker. I need to give thought to the timing of your action and to the effect it might have on other aspects of our endeavor."

"I'll move the matter forward whenever you decide, sir. And I'll do it with pleasure."

Miss Lotus smiled brightly as Tucker hurried passed her desk. He detected no odor of alcohol.

Thursday, December 23, evening

DENVER, COLORADO

Janine looked at the front of Time magazine. Instead of the usual face of a man of the year, the cover showed the mere outline of a man's head. The lead article explained that the country was without a president-elect, and that fact itself was the most important story. Time then went on to report at length on the history and background of both Allen Ward and Jackson Tootell. The material for the Hobaugh portion was brief and seemed to come directly from the earlier writing in the Miles City Star, the article that was of no interest to the national media at the time of its publication. Janine finished going through the magazine and then threw it onto an end table in disgust. Without putting it in writing, Time made it clear that Jackson Tootell would be president, and his picture would appear on the cover when the election formalities were satisfied.

Brushing that thought aside, she smiled as she anticipated time to be spent with Ralph and hurried to pack for the flight to Billings.

Friday, December 24, evening

MILES CITY, MONTANA

It took all of Bobby's courage to ask Margaret to join him for Christmas dinner, and he was surprised when she accepted. They shared the task of preparing the meal in the spacious kitchen where, years ago, ranch hands gathered for their meals. Seated at the old maple table, covered by a linen tablecloth, they ate the turkey and accoutrements by candlelight. After clearing the dishes, they sat, side by side, on the large davenport to exchange gifts. Each had several for the other, none of them expensive or elaborate.

When all the gifts under the tree had been unwrapped and Margaret was sitting close to Bobby, he reached into the drawer of an end table and brought out one more small package. Margaret looked at him for a long time before she started to remove the wrapping. When the paper was gone, she waited even longer before lifting the lid on the box. At the sight of the ring, with its large diamond, she gasped and turned to Bobby with an inquiring look.

"Margaret, will your marry me?" His face had the appearance of a worried child.

"Is that what you really want?"

"I've never wanted anything more in my life."

"Of course, I'll marry you, Bobby Hobaugh. That's all I've ever dreamed of."

Monday, December 27, evening

BILLINGS, MONTANA

Ralph and Janine spent the day riding snowmobiles from Cooke City into Yellowstone Park to look at elk and buffalo. They even saw a small pack of wolves. They maneuvered the machines over trails that had been turned into washboards by the snowmobiles that had traveled ahead of them. They returned to Billings late, and both were tired.

After Ralph finished blowing life into a blaze in the fireplace and they had cups of hot chocolate in hand, their conversation turned, as it always did, to the election.

Janine sipped the warm liquid and then said, "Before Senator Blaine was killed, the campaign committee was certain he and Weldon would be elected. To make sure the senator's staff had a place to stay in Washington during the transition, we reserved a block of rooms at The Willard. In the turmoil after Governor Weldon died, I forgot to cancel the reservations. Then I decided to keep them, thinking that you, Lance, Roman, and I would want to be in the capital at the time the electoral votes are counted. And I decided we probably would want to stay there to watch what happens if Tootell doesn't get a majority of the votes."

"I've planned to be in Washington on the 6th of January. My curiosity won't allow me to stay here in Montana and miss something as momentous as the announcement of the results from the Electoral College. But I hadn't considered a place to stay." Ralph gave her an admiring glance. "As usual, your thoughts are way ahead of mine." He was quiet for a heartbeat and asked, "Are you saying that we four can use the rooms at The Willard?"

"Exactly. The campaign paid for them when the reservations were made, so we don't need to worry about the cost."

"We could have handled the cost, but it's nice to know we will have rooms." Then he raised his eyebrows and asked, "Have you told Lance and Roman?"

"Lance knows and is making arrangements to be away from his wife and new baby. He's reluctant—or at least he tells his wife that he is. But I think he's just like you and me. He isn't going to miss the opportunity to watch a historic event."

"And Roman?"

"I haven't told him yet, but I will."

"Well, we all need to be there. We ain't done pushing Bobby Hobaugh for president yet!"

Tuesday, December 28, afternoon

MILES CITY, MONTANA

Tucker's clenched jaw showed his frustration. Tootell, in his usual way, had indicated he should act without receiving a specific order to do so. It was time to initiate his plan.

He knew of Margaret's daily routine and made the arrangement accordingly. It had been her habit to return to her apartment at the end of the work day. She would park her car on the street, walk up the walkway, and unlock the door. She always stepped into the apartment entryway without a concern and shut the door behind her.

The abduction was planned to be clean and simple. The muscular, heavily tattooed man Tucker had selected for the task was tested and reliable. He would grab Margaret as she stepped through the door and clasp his hand over her mouth to smother any scream. At the same time, he'd inject the drug that would leave her awake but confused. She would become cooperative and compliant. The drug selected was thought by most people to be used only by sexual predators intent on rape. Tucker had found it to be ideal for purposes such as the one at hand.

At five o'clock, Margaret sat quietly in the car outside the office for a few moments just thinking of the man she'd agreed to marry.

He was at the ranch working with the others as they corralled cattle to be weighed and loaded onto trucks. Where they would be sent by the order buyer, she didn't know or care. She smiled, remembering that Bobby referred to the ones to be sold as "the barren, the old, the lame, the halt, and the blind." She smiled and turned the key to start the auto.

As she drove along, Margaret's mind was on her soon-to-be husband. He'd called to say that he was tired from sorting cattle and helping the crew shove the cattle up the chute and onto the waiting trucks. Would she like to meet him in town for dinner? Of course she would. So instead of turning onto the street that led to her apartment, she drove down Main Street toward the restaurant. God, she loved Bobby Hobaugh!

Margaret Lisa would never know the horror that awaited her had she followed her usual routine.

Wednesday, December 29, evening

ATLANTA, GEORGIA

"The attempt to move Bobby Hobaugh's thoughts away from the presidency wasn't successful, sir."

"You failed, Tucker?" Tootell stared at the man standing rigidly before his desk. "That's never happened before in our entire relationship."

"Allow me to explain, sir." Tucker spoke hastily. "As always, the plan was designed to be fail-safe. When the target changed her evening routine, any attempt to complete the mission by other means would have compounded the risk of exposure. Instead, our man did as he was directed by aborting the attempt."

"The man you mention, what of him?"

"He will disappear, sir."

Tootell stood, stuffed his hands in his pockets. "It may be just as well that the effort wasn't a success, Tucker. The electoral votes will be counted on January 6. My lead in votes over both Hobaugh and Ward will be apparent. The large lead will make it obvious that any further effort to stop me will be futile. I will be president in the end." After a moment's thought, he added, "There will yet come a time to cause grief to Mr. Hobaugh and the three men and one woman who made him a candidate in the first place."

Constitution of the United States

The person having the greatest number of votes for President, shall be President, if such number be a majority of the whole number of electors appointed; and if no person have such majority, then from the persons having the numbers not exceeding three on the list of those of those voted for as President, the House of Representatives shall choose immediately, by ballot, the President, the votes shall be taken by states, the representation from each state having one vote...a majority of all states shall be necessary to the choice.

The person having the greatest number of votes as Vice-President shall be vice president, if such number be a majority of the whole number of Electors appointed, and if no person have a majority, then from the two highest numbers on the list, the Senate shall choose the Vice-President...a majority of the whole number shall be necessary to a choice.

32

Thursday, January 6, afternoon

WASHINGTON D. C.

Early in the day, the Houses of the newly elected Congress convened separately to organize. With the Republicans in control of both the House and the Senate, Timothy Welch was re-elected Speaker of the House of Representatives. Senator Paul Wheeler was re-elected majority leader of the Senate. The Houses then adjourned to reconvene in joint session in the House chamber at one o'clock in the afternoon.

Egbert Hamilton, the president pro tem of the Senate, presiding in the absence of a vice-president, rapped the gavel for quiet and asked, "Have the tellers completed their task?"

Whitney Cabot, dean of the Senate, rose from his seat to respond, "We have, Mr. President."

"Please deliver the tally to me."

Senator Cabot strode with great dignity to the podium and handed the tally sheet to the president pro tem. Egbert Hamilton read silently from the sheet, then raised his head to read it aloud. "The tally shows the following: For President, Arthur Simpson, 257 votes; Jackson Tootell, 234 votes; Bobby Hobaugh, 23 votes; Allen Ward, 22; Thomas Lowell, one vote; one vote for Susan Washington."

The president pro tem paused and then said what each person in the chamber already knew. "No person received a majority of the electoral votes for president."

He looked down again at the list and continued to read. "The tally also shows the following. For vice president, Henry Larsen, 257 votes; Jackson Tootell, 101 votes; Bobby Hobaugh, 94 votes; Allen Ward, 87 votes; Susan Washington, one vote." The president pro tem smiled as he said, "Mr. Larsen, who would be presiding at this session, had he not resigned from the office of vice president only recently, received the most votes, but not a majority." The solemn silence was broken by the sound of laughter coming from the members of Congress. The president pro tem turned to look at the man standing beside him. "I yield the gavel to the Speaker."

The majority leader of the House of Representatives rose from his seat and announced, "Mr. President and Mr. Speaker, I move that the joint session of the House and Senate stand adjourned. Mr. Speaker, I also move that the House reconvene in these chambers at three o'clock this afternoon for further consideration of the election of a president."

The Speaker immediately responded, "It has been moved that the House and Senate stand adjourned and that the House reconvene at three o'clock this afternoon. All in favor?" Down came his gavel as he announced, "The joint session of the House and Senate is adjourned."

Ralph, Janine, Lance, and Roman were seated together in the gallery. After the tally was read, Janine poked her elbow in Ralph's ribs and turned to whisper in his ear, "By golly, Ralph, you did it. Not by much, but you did it. Bobby Hobaugh may very well be president of the United States. You're a kingmaker."

"Not by much is right. I'm surprised Allen Ward got as

many votes as he did. I thought we'd done a better job than that on his supporters."

"Well, no matter. Bobby's the one who's first behind Tootell. Now we have to change that so Bobby's in the lead."

"Yeah, I'd better call Bobby when we get back to the Willard and explain what happened. I just wish he were here."

Thursday, January 6, afternoon

WASHINGTON, DC

The face of Lawrence Rollins, the handsome NBC anchorman, was devoid of its usual placid countenance. Instead, his appearance reflected the serious manner in which he spoke.

> Those of us following the election have assumed that Jackson Tootell would receive enough electoral votes to achieve the presidency. Therefore, it isn't surprising that he received the largest number of the votes, although not the majority needed to win. What is surprising is that he also received the largest number of Republican votes for vice president. No one contemplated such an outcome. As a consequence, it is now certain that Tootell will be sworn in as the holder of either one or the other of the highest offices in the land. What is even more surprising—almost unbelievable—is that Bobby Hobaugh, a man no one had heard of only a couple of months ago, could become the president. Of all the extraordinary things that have occurred since Senator Blaine died in the auto accident three days before the November election, the result with which we find ourselves is most extraordinary.
>
> We must look to our constitutional beginnings to understand how this came about. In

the beginning there were no political parties, and the framers of the Constitution apparently didn't contemplate their creation. In a time when communication was delivered by stagecoach or horseback, public campaigns for national office would be slow and cumbersome, at best, and all but impossible at worst. For that reason, the framers conceived a system of electors, each chosen by the people in his state, who would, in turn, choose the president.

They perceived that those chosen as electors would be well known in their respective states. They would be men of unchallenged character and sound judgment. The chosen electors would then make their choice for president and vice president from men of national prominence who had the same qualities. The one receiving a majority of the electoral votes would be president. The one receiving the second highest number would be vice president. The country would be served by two of its best.

Then political parties came into being. The result under the original system could be the choice of a president from one party and the vice president from another party. That was soon deemed to be an impractical result.

Hence the Constitution was amended to avoid such an outcome. Successful candidates for the top offices now emerge from the nominating convention of each party and run as a team. The candidates for president and vice president will always get the same number of votes and will win or lose together.

However, with the death of both Forrest Blaine and Warren Weldon, there no longer was a Republican team of candidates. The scramble for the vote of each elector became a free-for-all with different individuals vying for that vote. It was thought from the beginning that Alan Ward or Jackson Tootell would be the logical choice. If Bobby Hobaugh was thought of at all, it was only as a character in a clever ploy by Warren Weldon to hang onto votes during the last days of the November campaign.

Now, Hobaugh, the oft-called "Cowboy from Montana" could possibly hold the highest office in the land.

The anchorman paused with his eyes focused on the camera.

Or, that could be the situation unless something even more strange should occur. Who knows? The way this election has gone to this point, it just might.

The usual smile, so familiar to America's television viewers, replaced the earnest look.

This is Lawrence Rollins wishing each of you a good night.

Janine punched the off button and grinned at Ralph. "Who would have believed it possible? You placed Bobby Hobaugh in a position where he could become the president of the United States. It's hard to believe you brought him this far, but you did it."

Ralph smiled in return and waved a hand. "We did it. You, Lance, Roman, and I." He stood. "Should we call them and celebrate?"

Janine rose and wrapped her arms around his neck. "No, Ralph. Let's celebrate. But just you and me."

Thursday, January 6, afternoon

MILES CITY, MONTANA

One of Bobby's long time clients was selling his ranch—a large ranch that straddled the Powder River and had been owned by his family for a couple of generations. The transaction involved—in addition to the sale of the land itself —water rights, reserved mineral interests, Montana state leases, BLM permits, as well as the transfer of ownership of cattle, horses, and machinery. Bobby was concentrating on the final revisions to the sale documents when Margaret walked into his private office to say, "It's time. You really should go to the house at the ranch in time to watch the members of Congress count the votes on your big screen television. The votes of the Electors, those of your friend Ralph included."

His face wore a hint of a frown. "I need to finish here, Margaret. This is important. The sale of Hugo's ranch is to close next week."

"Bobby, by next week you may be president-elect. If that happens, the sale of Hugo's ranch won't seem important to you. And Harrington will handle the closing." She stepped forward. "Face it. The count won't go away just because you want to ignore it." She smiled her warmest smile. "Come along, now. Let's go see who the Electors have chosen. Don't worry. It isn't likely that you'll be the one."

He heaved a sigh before stacking the sale documents carefully in a pile and rising from the chair. "You're right, as you always seem to be." After pushing his chair back into the kneehole in the desk, he added, "Jackson Tootell will get the entire 283 Electoral votes. Then we can put this whole foolish notion to rest once and for all."

The large television was in a small room off the living room that Bobby liked to call his den. Two comfortable chairs faced the screen. Franklin Gary on Fox News was speaking.

...It was widely believed that Jackson Tootell would receive enough Republican electoral votes to achieve the presidency. He did not. What is surprising—almost unbelievable—is that Bobby Hobaugh, a little known man from Montana, received the second largest number of Republican votes. It is now an actual possibility that he could become President.

Bobby Hobaugh was never really taken seriously as anything more than a scheme by Warren Weldon to hang onto votes during the last days of the November campaign. With Weldon's death, no one thought of Hobaugh as a contender.

Now, Hobaugh, who was often dismissed as the Montana Cowboy, might actually become President of the United States....

When the phone rang, Margaret clicked off the TV and Bobby answered on the third ring.

He spoke wearily, "I know all about it, Ralph. So does Margaret. I have this on a speaker phone so she can listen too."

"Bobby, can we persuade you to come to the capital? The congressmen and congresswomen want to meet you and learn more about you. It's important to them to know the people they're choosing."

"Ralph, I'm not leaving Montana. I didn't want to get mixed up in this matter in the first place. Besides, I have lots to do here. I don't have time to sit around in Washington while members of Congress make up their minds." His voice took on a hard tone. "Don't ask me again, Ralph. I ain't going."

"OK, buddy. I won't mention it again." Ralph's voice carried his smile as he added, "Hang in there, Bobby. This will be over soon." The click as the telephone connection was broken sounded loud in the room.

Margaret sat back in her chair and looked solemnly across the desk at the man she had agreed to marry. "Bobby, do you realize what that vote means? There's a chance that you could become the president of the United States."

"My God, Margaret. I don't want to think about that."

"But don't you think Ralph is right in asking you to go to Washington now?"

Bobby sat for a while, looking into space. Then he turned back to face his long-time assistant. "No, Margaret, I'm not going until I know how it all comes out." He paused and looked into her eyes. "And if I do go, I'm just glad that you will go with me." When Bobby stood, Margaret rose too. Bobby reached out, put his arms around her, pulled her close and said, "I need you. I can't do this without you."

Margaret reached up and stroked the back of his neck. "Whatever happens, Bobby, we'll do it all together, as long as that's what you want."

Thursday, January 6, afternoon

CAMBRIDGE, MASSACHUSETTS

Allen Ward massaged his forehead while he moaned, "How could I have been so stupid? Why in God's name did I ever suggest to my supporters that they should vote for Bobby Hobaugh. In the end, all I needed were two more votes, and I'd have at least been vice president. Those votes would have been there, if it weren't for that foolish Hobaugh suggestion."

Helene, his attractive secretary, smiled a wan smile. "You did it because you're impulsive. Too often you act without thinking things through. This is just one of those times."

The handsome man shook his head. "Right now I could shoot myself."

"Don't act on that impulse, for goodness sake! Your dreams of being president are at an end. Put them aside."

Thursday, January 6, afternoon

ARLINGTON, VIRGINIA

Jackson Tootell, in his townhouse at the Watergate, turned from the television to face Tucker. "The press had it wrong by fifteen votes. We've gained that many in the last few days." He looked at his man and added, "You know which members of Congress you are to work on. I'll deal with a couple of them myself. Let's get started."

Tucker turned to the door, but his employer stopped him by saying, "Bobby Hobaugh remains a problem."

"He does. But another arrangement has been made to take him out of the picture."

Tootell stood ramrod straight, staring at Tucker. When he spoke at last, it was in a subdued voice. "Deniability is more essential than ever."

"Yes, sir. It is always foremost in my mind."

33

Thursday, January 6, afternoon

WASHINGTON D. C.

All but two members of the House of Representatives were in attendance when the House reconvened at three o'clock. The majority leader, when he spoke, stood before his desk rather than at the podium as was customary.

"Mr. Speaker, the Constitution addresses the situation with which we are faced. It states that the House shall choose a president immediately from among the three having the most electoral votes. It further states that the vote shall be taken by states, with each state having one vote." He paused. "I'm not sure, Mr. Speaker, how *immediately* is immediately according to the Constitution. But I believe the framers of the Constitution would want the members to use their considered judgment in something as momentous as electing a president. I submit, Mr. Speaker, that the delegations from the various states require time to discuss among themselves the way in which each will vote. For that reason, I move that the House stand in recess until tomorrow afternoon at the hour of two o'clock and that the House reconvene at that time to vote, by states, for president—as required by the Constitution."

Looking down on the assembled representatives from his high podium, Speaker Timothy Welch held his gavel in his right hand, ready to strike. "Let me remind the members that the three who have received the most votes are Arthur Simpson, Jackson Tootell, and Bobby Hobaugh." He paused to allow each member to consider the import of his statement. After a brief silence, he went on, "It has been moved that the House stand in recess until two o'clock tomorrow, January 7. All in favor?" The gavel came down together with his final words. "The House now stands in recess."

Late in the afternoon, Hobaugh's four supporters gathered in the office of Will Langworthy, Montana's lone member of the House of Representatives. The congressman, Ralph, Janine, Lance, and Roman stared at the television set. Larry Morgan, a talk show host on CNN was questioning two political analysts, Ed Selby, a professor of constitutional law at Yale University and Mary Adams, a former United States senator.

> "Senator, how do you think the vote will go in the House of Representatives?"

> "Twenty-six states have more Republican members than Democrats," Mary said. "If all of those states vote for the same man, that man will be president."

> "What if they don't vote for the same man?"

> "That's the probability. If the Republican states split their votes, it's not likely that anyone will be chosen on the first ballot."

> "What about the Democrats?

"Don't count Arthur Simpson out. He's certain to have the votes of twenty states, the ones in which the Democrats have a majority of members. Four states have split delegations. All Simpson has to do is persuade one or two Republicans in each of those states to refrain from voting during that state's caucus, and he'd have the votes of twenty-four states. Then he'll look at the states where the Republicans have a one-vote majority, such as Maryland or New Jersey. If he can get a couple of the Republicans in each of those states to abstain, he's in."

"How does he persuade a Republican to abstain from voting?"

"The president has a lot to offer, such as ambassadorial appointments and cabinet positions."

"Professor Selby, do you really think the president would try to buy votes that way?"

"Presidents make offers to members of Congress all the time in order to get votes. But remember, it's not only Simpson who's in a position to make those offers. So can Tootell or even Bobby Hobaugh. After all, it's the next president who will be making appointments. It will not necessarily be Arthur Simpson."

"Senator, are there any other possibilities?"

"Yes, there is one other that's interesting. Let me use North Carolina as an example. That state has twelve members in its delegation. Seven of them are Republicans, five are Democrats. The Democrats will vote for Simpson. Suppose four of those Republicans vote for Tootell and three vote for Hobaugh. Who wins? I think Simpson gets North Carolina's vote."

"That's a good reason for the Republicans to make peace and decide who they really want for president."

"Obviously they should, but they may not."

"Doctor Selby, how do you think the voting will go?

"I agree with the senator that the twenty states with Democratic majorities will cast their votes for Simpson. I think Montana and Florida will vote for Hobaugh. Texas may do the same. The rest of the states with Republican majorities will vote for Tootell."

"Senator Adams, what about the states with split delegations?"

"It's unlikely that they will be able to agree on which man to vote for. I expect each of them to pass when it comes time to cast their ballots."

"What happens if no one gets the votes of a majority of states?"

"Then, I expect, the House will recess again so the states can caucus some more."

"What will happen in the caucuses?"

"The members will discuss the vote at length. But the real action will be outside the caucuses. That's where the offers we've discussed will be made."

Larry Morgan shook his head. "How long will this go on?"

Mary Adams smiled. "Until someone gets elected. The House will keep meeting, taking votes, recessing, then reconvening, voting, and recessing until someone gives. Then we'll have a president."

Congressman Langworthy switched off the television and turned to the others. "We know one thing. Bobby will get my vote, and I'll stick with it no matter how long, unless he tells me to vote differently."

Ralph nodded as he spoke. "I know Bobby. If Tootell has twenty-five states on the first vote, without Montana, then Bobby will want you to give him Montana's vote and that will elect him."

Roman, sitting next to Janine, said, "It isn't going to happen, Ralph. Tootell won't get Florida. I met with the Florida Republican caucus, and they assured me they would vote in a block for Bobby."

Lance sat forward in his chair. "Bobby'll get Colorado, too. Janine and I were told so by the senior member at breakfast this morning."

After they shared some speculation about the votes of other states, the congressman rose from his chair, indicating the meeting was over. "I've things to do before the House reconvenes. We'll get the answer to all of this tomorrow afternoon." As the others rose and walked to the door, Langworthy stood for a moment, lost in thought. When he spoke, it was with a huge grin on his face. "This is the first time Montana has as many votes as California. My vote is as good as the combined votes of all the congressmen and congresswomen from that state. By God! It sure feels good."

He followed them through the door and grasped Ralph's hand in a political grip, and then the others in turn. "Get some rest, my friends. We'll visit again after the vote."

Thursday, January 6, evening

MILES CITY, MONTANA

The knock on the door of the main house at the Hobaugh Ranch late in the evening startled Bobby. The well-dressed young man introduced himself and his associate and said, "We're from the Secret Service, sir. You are a candidate for the office of president of the United States. It's our duty to protect you."

34

Friday, January 7, 2 p.m.

WASHINGTON D. C.

"Mr. Speaker, I move that the States cast their votes for president at this time and that the vote be taken in alphabetical order."

"Members of the House, you've heard the motion. All in favor?" Almost instantly, amid a mumbling of "ayes," the gavel came down. "So moved. The chief clerk shall call the roll of the states, starting with Alabama."

The chief clerk shuffled some papers, looked out at the assembled congressmen, and then called out in a loud voice. "Alabama."

The senior Republican from that state rose to his feet and spoke in a thunderous voice, "Mr. Speaker, the great state of Alabama casts its vote for Jackson Tootell."

"Alaska." The chief clerk's voice rose to his task.

"Mr. Speaker, the largest state in the Union casts its vote for Bobby Hobaugh."

Arizona voted for Tootell.

Then the clerk called out, "Arkansas."

"Mr. Speaker, Arkansas passes."

The roll of states continued with those controlled by Democrats voting for Arthur Simpson, and the states controlled by Republicans voting for Jackson Tootell, until the clerk called out, "Colorado."

"Mr. Speaker, Colorado, the crown jewel of the Rocky Mountains, casts its vote for Bobby Hobaugh."

The voting went on, state by state. The chief clerk, his voice getting hoarse, at last called out, "Wyoming."

"Mr. Speaker, Wyoming casts its vote for a fine citizen of its neighboring state of Montana, Bobby Hobaugh."

The Speaker looked at the chief clerk and said, "Please read the results of the tally."

Since everyone in the chamber, congressmen and spectators alike, had been keeping count, the reading of the tally was nothing but a formality. But the clerk did as he was directed, after which the Speaker surveyed the assemblage and announced, "None of the candidates received a majority of the votes."

The House majority leader spoke again. "Mr. Speaker, I move that the House stand adjourned until tomorrow, Saturday, January the 8th, at two o'clock in the afternoon, at which time the House shall again vote for president of the United States."

Friday, January 7, afternoon

ARLINGTON, VIRGINIA

Jackson Tootell, seated at his desk, glared at Tucker. "What the hell does that guy from Alaska think he's doing? I had him down as a sure thing."

"Maybe he wants something for his vote."

"Find out."

Friday, January 7, afternoon

WASHINGTON D. C.

Ralph and the others joined Congressman Langworthy in his office. The congressman told them what they already knew.

"Simpson got twenty votes. That was expected. Hobaugh got the votes of Alaska, Colorado, Florida, Texas, Montana, and Wyoming. Tootell got all the rest of the Republican states, twenty in number. The four states with split delegations did not vote. Bobby Hobaugh has the votes to elect either Tootell or Simpson."

Janine's habit of rubbing her arm asserted itself as she asked, "Is there a chance that Bobby could get the votes of any of the states with split delegations? If that occurred, some of the Tootell people might begin to think of voting for Bobby."

Langworthy shook his head. "Not a chance. At least not right now. The greater possibility is that some of the states that voted for Bobby will switch to Tootell. Alaska is one we need to worry about. Tootell will promise to allow wide open drilling for oil and gas in the Alaskan National Wildlife Refuge. Wilson Weaver is the lone representative from Alaska. He wants that—bad. Such a promise from Tootell might persuade Weaver to vote for him."

Langworthy continued. "Well, the House is in recess until tomorrow afternoon when we'll vote again. I'm sure a lot of horse trading is going on right now. If President Simpson can get the votes of the states with the split delegations, he's only two votes away from holding the presidency." Langworthy chuckled and went on, "You can bet your boots he's going to try for 'em. He'll be making all kinds of promises to some of the Republicans in the states with the splits. Don't you wish we could listen to those conversations?"

Janine frowned. "I'd rather hear the promises Tootell is making. He's the one who's most likely to get enough votes by promising things." She stood and muttered, "Damn, I wish Bobby were here. None of the members of Congress, except you, have ever seen him. If they knew him, the ones voting for Tootell might change their minds. If the Democrats could meet Bobby Hobaugh, even some of the split delegations might vote for him."

Ralph rose to his feet. "You're absolutely right. But Bobby's not here and he isn't going to come. We just have to do the best we can without him. Maybe, if the voting goes on for several days without Tootell getting the necessary twenty-six states, his followers may decide they could accept Bobby. It's a long shot but it's what we're faced with."

Lance seldom entered into the discussion of strategy, limiting his role to the handling of reporters. He surprised them by saying, "Congressman, something you said interests me. You mentioned that Bobby Hobaugh has the votes to elect either Tootell or Simpson. Do you think there's a chance Tootell will offer something to Bobby to get him to release those votes?"

Ralph snorted. "He might try anything. But Bobby Hobaugh can't be bought. I suspect Tootell knows that."

The congressman nodded his head. "I agree. Tootell is capable of anything, but it seems unlikely that he would approach Hobaugh with such a proposition."

"Then how about Simpson?"

Ralph spoke again, "Simpson won't try. There's no way Bobby could deliver Republican votes to a Democrat, even if he wanted to. Simpson knows it."

The congressman again nodded his agreement.

Roman Burke cleared his throat and said, "There may

come a time when it's better to hand those votes to Simpson rather than have Tootell become president."

Langworthy laughed, "In your dreams! No Republican congressman will ever vote to put a Democrat in the White House. If you think I'm wrong, just try to imagine the Democrats voting to put a Republican in the White House. Something like that just isn't going to happen—ever."

That brought a laugh from all except Ralph. He looked around at the group and said, "You're probably right. But Lance is also right that either Simpson or Tootell could come forward with offers, and we should always keep that possibility in mind. We'd better keep Roman's thought in mind as well. Who knows what will happen before this is over?"

A moment of silence gave each listener time to consider the ramifications of Ralph's comments. When Langworthy stood, he surprised Hobaugh's supporters by saying, "The Speaker asked if he could meet all of you. I told him I'd bring you to his office. Do you mind going to see him now?"

Janine looked from Ralph to Roman and then to Lance. "Why, no. What does he want?"

"I think he wants to meet the people who turned an unknown cowpoke into a presidential candidate." As he ushered them out the door, he added, "And I think he'll ask you to get Bobby Hobaugh to Washington so he can meet the man."

Speaker Timothy Welch was all smiles as the introductions were made. After the visitors were seated in his spacious office, he politely offered them refreshments, which they declined. At last he walked to the chair behind his massive desk. He turned to Janine and said, "I met you with Senator Blaine last year."

"I didn't think you would remember."

"I remember you well, and the memory has been reinforced by the good work you've done for the man from Montana, Bobby Hobaugh."

"You may not agree, sir, but we think Mr. Hobaugh is preferable to Mr. Tootell."

"You've made that very clear by the work you've been doing." Speaker Welch turned to Ralph. "I understand that you are Mr. Hobaugh's best friend."

"Well, yes. Bobby and I certainly are friends."

"Those of us in the House, who must now choose a president, would like to meet him. To most of us, he's a mystery. Can you persuade him to come to Washington? If he were here, you could parade him around among the Republicans so they could see that he is a real human being."

"I've tried, sir, but he refuses to leave Montana—at least until the voting is completed and a president is chosen."

"Please try again. Tell him the members of Congress feel it would be extremely helpful. The minority leader tells me even the Democrats agree."

"All right, I'll try once again, Mr. Speaker, but I can't promise success. A woman named Margaret Lisa is his assistant. She's the one he might listen to. I'll talk to her again."

"Those of us in Congress would appreciate it." The Speaker's gaze swept the room to take them all in. "I'm truly impressed by the things you've done for your candidate. People with your ability are always needed around here. If, for any reason, you don't continue to work for Bobby Hobaugh, let me know. I'll have a place for you."

Friday, January 7, late afternoon

WASHINGTON D. C.

The first tentative approach was not long in coming. Silas Strong, the senior member of the Georgia delegation, stopped Congressman Langworthy in the hallway outside the House chamber.

"Let's have a chat, Will." He grasped the Montana congressman's arm and added, "Not here—down below in my quiet office."

Strong led Langworthy through a basement warren to a small hide-away office of the kind reserved for all senior members of Congress. After they were seated, and Strong had offered his colleague a drink that Langworthy declined, the man from Georgia said, "No sense in beating around the bush. Just tell me what that man Hobaugh wants, so that he'll get out of the way and we can elect Tootell and be done with it."

Congressman Langworthy leaned back in his chair in astonishment. It wasn't the question that surprised him. It was the blatant manner in which it was posed. Jackson Tootell obviously thought he could buy off Bobby Hobaugh, and Congressman Strong wasn't subtle in making the pitch. When Langworthy didn't respond right away, Strong scowled and asked, "Well, what about it?"

"I can't speak for Bobby Hobaugh."

"Maybe not. But that man, Ralph Phillips, and that woman, Janine Paul, seem to speak for him. Have them find out what he wants and let me know before the House convenes tomorrow. If he's reasonable, Tootell will accommodate him."

Langworthy leaned forward for emphasis as he spoke. "Listen, Silas, I don't take orders from you. And I sure as hell don't take them from Jackson Tootell." He stood, stared at his fellow congressman for a moment, "I'll convey your message to Mr. Phillips and Ms. Paul." He stared down at the other man and finished by saying, "Don't hold your breath while you wait to hear what they and Bobby Hobaugh have to say."

35

Saturday, January 8, morning

MILES CITY, MONTANA

"Margaret, this is Ralph. Please forgive me for calling so early in the morning."

"That's all right. We open the office at eight o'clock, even if everyone else is closed. You know Bobby. He's here for at least half a day most Saturdays."

"Margaret, I'll skip the pleasantries. Jackson Tootell has sent a messenger to ask what it will take to get Bobby to direct the states that have voted for him to vote instead for Tootell. We need to know Bobby's response."

"You mean Tootell's willing to offer something to get Bobby out of the way?"

"That's it. An ambassadorship perhaps. Maybe even a cabinet position."

Ralph heard Margaret's lilting chuckle before she spoke again. "Well, I'll tell Bobby. But, Ralph, you know him. Do you think he'll respond well to an offered bribe?"

Ralph chuckled in return. "He'll tell the one who made the offer to go to hell. But please tell him of the offer, anyway."

"I'll tell him, but you've already guessed what his response will be."

Ralph was silent for a moment. "We really need Bobby in Washington so the congressmen can get to know him. Is there any chance you could convince him to make the trip?"

"Ralph, Bobby has told you he won't go. Nothing I can say will change his mind."

"I'm calling now because the Speaker of the House of Representatives personally asked me to do so. He wants to meet Bobby, and so do the other Republicans. Even the Democrats are anxious to see him in person."

"You know, Ralph, Bobby didn't want to get mixed up in this presidential business in the first place. Right now, he just would like to put it out of his mind." She waited a moment before continuing. "That's a little hard to do." She paused again. "Let me tell you what it's like here. The job of the Secret Service is to protect Bobby, but their presence makes life almost impossible. The ranch house has security equipment inside and out, with agents around all the time. Bobby can't even drive to work from the ranch. He has to be chauffeured by an agent. When he gets to the office, he can't just walk in through the reception area as he has done all these years—he has to enter through the back door because the agents are worried that someone in the reception area might be dangerous. Ralph, do you realize what it's like for Bobby not to be able to walk down the street to have coffee with old friends?"

Before Ralph could answer, she resumed her monologue, "No client is allowed into Bobby's private office without first being carefully scrutinized. As you can imagine, the clients don't appreciate that kind of treatment. I know the Secret Service agents are doing what is necessary to protect a potential president, but it makes life a struggle for all of us."

Margaret took a deep breath and began again. "They've even caused problems for Clint at the ranch. Apparently, one of the ranch hands has a criminal record. He was convicted of breaking and entering a few years ago and served a short sentence in the penitentiary. The guy had worked for Clint for a couple of years and was a good hand. Well, the Secret Service learned of his background, and the next thing Clint knew, the guy was gone—just gone—no notice or anything. Clint was left shorthanded just when he needed the man for the winter work with the cattle. When Clint asked the agent about it, he was told the ranch hand was invited to leave—for security reasons. Bobby raised hob with the agents, but they don't seem to care about his personal affairs. It's as though he has become government property." Ralph heard the chair rumble as she moved.

"We can't even leave the office for lunch. We tell the agents what we want and they order it prepared and delivered. And then they inspect it before we can eat. Damn it! They wanted to monitor the office phone calls. How in the world can you run a law office if the clients' phone calls can't be held in private? Bobby did tell them they couldn't do it, but they may be listening anyway. There's not a bit of privacy, Ralph. Those men even have my apartment staked out and they follow me wherever I go. Russell Harrington is in the same fix. They tell us they don't want any of Bobby's associates to be targets. I suppose that makes sense, but it sure makes it almost impossible for all of us to go on doing the things we've always done and need to do now."

Ralph cleared his throat. "Look, Margaret, I..."

Margaret's tone hardened. "Frankly, Ralph, Bobby's ticked. He doesn't want his life upset this way."

When Margaret finally stopped speaking, he said. "He's a candidate for president. They have to protect him."

"I suppose. But remember, only two months ago Bobby Hobaugh was perfectly happy with a peaceful life here in Miles City. Then you persuaded him to go on a speaking tour just to help elect Warren Weldon. He never expected it to end up like this."

"Margaret, I'm sorry for the problems you're experiencing. But Bobby's a candidate. Unless he's willing to tell the states voting for him to vote for one of the other candidates, nothing can change that now. I really hope he doesn't do that, and I don't think he will—at least not in response to Tootell's blatant offer. If you can do anything to get him to travel to Washington, I will appreciate it. So will Janine Paul, Lance Caldwell, and Roman Burke. All of us believe it's important to the country and the world to keep Jackson Tootell from winning the presidency. The Speaker wouldn't have asked me to call you if he didn't think so too."

Margaret's voice was flat. "I'll tell him of our conversation, nothing more."

"Tell him we'll have a charter jet at the airport in Billings within six hours when he decides to make the trip."

Late in the morning, a Secret Serviceman knocked on the door to Bobby's private law office. He entered to find Bobby seated behind his old desk, microphone for his dictating machine in hand. "I'm sorry to bother you, sir, but you need to know that a creditable threat to your life has been uncovered."

Bobby's eyebrows raised in astonishment. He sat forward and motioned to a chair, but the agent remained standing.

"Mr. Hobaugh, as you know, our agents routinely patrol the area around your ranch home. What you may not know is that we also fly over the area using infrared equipment. For the past three days, that equipment has picked up warm body readings from a heavy growth of thorn bush around the spring just above your house. Because we received the readings only in the evening and on each occasion at about dusk, we thought it too regular to be an animal.

Yesterday morning one of our agents crawled into the thicket and found that someone had made room to lie down and had placed a rest for a rifle where there's a clear view of your kitchen window." He paused, looking intensely at Bobby. "We kept the place under surveillance, and last evening we watched an individual creep toward that location from the far side of the ridge. In camouflage clothing, he did a good job of concealing his movements through the sage. He carried a rifle. Agents surrounded the area and apprehended the man. He was lying flat on the ground at the site. His sophisticated sniper's rifle was rigged with a scope, and it was sighted on the window."

"He was trespassing on my property..." Bobby frowned. "And you think...?"

"We've looked into his background. He was a sniper in the US Army."

"Where is he now?"

The agent sighed. "In the county jail in Miles City with charges for trespassing—for now he swears he was deer hunting. He insists he had his rifle aimed at a four-point buck and didn't realize that it was in line with your house. He was just looking at the buck.

"The FBI is sending a professional interrogator. We'll get the truth, and then he'll be transported to a maximum security prison."

"Maybe he's telling the truth.

The agent paused, braced his hands on Bobby's desk. "Mr. Hobaugh, think about it. Night after night, this trained sniper watched your window, waiting for you to come into view. If you had done so, you could have been a dead man. It would have been a shot at a very long range, but not beyond the ability of an expert marksman."

Bobby leaned back in his chair and stared at the agent.

"You think that someone was trying to shoot me?"

"Yes, sir. That's exactly what he had in mind."

"But why?"

"You're a candidate for president, sir. A celebrity, so to speak. People in your circumstance are always at risk." The agent paused for a moment, then added, "The threat is real, sir, very real. More real than the ranch hand, who may or may not have caused a problem. We think this may be related to the incident at Ralph Phillip's pumping station. Someone either wants to persuade you to drop out of the race for president or, if that doesn't happen, to eliminate you."

"This is all hard to believe." Bobby stood, walked across the room and back. "When will you know for sure?"

"The interrogator will be here first thing in the morning. In the meantime, the sniper is under constant observation."

Bobby returned to the chair, leaned forward, put his elbows on the desk, and looked the agent in the eye. "Don't tell Margaret about this. She doesn't need to know."

"I'm afraid she does, sir. We need to increase the level of security for both of you, and for others who associate with you." The look that appeared on Bobby's face reflected the agent's own concern. "The threat was real, sir, and we don't know when or under what circumstances the next one will come." The agent hesitated before adding, "Sir, we must protect both you and Margaret Lisa. It would be easier if she were to stay at your house and travel with you each day to and from your office. Then we could escort you both at the same time. It would minimize the risk to both of you."

Bobby leaned back in his chair again and closed his eyes. Finally he opened them again to look at the agent, only to say, "Damn Ralph Phillips."

Saturday, January 8, afternoon

WASHINGTON, D.C.

"The chief clerk shall again read the roll of the states in alphabetical order, beginning with Alabama."

The senior member from Alabama called out, "Alabama casts its vote for Jackson Tootell."

"Alaska."

"Mr. Speaker, the state of Alaska casts its vote for Bobby Hobaugh."

The remainder of the states voted as they had the previous day. After Wyoming cast its vote for Bobby Hobaugh, the Speaker said, "The chief clerk shall now read the tally of votes."

"Mr. Speaker, Jackson Tootell, 20 votes. Arthur Simpson, 20 votes. Bobby Hobaugh, 6 votes. Mr. Speaker, four of the states passed and did not vote."

The Speaker nodded and said, "The members will note that no one received a majority of the states' votes."

Once again, the majority leader rose from his seat to intone, "Mr. Speaker, tomorrow is Sunday. For that reason, I move that the House stand adjourned until three o'clock in the afternoon, Monday, January the 10th, to allow the states time to caucus once again."

Saturday, January 8, afternoon

ARLINGTON, VIRGINIA

"That guy from Alaska is trying to play it cute, Tucker. Get him in here." Tucker turned on his heel to leave, but Jackson Tootell stopped him with a growl. "The botched attempt on Hobaugh's life could hurt us. What's being done about it?"

"The man they have in custody will be gone before he can talk."

"That better be correct, Tucker. Is that understood?"

"It's perfectly clear, sir. It always has been."

"Just be sure you continue to understand our arrangement." Tootell glared at Tucker as he added, "No mistakes." Then he growled, "And get that clown from Alaska in here today."

Outside the building, Tucker muttered to himself, "That bastard I sent to Montana was supposed to be the best. He'll have to be taken out."

Saturday, January 8, afternoon

WASHINGTON, D. C.

"Ralph? This is Margaret calling. Bobby was so angry at the attempt to bribe him that he refused to even talk to you about it. He doesn't often use profanity but this time he said, 'You should tell those bastards to go to hell!'"

Saturday, January 8, evening

WASHINGTON, D. C.

Congressman Langworthy looked from Ralph to Janine and then to Roman Burke. He smiled as he spoke.

"I let Silas Strong know that Bobby Hobaugh can't be bought. He wasn't pleased." The congressman laughed as he added, "He warned me that once Tootell is president, my time in Congress won't be pleasant."

Janine shook her head. "Tootell has nice people around him, doesn't he?"

"One of the reasons we don't want him in the White House." Then Langworthy added, "Tootell didn't get Alaska after all. What do you think is going on?"

Ralph stood, hands in pockets, at the end of the congressman's desk. "Well, I've learned that things work here in Washington pretty much the way they do in the Montana legislature. I'd guess that Weaver is holding out for something more than drilling in the Wildlife Refuge."

"I don't know what it would be. But, who knows, maybe we're wrong. Maybe Weaver just isn't willing to deal," Langworthy said.

Ralph grunted and said, "We'll probably find out the next time the House votes." He turned to Roman, "How secure is Florida? Will any of your people sell out?"

"You never know what might make a person change his or her vote, but the state is secure for Bobby so far, and I think it will stay that way."

"Janine, what about Colorado?"

"They're still loyal to Senator Blaine and Governor Weldon. I think they'll hold."

Ralph nodded as he mused aloud, "Wyoming should stick with Bobby. That leaves Texas. I'd better call Dick Saylor." He turned to Congressman Langworthy. "Could you talk to someone in the Texas delegation and get a reading on their next vote?"

"Sure. I'll do it right away. In the meantime, see what you can find out from your friend, Saylor. He may be able to tell you more than I can. In this place, everyone is trying to find out what everyone else is doing without giving anything away." He rose to his feet to signal the gathering was at an end and then added, "It would be nice to know where we stand before the House votes again."

Saturday, January 8, evening

MILES CITY, MONTANA

Bobby spoke to Margaret across the table in the kitchen of the ranch house. "I like to win. When I was in school, I was on the football and basketball teams, and I hated to lose. When a judge rules against me, I hate it. I suppose it's natural, once you're in a contest, to want to win. Last night, in the middle of the night, I woke up hoping just that."

"Hoping you would win the presidency?"

"Yes, isn't that idiotic?" Before she could answer, he went on, "Margaret, you know how I feel about this. I'm scared to death some crazy thing will happen, and I'll find myself with all the responsibility of the world on my shoulders. I'm not prepared for that. I'm not smart enough for it. I'm not mean enough for it."

"I'll agree you're not mean, but lack of intelligence is not your problem. If it happens, Bobby, you'll do a good job—and the country will be safe."

"Well, I'm not going to fly off to Washington just because Ralph and Janine want me to. Logic tells me that there's little chance I'll be elected, and all of this will just go away. Then you and I can have some peace again."

"I wish I could agree with you, but I don't. You may as well accept that you may be in Washington very soon. It seems to me you should be preparing for that possibility now, instead of wishing it wouldn't happen. If you do win, you won't have time to prepare before you have to go."

"How can I prepare?"

"For one thing, you can stop seeing clients and devote your time to going over your active files with your law partner and with the staff. You need to share your thoughts and ideas with them regarding all of the pending matters so they'll be able to take over completely once you leave. There's a trial scheduled for March, you know. You may not be here to handle it."

"I suppose you're right as usual." Bobby rubbed the back of his neck. "Would you arrange times for me to visit with each one in the office and have the correct files available for each conference?" Bobby stopped and put his hand on hers. With a smile he added, "And please sit in on all of them with me." His smile disappeared when he said, "Do you know that I've never been to Washington? I had never been east of Chicago until that campaign stop in Cleveland."

"Neither have I, Bobby. Maybe it's time we took a trip."

Bobby smiled across the table at his long time assistant. "With you, it would be pure pleasure." Then the smile disappeared. "The business of the guy with the rifle is worrisome. God, Margaret, I don't want anything to happen to you."

"It won't, Bobby. The Secret Service agents have it in hand. They deal with that kind of situation all the time."

"Why in hell am I letting this go on? I should just call Ralph and tell him I quit."

"No, you shouldn't. We can't let some lunatic with a rifle upset the whole election process." She reached for his hand. "We'll be all right, Bobby. Have faith."

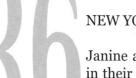

Sunday, January 9, morning

NEW YORK, NEW YORK

Janine and Ralph sat facing the television in their suite at the Willard. Senator Chris Harpstead, Democrat from California, was answering questions from Larry Morgan on CNN.

"Of course, the Republicans in the House of Representatives should get their act together. Nothing we will do during this session of Congress is more important than the selection of a president. The delay and appearance of disarray paints a horrible picture for the citizens of the country who expect the best of their representatives."

"Could the Democrats do better?"

"I know we could. Democrats may scrap among themselves when it doesn't matter, but when the chips are down, we gather together and make decisions. We Democrats in the Senate would have decided who should be president by this time."

"Would your Democratic colleagues in the House be as cohesive as you say the senators are, if they were in control?

"I'm sure they would, Larry." The senator paused for only a fraction of a second and then added, "Although, I must admit that the House of Representatives often acts with less solemnity, less sober-mindedness than the Senate."

"Some have said that the House is less stodgy than the Senate. Is that a fair characterization?"

Harpstead laughed. "That may be a fair characterization, all right." His smile disappeared. "The point is, the Democrats would never let something as momentous as the selection of a president turn into the circus we've been witnessing in the House of Representatives with the Republicans in control."

Sunday, January 9, afternoon

MILES CITY, MONTANA

"You mean the man with the rifle is dead?" Bobby's voice echoed his surprise.

"He was poisoned, sir." The agent stood stiffly near the entryway to the ranch house. "A woman claiming to be his wife—and carrying evidence that confirmed it—was allowed a supervised visit with him last night. This morning they found him dead in his cell." When Bobby just stared at him, the agent continued. "We don't know why she was allowed access to him. We can't explain how she managed to get the substance past our people when they conducted a full body search. We have no way of knowing how she administered it to the man, although we think it was an injection. The woman had dark hair that was so thick and curly as to be nearly matted. The investigators now speculate that she concealed an ampoule, to which a short hypodermic needle was attached, in that tangled mat. The ones who did the body search didn't comb out the hair as they should have. We think she used the needle and the ampoule to inject the man with some kind of fast-acting poison. We'll know more after the autopsy."

The agent cleared his throat. "Some of our people will be in for tough questioning." In an effort to redeem himself and his agency, he added, "We have an all-points bulletin out for her, of course."

"Did you get any information from him before he died?"

"None, sir. Agents specializing in interrogation arrived this morning to talk to him. Too late, obviously."

"How about information from her at the time she visited the jail?"

The agent shifted his feet and fidgeted. "None of consequence to the death, sir."

"Damn. I hope you find that woman."

Sunday, January 9, evening

ARLINGTON, VIRGINIA

"Listen, Weaver, I told you that unrestricted drilling will go forward in the Wildlife Refuge once I'm president, and you said you'd give me Alaska's vote. What the hell do you think you're doing, anyway, voting for Hobaugh the last time around?" Jackson Tootell stood with his hands on his hips while glaring down on the congressman from Alaska.

The smaller man didn't back away. "How do I know you'll carry through? How do I know you can get it done anyway?

Maybe you can get it through the House, but what about the Senate? All you have to do is mention the Alaskan Wildlife Refuge, and every Democrat in the senate genuflects." Congressman Weaver shook his head. "Senator Gentry is adamantly opposed, and he has lots of support. He's always been able to keep the issue tied up in the committee."

"Take my word for it, Gentry won't be a problem. He's like everyone else. There is something he needs, and I can provide it. He'll deliver the Senate votes when the time comes."

"That may be so, but no one knows about this conversation except you and me. Unless you're taping these sessions. If you're doing that, you're putting the noose around your own neck. You may think you don't need to carry through once you're in office." After the shortest of pauses, he continued, "I have no reason to trust you."

The big man's face reddened in anger. "I do what I say I'll do. That's all the assurance you need. Next time the House meets, you damn well better cast Alaska's vote for me."

Congressman Weaver's voice rose. "Don't try to bully me, Tootell. I'll decide when it's the right time to vote for you." He pointed a finger up at the candidate's face and growled, "Remember, I'm the senior Republican on the Interior Committee and have seniority on other committees. You cross me, and you'll pay for it the entire time you sit in the White House."

"I don't take kindly to threats."

"Neither do I." Weaver started for the door, then turned back and said, "I believe we finally understand each other."

Sunday, January 9, evening

WASHINGTON, D. C.

The approach that came from the Democrats was more subtle. A woman who looked familiar stopped Janine in the lobby of the Willard. "I'm Sybil Marlowe. May we visit for a moment?" Without waiting, she turned and strode toward a group of chairs arranged in a quiet corner. Janine followed, more than a little curious to learn what the woman wanted. Trailing behind Ms. Marlowe, she tried to remember why she should recognize the woman. She was slender, middle-aged, and carefully dressed in a classic black skirt and sweater.

When they were seated, Sybil Marlowe leaned toward Janine and spoke in low tones. "I'm here on behalf of some Democrats who think it would be a tragedy if Jackson Tootell were to become president. We understand that you and the other supporters of Bobby Hobaugh feel the same way."

The voice brought it back to Janine. The woman was President Simpson's assistant press secretary. Astonishing! But she responded in a neutral voice. "We're backing Bobby Hobaugh because we think he'd make a great president."

"But Mr. Hobaugh can't win. You must realize that. It's only a matter of time—a short time—until you begin to lose states that have been voting for your man."

Janine shook her head. "I disagree with that assessment. As time passes and congressmen begin to realize that Hobaugh's supporters are firm, the votes will begin to shift our way."

Ms. Marlowe smiled. "I doubt that you really believe that, but I understand why you say it." Her voice turned quietly serious. "With the votes of the states Hobaugh has been getting, President Simpson can be re-elected. That's a better outcome for the country than a Tootell presidency. Wouldn't you agree?"

"Whether I agree or not doesn't really matter, does it?"

Sybil Marlowe leaned back in the chair, crossed her legs, and ran her hand down her skirt as though to straighten a wrinkle. At last she said, "Bobby Hobaugh can be Secretary of the Interior of a new Simpson administration. Please convey that message to him." That said, the woman rose from the chair and strutted across the lobby and out the door. Janine sat for a minute, then laughed silently as she walked to the elevator. She could hardly wait to tell Ralph. She already knew what Bobby's response would be to yet another attempt at bribery.

Sunday, January 9, late

ARLINGTON, VIRGINIA

Tucker knocked and entered when Tootell grunted the invitation. "The rifleman is dead, sir."

"I heard that on the radio. What about the woman?"

"She will never be found."

37

Monday, January 10, morning

WASHINGTON, D. C.

Ralph and Janine rested quietly in their suite at the Willard, each in a comfortable chair. Ralph had just clicked on the TV to see House Minority Leader, Lawrence Little, responding to talk-show host, Howard Evans, on MSNBC. Evans, it seemed, had given Little the opportunity to blast the Republicans.

"Howard, the inability of the majority party to carry out their constitutional responsibility is appalling. We've been in session now for four days and aren't any closer to choosing a president than we were on January 6".

"What has your party done, Congressman, to move the process along?"

"There's nothing we can do. We don't have the votes. But, believe me, if we were in the position of the Republicans, we'd have our act together. The president would have been chosen long before this."

"Will you try to make an issue of it in the next election?"

"We won't have to. The people will remember and know how to vote. The country will not only have a Democratic president but a Democratic Congress as well. And it will be about time."

When the show ended, Ralph sat for a moment with his elbow on the arm of the chair and his chin in his hand. He turned to his companion and said, "The Democrats' effort to get Bobby to release his states to Simpson was interesting. I guess you let that woman know about Bobby's response to their attempt at bribery.

Janine smiled. "I did, and she wasn't happy about it." After a trice she added. "I've now been told that Ms. Marlowe doesn't speak for President Simpson. It's his Chief of Staff, Tracy Wheat, who's behind that offer of a cabinet post. His interest is in saving his job. The president has refused to have anything to do with attempts to solicit Republican votes."

Ralph nodded. "Well, I think it's time that you and I should try to shake things up. The Democrats control the California delegation by only one vote. In the morning, let's get a list of those Democrats and choose one who might be susceptible to persuasion."

Monday, January 10, afternoon

WASHINGTON, D. C.

Roman Burke and everyone else recognized that Janine and Ralph were now a couple. Roman found it interesting that Ralph felt no need for elevator shoes when he was with Janine and that she continued to wear heels. Apparently the height differential was of no importance to either of them. Today, they were sitting to his left in the gallery of the House as the states cast their votes. He found himself holding his breath as the chief clerk called out, "Alaska."

"Mr. Speaker, the state of Alaska casts its vote for Bobby Hobaugh."

The rest of the states voted as they had during each of the preceding sessions.

Burke rose from his seat and gestured for the others to follow. Outside in the corridor he faced them and said, "Well, we still don't know what's happening with Alaska. Maybe Tootell won't get that vote after all."

Ralph put his hand on Janine's back as they started walking. "Let's get down to Langworthy's office. We must do everything we can to hold the states we have and try to figure out a way to get some more."

Monday, January 10, evening

NEW YORK, NEW YORK

Timothy Welch, the Speaker of the House of Representatives smiled at his Fox news host, Peter Brown, and then turned to face the television camera as he answered the question.

"I'm aware, of course, of the criticism from the Democrats about the way the selection of a president is going. As you can guess, I don't share their belief that the sky is falling. The people expect us to act in a deliberate manner in making this momentous choice, and we're doing just that.

"But, Mr. Speaker, the Democrats are saying that they would get together and decide who should hold the office and then cast the votes to get it done. If we were to believe what they're saying, they would have finished the job by now."

"I doubt that, Peter. You know as well as I that the Democrats are even more contentious and more susceptible to infighting than we Republicans."

"But aren't they correct in their criticism? Shouldn't your party get itself together and choose a president without delay?"

"This is not a burden to be taken lightly or to be decided hurriedly. Please remember that the supporters of both Jackson Tootell and Bobby Hobaugh have deeply held beliefs. They aren't playing games. Each has a real concern for the future of the country."

"Have you used your influence to try to persuade the members from the states voting for Hobaugh to give their support to Tootell?"

"No, Peter. I haven't tried to persuade any member to vote any particular way."

"Why not? You're the Speaker. The Democrats are criticizing you for your failure to act decisively to end the stalemate."

Congressman Welch frowned. "This isn't a time for such legislative tactics. The stakes are too high. Each member of the House of Representatives must search his or her conscience and decide how to vote. History will remember what each of us does. Every member is burdened by that thought. Peter, both you and your viewers need to know that we Republicans will continue to act with due deliberation. We will not be stampeded."

Roman Burke, alone in his room at the Willard, punched

the remote and watched the screen grow black. Then he sat back and muttered to himself, "Timothy Welch, you can help to end this deadlock if you really want it ended. All you have to do is let it be known that you don't think Jackson Tootell should become president." He thought a moment, scowled, then added, "But for God's sake, don't say that you could accept him!"

Tuesday, January 11, morning

WASHINGTON, D. C.

Congresswoman Audrey Sanders from San Jose, California, had a record as a consummate liberal but with an independent streak. She agreed to meet with Ralph and Janine only at the personal request of Congressman Langworthy. She rose from behind her desk to greet them with a solemn face as she directed them to chairs. "I'm flattered to be visited by two such prominent political operatives." Her voice held little inflection.

Janine graced her with a smile. "We didn't realize we were either prominent or political operatives."

"Oh yes. Everyone in Washington knows that Jackson Tootell would be president-elect right now but for you two."

Ralph decided they might as well get right to it. "Congresswoman Sanders, we believe that Jackson Tootell is wrong for the country. That's the reason we've worked so hard for Bobby Hobaugh. We're here because we think you may share our concerns about Mr. Tootell."

"Of course I think Jackson Tootell is wrong for the country. What thinking person could believe otherwise? Let's be blunt. He's not only wrong for the country, in my view he's a menace to the country."

Janine spoke quickly. "That might be true. But he has the votes of twenty states and may be on the verge of getting some more."

"Well, what about it?"

Janine answered, "In order to stop him, we need some change in the vote, a change that indicates there is weakness in his support."

"So?"

"Would you be willing to vote for Bobby Hobaugh the next time California caucuses?"

The congresswoman snorted. "Not likely. But what good would that do anyway?"

Ralph responded. "Your vote for Hobaugh, a Republican, gives the California Republicans more votes than the California Democrats. We don't know how the Republicans from California are voting. But even if they all have been supporting Tootell, they might agree to shift to Hobaugh in order to get your vote. It would be a monumental change in the way things are at the moment."

He stopped to allow Audrey Sanders to consider the implications and then went on. "It might cause some of Tootell's supporters in the Republican states to reconsider their position and vote for Hobaugh." He paused again. "We think you could start a ground swell that would deprive Tootell of the presidency, all to the good of the country."

The congresswoman looked from Ralph to Janine and back again. At last she took a deep breath and said, "It's an intriguing idea. I'll think about it. But I'll be truthful. You should leave here understanding that it isn't likely that I'll ever vote for a Republican."

Tuesday, January 11, afternoon

WASHINGTON, D. C

From the gallery, Ralph and Janine watched the hubbub on the House floor before the session convened. Lawrence Little, the House minority leader, and Congresswoman Audrey Sanders stood face to face while engaged in a vigorous conversation. After an exchange that seemed to culminate in a quiet but angry declaration by Little, the congresswoman nodded her head. As the minority leader stalked away, Janine turned to Ralph to say, "That's the end of our attempt to get a Democratic vote for Bobby."

When the House convened and cast ballots again, the tally did not change. Alaska voted for Hobaugh, as did the other states that had given him their votes in past sessions. California voted for Simpson. The majority leader raised some eyebrows among those on the House floor and in the gallery when he moved that the House adjourn for two days and not reconvene until Friday, January 14. Hobaugh's supporters soon found out the reason. They were again summoned to the Speaker's office.

Speaker Welch's eyes moved from Ralph to Janine to Roman and finally to Lance. At last they settled back on Ralph as he spoke. "The majority leader and I believe it's essential that we meet your man, Hobaugh. If he refuses to travel to Washington, perhaps we should go to him." He turned to face Ralph directly. "Will he meet with us if we fly to Montana?"

"I'm sure he will. Bobby's a gentleman. He wouldn't refuse to talk with someone who traveled that far."

"Please call him to be certain. If he agrees, we'll fly to Billings Thursday morning. I assume all of you can travel with us."

Ralph answered for all of them. "Yes, sir, we can. I suggest we get together in the conference room at my offices in Billings. It's private so we won't be bothered by the press. I'm absolutely certain Bobby will come to Billings from Miles City to meet you."

"It's kind of you to offer the use of your facilities." The Speaker glanced from one to the other. "It's agreed then? We'll go to Billings on Thursday?" When they all nodded, he added, "Very good. I've already chartered the plane for the trip." He stood to let them know the meeting was ended but then continued, "I may ask the minority leader to go with us. It wouldn't hurt if the Democrats knew a little about Bobby Hobaugh, too."

Democrat Lawrence Little, the House minority leader, smiled at the Speaker. "Timothy, you Republicans are the ones with the problem. We Democrats know who we're going to vote for each time the House convenes. If you want to fly off to Montana to meet with this invisible man, it's fine with me. But I'm not going with you and lend legitimacy to him as a candidate."

"I thought I'd ask, just as a matter of courtesy. If you don't want to go, that's your privilege." Welch reached out to shake Little's hand and added, "We'll be back Thursday night and available for the vote Friday afternoon."

Little gripped the Speaker's hand with both of his. "As a matter of courtesy, you might share your impressions of Bobby Hobaugh with me when you get back. I must admit, I'm curious."

38

Margaret was astonished, and Bobby was chagrined to find that they would be in an armored limousine that traveled in the middle of a caravan of vehicles on the 135-mile trip from Miles City to Billings. He had wanted to make the drive in his SUV, but the Secret Service agents had been adamant. Bobby was even more chagrined to find that the streets around Ralph's office building were sealed off and that it—both inside and out—was alive with sheriff's deputies. He refused to believe either he or Margaret was at any serious risk. It all seemed a waste of money and manpower. Even on the elevator ride to the fourth floor, they were accompanied by three Secret Service agents.

Margaret Lisa sat at Bobby's right hand and across the table from the House majority leader who was seated next to Timothy Welch. Welch and Bobby were directly across from each other. Ralph Phillips, Janine Paul, Lance Caldwell, and Roman Burke made up the rest of the gathering.

Following introductions, the Speaker thanked Bobby for making the long drive from Miles City.

Bobby replied, "Our trip wasn't nearly as long as yours, sir."

"Mr. Hobaugh, we made the journey from Washington because we believe it's important to learn more about you. You are one of only three people from whom we in the House of Representatives must choose a president. We know a great deal about the incumbent president and about Mr. Tootell. You, however, are something of a mystery to us."

"Well, I'm willing to answer your questions. That should solve any mystery about me."

"We know that you are a lawyer and a rancher. We know you are also a state senator. But we don't know your thinking about matters of national importance. Do you mind if we ask about such matters?"

"Not at all. But please realize that my only sources of information about national affairs are the newspapers, magazines, television, and blogs."

"Understood." Welch shifted his weight in the chair. "Let's start with one of the difficult issues. As you know, the president appoints Supreme Court justices, and one of the contentious questions that arises when a court vacancy occurs relates to abortion. If you become president, would your position on that issue be paramount in your selection?"

Bobby smiled at Margaret and then turned back toward Welch. "Mr. Speaker, Margaret and I have different views on the abortion issue. I'm a right-to-life guy and she's for a woman's right to choose. We differ on that and many other things." His face turned serious. "Choosing a justice of the Supreme Court may be more important than choosing a president. The choice should not be made on a single issue, no matter how important that issue may seem. If I were president and had to choose a person for the Court, I would look for someone who understands that the proper role of the court is to interpret the law, not make the law. Activist judges have, in my opinion, fostered a belief in our country that litigation to achieve social justice is not only acceptable, but admirable. But whose idea of social justice are we to accept? All too often it's the idea of one judge who wants to shape the world as he or she thinks it should be, regardless of precedent."

Bobby turned to Margaret. She said, "I assure you, if Bobby has to choose a justice, he will carefully consider all sides of the abortion issue—and every other issue."

The majority leader smiled at her and said, "Abortion leads to thoughts of health care." He turned to Bobby. "We all know that the cost of health care has skyrocketed in recent years. The cost can be so high that some people simply can't afford to do the things they should to maintain good health. Or to treat themselves when they're sick. What do you think of all the legislative attempts to address that problem?"

"Universal health care services provided by the government seem only to lead to excessive demand. If a person doesn't have to pay, the tendency is to use the service to the maximum. That's true with anything that's free. Then the only way to control costs is through some kind of rationing, and we all dislike that notion." Bobby paused in thought. "It seems to me that government should, as a general rule, provide cost-free medical service only to those who really can't afford to pay. It's in the nature of welfare. Those who can pay, should pay. I recognize that there are some who are in between—who could pay but only at the expense of depriving themselves of other necessities. Recent changes in the care that government provides seem to help. But the governmental cost has been way beyond projections." He turned back to the majority leader. "Higher deductibles? A health care tax? Reduced benefits? There have been many proposals, but none of them has been acceptable to a majority of Congress, and, I guess, to a majority of the people as well. It appears that something must be done, but I simply don't know what that might be."

"At least you're honest. Some in Congress won't admit that they don't know everything about everything," the majority leader said.

The Speaker nodded his agreement and then asked, "What about missile defense? Should the United States create a comprehensive shield against intercontinental ballistic missiles?"

"Sir, I can't answer that because I don't know if a complete defense is possible. If it is, I don't know the cost. I've read that experiments have been conducted. So far, those experiments have not been universally successful in destroying an incoming intercontinental missile with either another missile or with a laser burst. It seems to me, however, that if such a system can be built, some country will build it. The U.S. should not let some other country with intercontinental missiles get ahead of us on that one, no matter what the cost."

"Who would you rely upon for advice if you are chosen as president?"

"Mr. Speaker, that's one of the reasons why the idea of me as president is so unrealistic. My friends and associates are here in Montana, and they have no more national experience than I do. But to answer your question, sir, I suppose that if I were president, I would rely for advice on people such as you, people who have experience in national affairs. I would also expect you and other knowledgeable people to help me select members of the cabinet—help me find competent people for all positions of responsibility."

The majority leader raised one hand slightly off the table as though asking permission to speak. "The troubles in the Middle East seem to be unending. Do you have any thoughts about how they might be addressed?'

Bobby stared off into the distance as he thought. "Well, at least the radical Islamist terrorist threat has diminished to some degree, and our involvement in Iraq has ended. Osama Bin Laden is dead. Afghanistan no longer seems to be the chief training ground for those who would attack our shores. The actions taken after the World Trade Center disaster were at least partially effective in allowing us to identify and capture potential terrorists—domestic and foreign." Then he added, "But this country can't dictate the way others act. We can't, for example, force the Arabs to embrace the Jews. Because of the importance of the Middle East to our own interests, however, we should do the things that we can do to lessen the tensions that continually grip that region. Past administrations of both parties have been consistent in doing just that and so far have forestalled outright regional war. Future administrations should continue the effort."

The two congressmen and Bobby exchanged questions and answers until noon. Ralph's secretary knocked on the door and delivered sandwiches, chips, soda, and coffee. The party visited genially about nonpolitical matters as they ate. Sandwiches and soft drinks devoured and the residue removed by the secretary, the questioning resumed.

The majority leader spoke first. "Mr. Hobaugh, what is your view of the relationship between the president and Congress?"

Bobby pointed a finger at Ralph and laughed. "Once, when our legislature here in Montana had just defeated one of the governor's pet projects, the governor was on the fight. I can still hear Ralph reminding him that 'the governor proposes but the legislature disposes.' The governor didn't like to be reminded of it." Turning toward the majority leader, Bobby continued. "I believe the president must work with the Congress in an effort to achieve the best results. The veto, I believe, should be used sparingly. I realize it has been used sometimes purely for political purposes. I also realize there are instances when that may be proper, but those instances must surely be kept to a minimum."

It was the majority leader's turn to laugh. "Well, if you become president, we'll do our best to save you from the need to use the veto for any purpose."

The Speaker spoke next. "Mr. Hobaugh, the majority leader's question raises another question in my mind. If you were to find yourself as president, what programs—what legislation would you propose for Congress to consider during the coming congressional session?"

Bobby shook his head and looked first at the Speaker and then at the majority leader. "Gentlemen, I have no program. How could I? We're reminded again of how ridiculous it is to consider me as president of the United States."

Ralph was speaking almost before Bobby stopped. "Speaker Welch, the Republican Party has its platform. And Governor Weldon had his agenda. Both lay out a course that is right for the country. I know Bobby Hobaugh well. When he's president, he'll go back to the basic ideas set forth in the platform and in the governor's agenda and take the steps that are required to put them into action."

Roman Burke followed quickly, "That's right, sir. The Governor's program is categorized and compiled into manuals that make it easy for anyone to understand and follow. I know, because I put it all together for the governor's review. He gave it his approval just before the election. Bobby—and his cabinet—can use it at least as a place to begin."

"These two fellows make it sound easy, don't they?" Bobby shook his head again. "Well, I'm sure they're sincere, but I'm still just a sagebrush lawyer who knows the country would be much better served if someone with more experience is elected president."

The Speaker turned to Burke. "It's encouraging to know that Governor Weldon's proposals are preserved and in usable form." Turning back to Bobby, he said, "It appears you would have lots of help from your friends and associates as well as from those of us in Congress. Maybe you're too pessimistic about your ability to serve."

"No, sir, I'm not. It's not something you should even consider."

Ralph jumped in again. "Bobby's modest. But if he's president, he'll make us all proud. Take my word for it."

The questioning went on in a similar vein until three o'clock. The Speaker, at last, leaned back in his chair and said, "We've taken much of your time, and we must leave for the airport to return to Washington." He stood and reached out to shake Bobby's hand. "Mr. Hobaugh, you have been most forthcoming in your response to our inquiries. It's been a pleasure to spend time with you." Turning to Margaret with a smile, he asked, "I don't suppose it would do any good to suggest you try again to persuade your employer to travel to Washington so other congressmen can have the opportunity that we've just enjoyed?"

Margaret shook her head. "Sir, he says he won't go. Nothing I can do will change his mind. But you can try yourself. There he stands."

They both looked at Bobby, who was shaking his head. "Mr. Speaker, I'm not going to Washington and be paraded around for inspection like some exotic animal. If I did go to Washington, the assumption would be that I was there in an attempt to gather votes for myself. I'm not going to be put in that position."

"Well, it didn't hurt to make the suggestion one last time. While I don't agree with your decision, I respect it. We won't ask again."

As the Secret Service agents chauffeured Bobby and Margaret along the interstate highway leading back to Miles City, she reached out and patted Bobby's arm. "That wasn't too bad was it? Those were nice people."

"Nice, yes. And, no, it wasn't too bad." He was silent for a time, seeming to concentrate on the passing scenery, and then looked sideways at Margaret. "It just doesn't seem possible that all of this could have come about simply because I went to Billings to listen to Senator Blaine make a speech. It seems no more real to me than a bad horror movie."

After the plane leveled off at cruising altitude and drinks had been distributed to the little party, all but Timothy Welch engaged in lively chatter, most of it having to do with the problem the Republicans had in the selection of a president. The Speaker quietly sipped his drink, apparently lost in thought.

Finally, he said to no one in particular, "I liked him. He's obviously intelligent. He's thoughtful. He isn't afraid to admit he doesn't have all the answers and doesn't try to be more than he is." He looked across the aisle at Ralph and said,

"Your friend is a nice person." Then the Speaker stared off into space and seemed to speak to the world in general.

"I'm reminded once again that people of good judgment live in places outside the Washington D. C. beltway."

Friday, January 14, morning

WASHINGTON, D. C.

Speaker Timothy Welch picked up the phone to hear Lawrence Little say, "Well, you met the mystery man. What can you tell me about him?"

"Lawrence, you weren't interested enough to go to Montana to meet him. Why should I tell you anything?'

"Ah c'mon, Timothy, we've been friends a long time. I'm just curious, that's all."

The Speaker relented and said, "I like him. For a president, we could do worse."

"That's all? Are you supporting him instead of Tootell?"

"Friendship only goes so far, Timothy. I can't tell you that, and you know it."

"Well, let me ask you this. If your vote made the difference, would you feel comfortable voting for Hobaugh?"

The Speaker waited a long time before answering. When he did, it was with a heavy voice. "Lawrence, sometimes we just need to be honest—with ourselves and with others. The answer is yes. I'd feel comfortable voting for Hobaugh if my vote made the difference."

He paused. "But Lawrence, you never heard me say that."

Friday, January 14, afternoon

WASHINGTON, D. C.

The House convened at three o'clock to embark once again on the voting routine. The Clerk read out the names of the States, starting with Alabama. When Alaska's name was announced, Congressman Weaver rose from his seat and said, "Mr. Speaker, the State of Alaska casts its vote for Jackson Tootell."

A murmur arose on both the House floor and in the gallery. Tootell had at last taken one of the states that had been voting for Hobaugh. To many it foretold the end, the inevitable time when Tootell would be elected. There was a sense of expectation as the voting went along, each person in the chamber wondering if Tootell would get the votes of any of the other Hobaugh states. Colorado, Florida, Montana, Texas, and Wyoming all cast ballots for Hobaugh, just as they had been doing.

When the voting came to an end, the House adjourned until Monday, January 17.

Over the phone, Dick Saylor's familiar voice sounded worried. "Ralph, it appears to me that Tootell has pushed every button that is dear to the heart of a Texan. I'm afraid he'll get the Texas vote next time around."

"Have you been urging your congressmen—at least the ones you can work with—to hold the vote?"

"Sure have. But there's only so much that can be done from here. All the action is in the back halls of Congress. That's the kind of situation that Tootell thrives on."

"Well, we'll continue to do what we can. Our Montana congressman is talking to some of your people right now. I hope Texas hangs tough. If it doesn't, the groundswell for Tootell may carry over to the other states that are holding out for Bobby Hobaugh."

"Do your best, Ralph. And I'll keep making calls from here. I haven't changed my mind about that man, Tootell. God help the country if he's elected."

Ralph looked across at Janine as he put down the phone. "Dick Saylor is afraid we'll lose Texas. I'm tired of waiting and watching without doing something to affect the outcome of this election. Tennessee has been voting for Tootell, and the Republicans control Tennessee by one vote. Let's see if we can find out if they're solid for Tootell. They may not be. If one or more of their congressmen would threaten to vote for Simpson unless the others voted for Hobaugh, we might just swing Tennessee to our guy."

Congressman Langworthy shook his head. "Won't happen. That kind of threat is empty, and they'd all know it."

Roman Burke asked, "How are the members from Tennessee lined up? Do you know?"

"Nope. I haven't had any reason to ask." Langworthy looked around the room at Hobaugh's supporters. "I know Lester Botham fairly well. We came here as freshman together. I could talk to him. He may be willing to tell me what the situation is."

"Do it, please." Janine seemed to be pleading.

Friday, January 14, evening

WASHINGTON, D. C.

Langworthy stood in his office as he reported. "Botham was perfectly willing to share his contempt for Jackson Tootell with me. He's the only one in his delegation who would rather vote for Hobaugh. The rest, he tells me, are all firm for Tootell."

"Will he agree to do anything to try to change the minds of some of the others from Tennessee?"

"No, he won't. He made it plain that he would take offense and so would the others from that state if we tried to interfere in their affairs." Langworthy added, "Ralph, I understand how strongly you feel about your friend. We all share that feeling. But you better forget trying to get the vote of Tennessee. You'll only make some people mad."

Janine patted Ralph on the arm. "The congressman's right, Ralph. Let's think of something else."

Friday, January 14, evening

NEW YORK, NEW YORK

The face of Thomas Hickman, the craggy-faced CBS anchorman, was devoid of its usual placid countenance. Instead, his appearance reflected the serious manner in which he spoke.

> In the last round of voting by the members of the House of Representatives, Jackson Tootell received the votes of the same twenty states that he's been getting—but this time he got Alaska as well.

It seems probable that Tootell will, sooner or later, receive the votes of the remainder of the states that have been voting for Bobby Hobaugh. He will either make a deal with Hobaugh under terms of which Hobaugh will agree to release the votes to him—or the congressmen voting for Hobaugh will eventually accept the inevitable and vote for Tootell.

The United States Senate is required by the Constitution to choose a vice president from the two—just two—receiving the most electoral votes for that office. Henry Larsen, the Democratic candidate for vice president received the largest number of electoral votes for the office. Jackson Tootell received the most Republican electoral votes. The members of the Senate must choose one of them for the vice president. Assume that the House of Representatives chooses Jackson Tootell for president. Logic tells us that the man can't be both president and vice president at the same time. But would they follow the Constitution and vote for the Democrat? Or would they ignore the Constitution and vote for Bobby Hobaugh who had the third most votes? Only time and the votes in the House of Representatives will tell.

Thomas Hickman swiveled a quarter turn to his left to face a different camera.

The members of the House of Representatives will continue to cast their votes, and eventually a president will be chosen. If Jackson Tootell is the choice, the Republican members of the Senate must then face their difficult decision." The commentator paused for effect. "Will they follow the constitutional requirement and vote for Henry Larsen, the Democrat? Or will they choose party loyalty over the Constitution and vote for Hobaugh, the Republican?... Or might they just avoid the need to make that choice by refusing to bring the matter up for a vote at all? They could let time pass until after January 20. After that date the office would be vacant and newly elected President Jackson Tootell could nominate a person of his choice who would then be immediately confirmed by the senate.

Another pause before his customary warm countenance and shining smile re-appeared.

It's just one more extraordinary possibility that has arisen from the most extraordinary of all elections. This is Thomas Hickman speaking from CBS headquarters in New York. Have a pleasant evening—and good night.

Roman Burke slammed the off button of the remote. "If those Republican senators had any sense, they'd be working as hard as they can to persuade their House counterparts to elect Bobby Hobaugh. Then they wouldn't have to face that choice."

40

Saturday, January 15, afternoon

WASHINGTON, D. C.

Ralph listened as Janine read from the New Yorker magazine. Its lead commentary was in the usual form, replete with understated sarcasm.

The Wild West Gang of Four managed to steal the election. Like train robbers of old, the hijackers burst through the doors of the election process and heisted the opportunity for Congress to vote for the one Republican truly qualified to be president. Allen Ward's political philosophy is attuned to the majority of the people, and he has the intellect and experience to properly serve the country as its chief executive. The same cannot be said of Jackson Tootell. At best, Tootell reminds one of the robber barons of another century. But, because of the

Gang of Four, the only alternative to Tootell is someone named Bobby Hobaugh, a nonentity from somewhere in the nether regions of the West. We understand that Mr. Hobaugh had never been east of the Mississippi until the day before the election in November. It is ridiculous, or worse, to ask members of Congress to believe that riding the range on a Montana cattle ranch qualifies him to be president.

But the Gang has presented the members of the House of Representatives with a bitter choice—a choice between a man of questionable integrity and a nonentity. Who are these Gang members who have wreaked havoc with the election? Ralph Phillips, the apparent leader, is a small man with a big ego, obviously burdened with a Napoleonic complex. One expects to see him with his hand tucked into the front of his suit coat. Janine Paul towers over Phillips like an Amazon, determined to ensure that their quixotic schemes come to fruition. Lance Caldwell sees himself as the righteous messenger, spreading the word that Hobaugh is the savior. The presence of Roman Burke in the Gang puzzles the observer. He was the pragmatic tactician who managed Governor Weldon's successful campaign. It is difficult to understand how he became associated with the other three in their foolish quest to

```
elect a cowboy to the highest of-
fice in the land. But there he is,
standing shoulder to shoulder with
the others, expecting congressmen to
believe they should vote for the man
from Montana.

    Burke, because he is a pragma-
tist and because he obviously be-
lieves Tootell is wrong for the coun-
try, should persuade Phillips and the
others to ask the congressmen who are
voting for Hobaugh to give their votes
to Simpson. By doing so, he could
save the country from Tootell.

    But this Wild West Gang seems
bent on continuing their attempt to
secure the election of Hobaugh even
though it is apparent that their ef-
fort will only result in the elec-
tion of Tootell. Why are we remind-
ed of the Gang That Couldn't Shoot
Straight?
```

Janine stopped reading and looked at Ralph with eyebrows raised. "Well, Napoleon, what do you think of that?"

Ralph leaned back in his chair and laughed. "I like the part where they called you an Amazon."

Janine's voice turned serious as she asked, "Are they right though, Ralph? Did we steal from the Congress the opportunity to vote for someone they might have chosen?"

"Who knows what might have been? I think our intentions have always been proper. We weren't satisfied with either Tootell or Ward and neither were a majority of the electors."

"But our efforts may bring about the worst result—the election of Tootell."

"It could happen. But then it might have happened no matter what we did." Ralph leaned forward, elbows on his knees, chin resting on his fists as he smiled at his companion. "I haven't given up, Janine. There must be a way to convince enough congressmen to vote for Hobaugh. When that's done, we really will have stolen the election from Tootell."

Janine lapsed into thought, then straightened to say, "What about Allen Ward? Would he try to influence some congressmen to change their vote from Tootell to Bobby?"

"Ralph's eyebrows went up. "Maybe. Let's try him."

Twenty minutes later Ralph dropped the cell phone in his lap, smiled at Janine and said, "Mr. Ward really doesn't like Tootell. He'll start making calls right away."

"I hope it isn't too late. The dike may have been breached when Alaska changed its vote."

Laws of the United States

The term of four years for which a President and Vice President shall be elected, shall, in all cases, commence on the 20th day of January next succeeding the day on which the electors have given their votes.

41

Monday, January 17, afternoon

WASHINGTON, D. C.

Colorado voted for Hobaugh as did Florida and Montana. Then the senior member from Texas rose from his chair to intone, "Mr. Speaker, the great state of Texas casts its vote for Jackson Tootell." Wyoming voted for Hobaugh. As the House adjourned until Tuesday, January 18, ultimate victory for Tootell appeared to be in sight.

Monday, January 17, afternoon

ARLINGTON, VIRGINIA

Tootell smiled a wisp of a smile and said to Tucker, "Colorado will be next and then it's over."

Monday, January 17, evening

WASHINGTON, D. C.

Late in the evening, four Democrats gathered in the office of Lawrence Little. The House minority leader was joined by the House minority whip, the Senate minority leader, and Senate minority whip. Lawrence Little was speaking. "It's agreed that we have to stop Tootell?" When the other three nodded their concurrence, he rose from his chair and said, "All right, let's go see the president."

When welcomed into the oval office, the minority leader spoke, "Mr. President, Jackson Tootell got the votes of twenty-two states today. I'm told he'll get the vote of Colorado tomorrow. After that, Florida will change and vote for him. Then Wyoming and Montana will concede the inevitable. When that happens, Tootell will have the votes of twenty-six states and will be the next president."

President Simpson grimaced and shook his head. "God, what an awful thought."

"We're here to suggest that we should not let it happen."

"How can you stop it? If Tootell gets the votes, he's in."

"Mr. President, we can stop it by giving Bobby Hobaugh the votes that you've been getting."

Arnold Simpson's eyebrows went up in astonishment. He leaned back in his chair before he asked, "What do you mean?"

"Just that, sir. The Democrats can elect Bobby Hobaugh."

"My God, will they do it?"

"They'll do it with your permission, sir. None of us like it, but we can't bear the thought of Jackson Tootell sitting in this office as president of the United States."

"You're asking me to direct the congressmen who have been casting their ballots for me to vote for Hobaugh instead? When the House convenes tomorrow?"

"Yes, sir, that's exactly what we're asking."

Arthur Simpson leaned back in his chair and blew out a long breath. "Gentlemen, I have to think about this. It's the most unusual thing imaginable."

"Not quite, sir. This whole damn election is beyond imagination. Be that as it may, now it's time to do the thing that's right for the country."

"What do we know of this man Hobaugh? Will he be better than Tootell?"

"Sir, Timothy Welch went to Montana to meet him. Welch told me that Hobaugh is honest, thoughtful, and intelligent. I believe Welch." Little smiled, "That's really all we know. But, sir, that's better than Tootell—especially the honest part."

"But how will we ever explain it to the Democratic Party faithful—the ones who worked so hard to get me elected? They'll scream to high heaven that we sold them out."

"Sir, we'll simply tell them that the Republicans may have thought they won the election. But in the end we Democrats chose the President."

The President nodded his head in silence as he thought about the proposal. Then he spoke again to say, "This is something that will take time to digest." He leaned forward, rubbed his hand across his brow, and shook his head. Shifting in his chair, the president lifted his eyes to the ceiling as though asking for divine guidance. Finally, he looked back at Lawrence

Little. "I've got to discuss this with the First Lady. Can I call you later tonight to let you know what we decide?"

"Of course, sir. We are asking you to make a decision that is not only difficult but also momentous. Please take time to think it through."

The minority leader was awakened by the ringing phone at three o'clock in the morning. "Lawrence, this is Arthur Simpson. The First Lady and I agree the Democrats should vote for Hobaugh. You may convey that as my request to the Democratic caucus."

"Thank you, sir. I'm convinced it's the right thing to do."

42

Tuesday, January 18, afternoon

WASHINGTON, D. C.

Both the members of the House and the people in the gallery were becoming accustomed to the procedure and to the way the spokesman for each state would announce its vote. Even the chief clerk had stopped calling out the names of the states as though proclaiming a royal visit. Today he was all business, reading the name of each state immediately after the previous state had voted. The silence that had prevailed in the chamber at the time of the first vote was now replaced by the sounds of members moving about and visiting quietly among themselves. In the gallery, it was the consensus that Tootell would get the vote of Colorado today and the votes of the remainder of the states that he needed tomorrow. He would then be sworn in as president on January 20, the day set forth in the Constitution.

Alabama, Alaska, and Arizona voted for Tootell, as expected. Then the chief clerk called for the vote from the state of Arkansas. The senior member from that state rose and said in a quiet voice, "Mr. Speaker, the state of Arkansas casts its vote for Bobby Hobaugh."

For a moment the fact that Arkansas had voted rather than pass didn't register with those on the House floor or those in the gallery. When it did, there was a brief period of absolute silence. When it penetrated the minds of the throng that Arkansas had not only voted, but voted for Hobaugh, the noise level began to rise. The Speaker pounded his gavel and called for quiet. He looked at the man who had spoken as though he'd gone out of his mind. Then he asked, "Did I hear the gentleman correctly? Did you say Arkansas votes for *Hobaugh?*"

"You did, Mr. Speaker. Yes, sir."

California was next, and when it too cast its vote for Hobaugh, everyone in the chamber realized that something extraordinary was happening. The Republicans on the floor looked puzzled. The Democrats wore smug expressions. When Connecticut also cast its ballot for Hobaugh, all of the members and most of those in the gallery had figured it out.

Janine reached for the man on her left, squeezed his arm, and whispered in his ear. "You did it, Ralph! You're the master politician! You're better than any of those old ward bosses we've read about. The Democrats aren't going to let Tootell win. They're going to elect Bobby." Ralph smiled, reached an arm around her shoulder, and gave her a hug.

The voting continued, state by state. Each state that had been voting for Simpson, as well as the states of Colorado, Florida, Wyoming, and Montana, voted for Hobaugh. Another state with a split delegation also voted for him.

The Speaker asked the chief clerk to announce the tally, even though every person in the chamber knew the outcome. "Mr. Speaker, Bobby Hobaugh received 26 votes, Jackson Tootell received 22 votes, two states passed and did not vote."

"Members of the House, you've heard the tally. Does any-one contest it?" The Speaker waited for a full minute before continuing. "Hearing no contest of the tally, Bobby Hobaugh has been elected president of the United States of America."

Amidst the clamor that followed the announcement, the majority leader moved that the House adjourn. The Speaker banged his gavel and the session came to an end.

Outside the chamber, The Gang of Four whooped and hollered and exchanged gleeful high fives.

Tuesday, January 18, afternoon

ARLINGTON, VIRGINIA

Jackson Tootell's face was crimson as he stared at Tucker. "How the hell did this happen?"

"I don't know, sir. It never occurred to me that the Democrats would give their votes to Hobaugh."

Tootell turned his gaze back to the TV that showed members of the House hurrying out the door to go to their offices.

As he watched, his face became impassive. He said to Tucker in a quiet voice, "Hobaugh will be sworn in as president. We must change our plans once again."

Tuesday, January 18, afternoon

MILES CITY, MONTANA

In the den of his ranch house, Bobby stared at the television screen without saying a word. Margaret moved closer to him on the davenport, grasped his hand, and said, "You're president now. You won."

"Margaret, this can't be. I'm sure I'll wake up and find it's all a nightmare. It just can't be happening."

"It happened."

Before she could continue, the phone rang. She answered and then quietly handed the phone to Bobby.

"Mr. President, this is Ralph. Congratulations."

"Ralph, this isn't right. I can't be president. God, man, you know me. I'm just an ordinary human being. I haven't any knowledge of national affairs. I won't know how to begin."

"Bobby, the first thing is to get you here. The next thing is to get you sworn in. The chief justice customarily does it."

"Look, don't make any more plans for me. I have to digest all of this. It will take time." Bobby thought for a moment. "Any federal judge can swear me in. I may have Judge Wilson do it in Billings."

"Don't do that, Bobby. It's a national event. Like it or not, you are now the president of the United States. The people deserve the ritual and some ceremony now that the uncertainty has been eliminated."

"I'll talk it over with Margaret and decide." Bobby started to put the phone down, then stopped, and spoke again. "Thanks for calling, Ralph. You're a good friend, and I know you want the best for me. Please do me a favor. Talk with Janine and Roman about possible cabinet members and presidential advisors. I'll need to visit with Speaker Welch about the same things. Would you arrange a time for that, please?" Bobby took a deep breath, "And Ralph, you, Janine, Lance, and Roman will be the ones I rely on the most. I don't know what your titles should be." He dropped the phone in its cradle before Ralph could respond.

The phone rang again. When Bobby picked it up, he heard a woman's voice say, "Please hold for the president."

Bobby clasped the phone to his chest and said softly to Margaret, "It's the president."

"This is Arthur Simpson speaking. I'm calling to congratulate you and to offer my cooperation during the transition."

"That's kind of you, sir, and I appreciate it very much. I'll need all the help I can get."

"Don't worry too much. What this job requires is common sense, and, from what I've been told, you have it in abundance." Simpson laughed and added. "Perhaps if I'd demonstrated more common sense, the people would have re-elected me."

"Right now, I wish they had."

"Well, you're the chosen one. Now we have to get you here for the swearing in. I've dispatched Air Force One to Billings to pick you up. As you surely know, the chief justice usually gives the oath. Justice Butterfield has set aside the entire day on the twentieth to be available to do the job."

"Mr. President, I would rather have Judge Wilson here in Montana administer the oath. He's an old friend, and I'll be more comfortable among familiar surroundings."

"It's your choice, obviously. But let me suggest that Washington is the proper place to hold the ceremony. The people of the country expect it, and you'll soon learn that public perceptions govern much of what you do." Simpson waited a moment and then added, "You could take the oath on the steps of the Capitol building. That's where it's customarily done. But there isn't time to arrange all the usual pomp and circumstance. Besides, it's colder than hell here. I suggest you gather a few of your closest friends and do it here in the White House. The media will attend in force, of course, to record and report. That's their job."

"I haven't any staff to make the arrangements you've described. That's another reason to do it here in Montana, sir."

"I still have the reins of government in hand, and I'll make any arrangements that you wish. Just let me know your decision. And please call me Arthur. If it's all right, I'll call you Bobby. You and I are members of the most exclusive club in the world. You'll soon find yourself calling all the living ex-presidents by their first names. You'll appreciate and respect them all, Republican and Democrat alike."

"I suppose you're right about the public need for some ceremony. All right, I'll fly to Washington as soon as possible. If you'll arrange for the swearing in day after tomorrow, I'll be thankful. You are willing to hang onto the job for another couple of days, aren't you?"

Simpson's laugh was hearty. "Just tomorrow. The day after that, I'm out, whether you're sworn in or not." Then, as though he had almost forgotten, he said, "By the way, my wife and I have known we'd be leaving, so most of our belongings are gone from the White House. You can plan on moving in when you get here. We'll stay at Blair house until I'm done with this job."

"You've been most kind and helpful, Arthur." Bobby took a breath. "Sometimes I wish you'd never allowed the Democrats in the House to vote for me."

"I was convinced—and I still am—that it was the best thing for the country."

"Well, it's done." Bobby paused. "I'll depend on my friends Ralph Phillips and Janine Paul to work with your people to coordinate things. Who should they call?"

"Have them call my chief of staff. I'll alert him to expect it." He paused. "I'm anxious to meet you. And remember, if I can help at any time along the way, all you have to do is ask.

I've called for help from my predecessor more than once."

When he put the phone down, Margaret patted his knee. "It's the right thing to do, Bobby. A president should take the oath of office in the nation's capital, not in Billings, Montana."

Bobby pulled her close and held her silently for a long time. Then he rose from the couch with a sigh and said, "I'd better tell the Secret Service guys about our plans. From now on, they enter into everything we do. Privacy, I'm afraid, is a thing of the past for us."

Before he could say more, there was a knock on the door. When Bobby opened it, the Secret Service agent in charge said, "Good day, Mr. President. We've arranged secure transportation to the airport in Billings. Air Force One will be ready to depart for Andrews Air Base at ten hundred hours tomorrow morning, local time. And, sir, the security from now on must be even more stringent. There will be at least four of us with you at all times."

43

Wednesday, January 19, afternoon

WASHINGTON, D. C.

President Arthur Simpson and his wife, Penny, met Bobby and Margaret as they stepped from the limousine. The two men exchanged pleasantries and a formal handshake. Bobby put a hand on Margaret's back as he introduced her. The First Lady's smile was warm. She grasped Margaret's hand in both of hers. "I've been anxious to make your acquaintance—anxious to meet a woman whose life has been something other than constant politics." The smile widened. "But, from today on, you'd better expect politics to govern much of what you do."

The president laughed his patented laugh. Eyes on Bobby, he said, "From here on almost everything that you do will be governed by politics, like it or not."

Mrs. Simpson released Margaret's hand and her face sobered. "I'm still dealing with matters related to our move back into private life. Will you excuse me if I leave Arthur to conduct the White House tour?"

Margaret returned the smile. "Of course. You must be terribly busy. We understand."

"Please join us for dinner this evening at Blair House. Perhaps I can answer some of the questions you might have about the life you're about to live."

"Thank you for the offer. I will have a lot of questions."

The Oval Office was much smaller than either of them expected. Nonetheless, it was impressive as the place where momentous decisions affecting the world had been made over the generations. Simpson said, "Try the chair." When Bobby was seated behind the desk, he added, "You will want different decorations and appointments than the ones I have in here. The White House staff will help with that. They've seen presidents come and go and know the routine."

Bobby rose and asked, "When will the swearing-in take place?"

"It's scheduled for tomorrow morning at ten o'clock in the East Room. Chief Justice Butterfield will administer the oath. You'll need a bible and someone to hold it." He smiled at Margaret. "I assume you can handle that job."

"We brought a bible that Bobby's mother cherished. If I'm asked to hold it, I will."

Bobby spoke to Simpson while smiling at Margaret. "Of course she'll hold it. Who else would I ask?"

Simpson gestured for them to sit in chairs in front of the desk as he, from force of habit, took the one behind. "After you've taken the oath, the press will expect you to make a speech."

"I'm prepared to make a few remarks but they can hardly be considered a speech."

"Generally we politicians speak too much and too long. You won't offend anyone by keeping it short."

"What happens then?"

"My cabinet members will be here to meet with you and answer any questions you may have. You're lucky. There are no major crises facing the country right now. The Secretaries of State and Defense and the National Security Advisor will tell you of the minor crises. Each of them has agreed to stay on board until you've had time to choose your own people."

"I'd be in a tough spot if they all quit tomorrow."

"Well, as I said, they won't."

Bobby asked, "What happens after the swearing-in?"

"You'll be president of the United States. You're on your own. You'll immediately receive calls from other heads of state, demands from members of Congress, petitions from irate citizens, and you'll be expected to be ready to handle them all. One call will be from the Senate majority leader to discuss the voting for vice president. It will be a courtesy call. The senators can vote any time they wish, but they would like to accommodate your schedule."

"How does my schedule affect their activities?"

"They don't want to be voting while you're taking the oath. They'll probably wait to vote until tomorrow evening to give you some time to settle in. After all, there's no hurry. The voting is a formality. There are only two people they can vote for. One is Henry Larsen—and they won't vote for a Democrat—unless they just want to repay a favor. After all, the Democrats elected you. Perhaps the Republicans will elect a Democrat." Simpson laughed before he continued, "That won't happen, of course." The president's face turned serious again. "Jackson Tootell is the other one. He'll be your vice president."

"I hadn't given any thought to that. Or about any of the many other details that must go with the job." Bobby smiled at Arthur Simpson. "Now I know why you offered help. I hope that offer was sincere because I may need you tomorrow."

"You'll do fine. Just remember what I said. All this job requires is common sense. Use common sense right from the start, and before you know it, you'll feel comfortable in the position." Simpson rose from the chair, walked around the desk, and put his hand on Bobby's upper arm. "Harry Truman didn't do badly, and he got stuck with the job in the middle of a war."

"I hope you're right, and I'll take your advice. Now, if you don't mind, we need to rest a bit."

"Your belongings should be in the living quarters by now. I'll be here in the Oval Office until five o'clock, and then I'll be at Blair House. If you have any question, the staff can't answer, please don't hesitate to call."

As the president-elect and his bride walked through their new surroundings, Margaret mused, "He's a nice man. Why didn't we re-elect him?"

Thursday, January 20, morning

WASHINGTON, D. C.

Bobby wore the dark gray suit that Janine had chosen for the speech in San Francisco. Margaret was dressed in the same suit she'd chosen from her office wardrobe for her recent wedding day—the stone-gray suit with a belted jacket over a scarlet turtle-neck sweater, accessorized with only the beaded hair comb that had been her Native American grandmother's. She held the Bible, with Bobby's right hand resting on its top, as he repeated the oath. His face was solemn, and his voice was firm as he concluded with the words, "...so help me God."

The chief justice shook his hand, after which Bobby and Margaret shared a long embrace. Arthur Simpson, next in line, grasped Bobby's hand with both of his, smiled and said, "It won't seem so intimidating after a few days."

Bobby whispered, "I hope so." He turned back toward the microphones and television cameras, looked at the throng gathered in the East Room, took a breath, and began.

"Thank you all for coming today. As you know, I have just accepted an office I did not seek. I'm here only because of a series of events no one would ever have contemplated. We are about to test the theory that anyone can serve reasonably well as president of the United States. It would be untruthful to tell you that I feel confident of my ability to fulfill that role. Nevertheless, the system our forefathers devised has brought me here, and I will do my very best for the people of this great nation." He gestured toward the now ex-president. "I want to thank President Simpson for the kindness he has shown me. His behavior speaks well of his character, and it reaffirms the peaceful way in which executive power transfers in our country."

"Holding the Bible for me today is a lady of long acquaintance who, only five days ago, became my wife. Margaret is possessed of all the womanly virtues, and I love her dearly. Her judgment is unexcelled, and it is upon her that I will rely for advice and counsel.

"Finally, this nation was founded on Christian principles, and those principles will guide me during the time I remain in the office of president. I ask that each of you pray for me."

He stood for a moment as the flashes of many cameras bombarded him, then drew Margaret to his side so more pictures could be taken. At last, they stepped away from the podium to be surrounded by people anxious to reach out to them. First in line, of course, was now former President Simpson. "Thank you for the kind words. Remember, I want you to succeed."

Next was Ralph. "Congratulations, my friend. Or I should say, Mr. President. And congratulations, too, on your marriage. That was a surprise." Ralph poked a finger at Bobby's midriff and said, "I wasn't sure Margaret would have you."

"Neither was I, but thank God, she said yes."

Janine gave Margaret a hug and said, "I envy you. You got a great guy who will make a wonderful husband and president." Turning to Bobby, she said, "We need to talk about a lot of things as soon as you can escape this crowd. We're getting calls from hundreds of people wanting appointments."

"We'll stay here for a while, doing the reception line routine, and shake hands with as many of these people as possible. Then I'm scheduled to meet with President Simpson's cabinet members." Looking from Janine to Ralph, he said, "Can both of you, as well as Roman and Lance, be there?"

Janine smiled. "It's on our schedules too."

Ralph added, "You're off and running as president. The rest of us will go along for the ride."

44

Thursday, January 20, morning

ATLANTA, GEORGIA

"Tucker, you remember when the anti-trust people were after us?"

"Yes, sir, I remember well."

"The first federal judge assigned to the case was biased against us."

"Yes, sir."

"We had to do something about it. Isn't that right?"

"That was your conclusion, sir."

"That judge had an unfortunate accident, didn't he?"

"Yes, sir, he did."

"The judge that succeeded him was more reasonable, and he dismissed the case. Had that not happened, I would never have achieved the business success that I've enjoyed."

"That's probably true, sir."

"Now another man is standing in my way."

"Do you mean Bobby Hobaugh, sir?"

"I do. Just like the judge, he must be removed."

"The president is different from a judge, sir."

"Do I detect some reluctance on your part, Tucker?"

Tucker stiffened. "In line with our agreement, I'll do my part, sir."

Jackson Tootell remained impassive as he stared across the desk. "Of course you will. Let's review the arrangement. Eight years ago you agreed to work for me for ten years. During those ten years you would do things for which you have a peculiar talent. In exchange, I agreed to deposit a substantial amount of money each year in an offshore account in your name. I've upheld my part of the bargain, haven't I?"

"Yes, sir, you have. And so have I."

"Indeed you have. But your evident reluctance causes me concern. Do you want out of the agreement, Tucker?"

"No, sir. At the end of ten years I will have enough money to disappear and enjoy the life I've always wanted."

"It's heartening to hear that, but I'm willing to change the bargain for your benefit. Use your talents one last time, and I'll deposit the entire amount of money I owe you, including the last two years' payments, in the offshore account. When this final assignment is completed, you are free to disappear. You will never hear from me again."

"Sir? Won't you have further need of my services?" Before Tootell could answer, Tucker continued. "Once you said you wanted to repay Ralph Phillips for the trouble he caused. I have something special in mind for him. "

"Tucker, after you are finished with the last task, I'll be president. I'll have all of the agencies of the United States government at my disposal. No, I won't have any further need of your services."

"Sir, aren't you concerned that I may at some time tell more than I should? Or threaten to do so?"

"Tucker, we both understand the nature of our relationship, and we have done so right from the beginning. Neither you nor I can threaten the other. If one of us goes down, we both go down. That mutual interest is all the protection either of us needs."

"Yes, sir, you're correct. That's the reason I believe you when you say that I will never hear from you again."

"All right then, we still understand one another?" When Tucker nodded his agreement, Tootell continued, "The Senate will meet at seven o'clock this evening to elect a vice president. They will elect me. Should anything happen to the president after that, the vice president will become president."

"Yes, sir, that's the way it works."

"I will be sworn in as vice president immediately after the vote. That's the schedule. Before nine o'clock tonight, I'll hold the office." Tootell rose from his chair and walked across the room to look out the window. "Mr. and Mrs. Hobaugh will be receiving hundreds of cards and gifts. They will also get numerous bouquets of flowers from well wishers. The flowers will be delivered to the White House this afternoon." Turning to face Tucker, he said, "Among the bouquets will be one consisting of several giant amaryllis. In one amaryllis stem there will be three tablets. Your job is to arrange for the delivery of flowers—flowers in profusion—and ensure that the tablets are in place in the amaryllis. Use any names that seem appropriate—party regulars, lobbyists, whatever—on the cards that accompany the flowers."

"Yes, sir. I can ensure that the flowers will be delivered, but how do you know they will pass inspection and be allowed into the White House?"

"That has already been arranged. They'll be accepted for display in the White House. As you must have guessed, I have people who are...ah..., how to say it,...responsive to me on the White House staff."

"May I ask, sir, how the tablets will be used?"

"Why not? The president and his new wife are coffee drinkers. The tablets will be in the last cups of coffee they drink before retiring."

"Why three tablets, sir? Aren't two enough?"

"Insurance. One will be left in the fabric of the carpet in the bathroom that was used by President Simpson. When it's found—and it *will* be found—suspicions will move in his direction. After all, his own party abandoned him for Bobby Hobaugh. Who could have more reason than he to hate the man?"

"No one, sir." He paused. "And afterward?"

"The money will be deposited automatically in your offshore account as soon as the flowers are in the White House. You should be on your way to wherever you plan to go by that time." Jackson Tootell smiled. "I'll be sworn in as president, probably tomorrow afternoon, having served as vice president for only a few hours."

Walking through the small outer office, Tucker glanced at Miss Lotus. He wondered why Tootell kept a woman with a drinking problem for a secretary. Then he realized that she, like he, knew too much. Tootell kept her where he could watch her.

Thursday, January 20, afternoon

WASHINGTON, D. C.

"Mr. President, this is Senator Wheeler calling."

"It's nice to hear your voice, Senator."

"The reason for my call, sir, is to discuss the vote for vice president. We've tentatively scheduled that vote this evening at seven o'clock. Is that acceptable to you, Mr. President?"

"It's sooner than I expected. Could it be delayed until tomorrow? I'd like the chance to visit with Mr. Tootell about the workings of the new administration."

"Actually, Mr. Tootell was the one who asked us to schedule the vote for today."

"I am having a call placed to his town house in Arlington. I believe we should at least speak to one another before he and I become an administration. I would appreciate it, Senator, if you would delay the vote."

"Mr. Tootell told me he is in Atlanta and expects to be sworn in by a federal judge in that city, immediately after the vote is taken."

"Then I'll try to reach him there."

"I'm somewhat reluctant to mention this, sir, but if Mr. Tootell isn't sworn in today, the office of vice president will be vacant tomorrow. We don't want another constitutional crisis, do we?"

"Of course not, but I'll simply nominate him to fill the vacancy and the Senate can approve the nomination. Not much will have changed." Bobby heaved a sigh. "Senator, I'm not accustomed to the activities I've been through the last couple of days. I'm staring at piles of paper on the desk, each of which demands my attention. Frankly I need to catch my breath. I really would appreciate it if you would honor my request and delay action on the vice presidency until tomorrow."

The tone of the majority leader's voice told of his reluctance. "I suppose I could ask what assurance we have that you will nominate Jackson Tootell. After all, if the position is vacant, you can choose anyone you want." There was a brief pause, as though his own statement embarrassed him. Then he quickly went on to say, "But we in the Senate want to begin our relations with you on a positive note, so we'll delay the vote at your request, Mr. President. I'll assume you will square it with your vice president."

"Yes, of course. I will nominate Mr. Tootell as one of my first acts. Please accept my word for that. His confirmation by the Senate should be a certainty." When the senator made no further comment, Bobby finished by saying, "Thank you, Senator, for the accommodation."

Thursday, January 20, evening

ATLANTA, GEORGIA

"They've done what?"

"The Senate has delayed the vote for vice president until tomorrow." Tucker stood beyond the desk with his hands clasped behind his back.

"What about the flowers? Have they been delivered?"

"Yes, sir, just as you directed."

Tucker detected a note of desperation in Jackson Tootell's voice when he said, "We've got to get word to the woman in the White House to delay the coffee matter until tomorrow night." He turned away from Tucker toward the window, hands clenched at his side.

Behind him, Tucker said, "I'm afraid there isn't time for that, sir." With gloved hands, he drew a small handgun, silencer attached, from his jacket. Just as the big man was turning, he pointed it at Jackson Tootell. All Tootell had time to exclaim was, "What?"

The first shot struck the creator of *Tootell Nationwide* squarely in the middle of his chest, driving him backward. As he fell, the second shot entered his throat and exited the back of his neck, severing his spine. Tucker waited only a moment to be certain Tootell was dead. Then he carefully placed the gun on the desk. Under the gun he left a slip of paper on which was written, in feminine hand, "You deserve this, you bastard! You killed the president." Miss Lotus's penmanship had been perfectly forged.

Tucker stared at the body without expression. "There was no way you would have allowed me to live. I know too much. I just moved first—before you could hunt me down and kill me." He turned to leave, then looked back with a crooked smile, "Thanks for the money—all of it."

As Tucker exited the building, he didn't glance at the Secret Service man who was standing outside the door. The agent ignored him as well. Since Tootell became a presidential candidate, Tucker had been passing in and out of the building. He was known to be trustworthy.

Miss Lotus lived in a small town house in Smyrna, a quiet community on the outskirts of Atlanta. She opened the door only as far as the safety chain would allow, looked at Tucker and exclaimed, "What brings you here?"

"Please let me in." The look on his face and the tenor of his voice indicated something was terribly wrong. She unlatched the chain and moved away from the door. Tucker closed it quietly and again secured the locks. Miss Lotus sank in the worn chair that provided relaxation for her after each day's work. She gestured for Tucker to sit in another nearby.

Tucker seemed to hesitate, then blurted out, "Tootell's dead. I just came from his office. I found him lying on the floor in a pool of blood. Someone shot him."

Miss Lotus gasped and put her hand to her mouth. Her

eyes were wide as she stared at Tucker. No sound escaped her covered lips.

"Miss Lotus, do you have something to drink? I need to calm my nerves."

Without speaking, she pointed to a cabinet near the door to the kitchen. He moved a bottle of inexpensive bourbon and two small glasses to the cabinet top, turned to her and asked, "Will you join me?"

Miss Lotus was starting to cry. She nodded her head to indicate she would like a drink, then reached for a handkerchief and used it to cover her eyes and nose. Tucker poured the whiskey neat and, after a quick glance over his shoulder, emptied the caplet into one glass. He handed the glass to her and returned to the chair. "Do you know anyone who might have done it?"

She shook her head as she sobbed. When she found her voice, she said, "He has lots of enemies. Who knows?" She began sobbing even more. After a minute, she shuddered and looked at Tucker with terror in her eyes. "They'll be after us— you and me. The police will find out all the terrible things that Mr. Tootell made us do, and they'll be after us."

Tucker took a sip from his glass and said, "I've been thinking the same thing." He shook his head. "I'm not sure what we should do." Then he lifted his glass and said, "The whiskey will help. Try some."

She nodded, wiped her eyes and nose, picked up the glass, and downed the liquid in one gulp.

Tucker didn't stay to watch her die.

44

Thursday, January 20, evening

WASHINGTON, D. C., THE WILLARD

The so-called Gang of Four, weary but jubilant, rested in the hotel suite with drinks in hand. They paid little attention to the television set tuned to one of the major broadcast channels until an old familiar face appeared. The commentator, a Washington hand of many years, displayed a solemn expression as he spoke.

Nothing that I've seen in all my years of watching the national political process can compare to the happenings of the past two days. Both we, the Beltway insiders, and the public at large, are confronted with the reality of a president about whom virtually nothing is known. How did it come to this?

That question leads us to those four individuals who somehow catapulted an unknown man from Montana into the presidency.

Who are they, these three men and this woman who performed the impossible?

Well, there is Lance Caldwell, who never tired in his efforts to portray an unknown as the one whom the electors should choose as the next president, even when those efforts must have seemed futile. There is Roman Burke, an established political operative. How was he persuaded to attach himself to such a quixotic endeavor?

But most of all, we have to admire the imagination, persuasive ability, and resourcefulness of Ralph Phillips and Janine Paul. They were able to convince a small number of electors to consider Bobby Hobaugh as a potential candidate—and to hang on to that core of electors to the end. Then they persuaded Allen Ward—a truly creditable candidate—to withdraw from contention and throw his support to Hobaugh. At that point they had ensured that their man could become president. Finally, these two somehow convinced the entire Democratic caucus to do what no one would ever have believed possible—elect a Republican.

Incredible!

About Bobby Hobaugh we know almost nothing. Soon enough, however, the press will dig hungrily into his past life, searching for any mistake, any error, any blemish. For now, however, we can only rely on the few words we heard him speak today. From those words we can conclude he is modest and well aware of the burden he has assumed. His statement that his wife is "possessed of all the womanly virtues," already the target of caustic comment from some feminists, tells us that he is of a world in which the old verities still apply. And he spoke of prayer without apology. Are these not admirable attributes?

Now all of us must hope that President Hobaugh will rise to the challenge—a challenge that

bested even some of those who came to the office
with the apparent background, talent, and prepa-
ration to succeed.

The old commentator paused for a long moment, eyes
first on his hands, folded before him on a tabletop, then back
to the camera.

The new president asked that we pray for
him. Perhaps we should simply do as he asked—
pray for his success—and add a prayer for the
rest of us and for the continued well-being of this
great country.

Lance Caldwell, standing alone at the back of the room,
listened to the last of the commentator's words and thought
of his infant son. What would the future of the country be like
for him?

He whispered a quiet, "Amen."

Thursday, January 20, evening

WASHINGTON, D. C.

"It's been a hectic day. I had no idea there could be so many
demands on the president. The United States' entanglements
in the affairs of foreign countries are far greater than I ever
realized." Bobby and Margaret sat side by side in their private living quarters, having just returned from dinner at Blair
House. "I've learned more about the nuclear capability of
the United States and other countries than I ever wanted to
know. It's frightening." Bobby put his arm around Margaret's
shoulder, pulled her close, and gave her a squeeze. "Enough
of that. How was the afternoon for you?"

"I spent most of it with the White House staff, trying to learn how things work around here." She sighed and shook her head. "There are more people employed in this building than live in many towns in Montana. Most of them have been here for a long time, and all of them seem to know what to do." She leaned her head onto Bobby's shoulder. "I won't be cooking any meals, I guess. They'll even buy our clothes."

Bobby held her close and rubbed his chin gently along the side of her head. "Speaking of clothes, I need more suits. My old brown one won't do in this environment."

"We both need clothes. I need them more than you. When the news people report on the activities of the First Lady, the most important thing seems to be the dress she wore." Margaret laughed and straightened up. "Think about our situation. We've never even seen the Washington Monument and here we are, living in the White House. It's hilarious!"

Bobby chuckled in response. "It's more ridiculous than hilarious." He pulled her to him again. "We won't be taking any of the public tours, that's for sure. But I guess we'll get to see all the important places as time goes along."

Their conversation was interrupted by a gentle knock on the door and the entry of a staff member, carrying a silver carafe. She stopped briefly and said, "Excuse me, please." Then she moved to the table in front of the davenport and added, "I'll freshen your coffee before I leave for the evening."

Bobby started to rise and then sat back, smiled and said, "I'm sorry I can't remember your name quite yet. In time Margaret and I will know the names of everyone who works here. But we appreciate your kindness."

"Thank you, sir. I'm told the coffee was brewed just the way you like it." Margaret, too, thanked the woman, who quietly left the room carrying the carafe.

Bobby yawned and reached for the cup, steam drifting upward from its hot contents. "I still can't believe all of this has happened." Turning to Margaret, he lifted his cup and sniffed the aroma. "Smells like almonds. I wonder how anyone got the idea that's our special kind. I don't normally drink flavored coffee, do you?" He took a sip, raised the cup in a salute and said, "Well, never mind. Here's to us. Despite our wishes, we've been chosen to serve the country. May we serve it well."

Laws of the United States

If, by reason of death, resignation, removal from office, inability or failure to qualify, there is neither a President nor a Vice President to discharge the powers and duties of the office of President, then the Speaker of the House of Representatives shall, upon his resignation as Speaker and as Representative in Congress, act as President.

45

Friday, January 21, morning

WASHINGTON, D. C.

CNN announced it first, at nine o'clock in the morning, Washington time.

Breaking news just in. President Hobaugh and his wife are dead. It has just been reported that President Hobaugh and his wife, Margaret, were found dead in their quarters in the White House early this morning. A member of the White House staff entered the quarters to begin her morning cleaning duties and found the couple seated side by side on a sofa. There was no evidence of injury to either the President or Mrs. Hobaugh. Initial reports indicate that they may have been poisoned. At this time we are attempting to confirm the deaths and learn more about the situation. Stay tuned for further information as it becomes available.

Within minutes, word of the deaths spread throughout the country. In Washington, the report took on special importance. The country was without a president and, because the vote by the Senate to elect a vice president had not been held, the country was without a vice president as well. For the first time in history, there was a vacancy in both offices.

Late in the evening, Timothy Welch, just resigned from his position as a member and Speaker of the House of Representatives, stood in the East Room of the White House where Bobby Hobaugh had sworn to uphold the Constitution only the day before. The chief justice once again administered the oath of office. Among the select few chosen by Mr. Welch to accompany him at the ceremony were Ralph Phillips, Janine Paul, Lance Caldwell, and Roman Burke.

Mr. Welch received not a single vote for president in the general election held on November 1.

He received not a single vote for president in the election held by the electors on December 13.

He received not a single vote for president during the long election held in the House of Representatives.

When Was Election Day?

ACKNOWLEDGEMENTS

Several people read the original and subsequent versions of the manuscript that became this book. Each provided comments and suggestions for improvement. My thanks to Dr. Aurora Mackey, Marcia Melton and—especially—Florence Ore, for their contribution of time and talent, the result of which is a much more engaging and readable story.

And special thanks to my niece, Kathleen Mohn, who utilized her professional editing skills to improve upon the often juvenile punctuation and word usage of her author uncle.

And, of course, thanks to Janet Muirhead Hill for her constant encouragement, clearheaded judgment about publication matters, her ability to produce a book that is both attractive to the eye and worthy of a read. Most of all, thanks beyond measure for her patience with a sometimes obstreperous author.

Jim Moore

*A discussion guide for this book is
available at www.ravenpublishing.net*